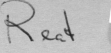

Megan sat up in bed. . . .

A breeze had come up, filling the room with life, and for a moment she didn't move.

She should lie down and pull the covers around her. She should close her eyes, close her heart, keep safe from phantoms of the night.

But he was calling for her. And she could no more ignore that call than she could stop her heart from beating.

The room was a shifting mass of shadows, but she knew he wasn't there. He'd been there, watching her. And then he'd left, for what reason she couldn't fathom. But deep within his tortured soul he was calling to her.

And she was answering that call, with a kind of dazed certainty. All that mattered was Ethan, calling to her to come to him. At last.

ABOUT THE AUTHOR

When the musical *Phantom of the Opera* debuted on Broadway several years ago, Anne Stuart was so fascinated by this unusual love story that she traveled down from her Vermont home to New York to see this play. Inspired by its passionate intensity, Anne sat down to write a story of her own and the result is *Night of the Phantom*. Anne tells us that "This book is merely a fantasy. It is not meant to do anything but entertain—and not to be taken too seriously."

Anne lives with her husband and young son and daughter in a small town in Vermont where she's a deacon and Sunday school teacher in her church.

Books by Anne Stuart
HARLEQUIN AMERICAN ROMANCE

Don't miss any of our special offers. Write to us at the following address for information on our newest releases.

Harlequin Reader Service
P.O. Box 1397, Buffalo, NY 14240
Canadian address: P.O. Box 603,
Fort Erie, Ont. L2A 5X3

ANNE STUART

NIGHT
OF
THE
PHANTOM

Harlequin Books

TORONTO • NEW YORK • LONDON
AMSTERDAM • PARIS • SYDNEY • HAMBURG
STOCKHOLM • ATHENS • TOKYO • MILAN

For my niece, Jennifer,
who knows a good phantom when she sees one.

Published July 1991

ISBN 0-373-16398-3

NIGHT OF THE PHANTOM

Prologue

He loved the night. It spread around him, a soft, comforting cloud of darkness that wrapped him in a warmth as vital to him as air and food. Daylight was a time to hide, a time to simply live through, but at night, he came alive. Blood pumped through his veins, his lungs filled with air and everything became possible, all under cover of the beneficent darkness.

He sat in his chair, utterly still, as he let the night drift around him. He could sit that way for hours, unmoving, not even blinking, absorbing the darkness into his very soul.

By tomorrow, his precious darkness would be violated. He'd never had the chance to pass judgment before, and he found the idea curiously seductive. In an unjust world, he was going to force justice. He was going to make Reese Carey pay for his crimes, and he expected to use his considerable creative powers to do so effectively.

And then he'd surrender to the darkness again. Triumphant in the inky black of night, he'd go back to being alone once more, content, a phantom to terrorize the narrow-minded people of Oak Grove. Ethan Winslowe, a creature to frighten children and gullible adults. A deformed monster, a specter of the darkness.

A phantom of the night.

Chapter One

Megan Carey told herself she had no reason in the world to feel guilty. For the first time in her twenty-seven years, she was going to do something irresponsible, romantic and wonderful. She was taking off with nothing but a brand-new matched set of luggage, a one-way ticket to Europe and a wad of traveler's checks that would choke a horse, not to mention enough unencumbered plastic to keep her going until she and she alone decided it was time to stop.

Her co-workers at Carey Enterprises were giving her a lavish send-off, out of keeping with her relatively few years on the job, but well deserved in terms of how well she was liked in the huge construction-and-development firm. The fact that she was the boss's only child was a drawback rather than an incentive, but her friends in the executive offices were partying up a storm anyway, throwing her a bon voyage party worthy of a veteran of fifty years in the company. Meg accepted it with good cheer and gratitude, wishing she could just get rid of this nagging little feeling of guilt.

It wasn't as if she were leaving her father in the lurch. She'd worked for the huge company founded by her grandfather since she was in high school, working during school vacations, doing every job imaginable as she learned the construction business from the bottom up. Not that Carey Enterprises was simply a construction company. Reese Carey had turned a run-of-the-mill organization into a multinational glamour business. He built mansions for millionaires, upscale office buildings, elite public buildings for wealthy municipalities. Carey Enterprises had a reputation for quality worth paying for, a reputation Megan viewed with justifiable pride, secure that she'd been partly responsible for it.

But she was tired of it. Tired of working every spare minute that wasn't spent on schooling, tired of being so tied to her father that she had no life of her own. Tired of squashing down her embarrassing, undeniably romantic yearnings for a life of adventure. And now, finally, she was going to give in to those yearnings, toss the common sense that had ruled her life to the winds and take off.

Her father hadn't taken her decision well. But for once, she was adamant. There wouldn't be a better time to leave. Her father was about to remarry after five years of widowerhood, and his fiancée was a sensible, attractive woman who knew as much about the business as Megan did. Her father would be so busy with his new bride that he wouldn't have time to miss her.

If only he hadn't been looking so worried during the past few weeks. So preoccupied and slightly desperate. Whenever she'd asked him what was wrong, he'd only insisted he was going to miss her, but she didn't think it was that simple, despite her immediate upsurge of guilt.

She'd even gone so far as to check the financial records of both the firm and her father's private accounts, wondering whether he was on the brink of ruin and didn't want to tell her. But both Carey Enterprises and

Reese Carey himself were not only solvent, they were flush, with the real estate and building slowdown not seeming to affect them at all.

She accepted a glass of imported champagne from someone in the accounting department, accepted a kiss from one of her father's secretaries and moved through the crowd. She was due to fly from New York in four days' time. She was allowing two days to drive from their home in Chicago to the East Coast, another day to shop, and then her adventure would begin. But it wouldn't start until she made one last-ditch effort to find out what was troubling her father.

He wasn't anywhere in sight. He'd circulated through the chattering employees for a while, his usual bonhomie firmly in place, and then suddenly, he was gone. He could be anywhere in the elegant office building they'd constructed seven years ago from plans by the great Ethan Winslowe, but she had a pretty good idea where he'd be.

His office door on the deserted twentieth floor was ajar. She could see a pool of light beyond, and for a moment, she hesitated, wondering whether she'd be walking in on a romantic moment between Reese and Madeleine. But no, Madeleine had been deep in conversation with the comptroller. Her father would be alone, ready for one last father-daughter talk.

The thick rugs muffled her footsteps, even in the high heels she wore to add to her miserly five-foot-two height. She pushed the door open, a warm smile on her face, and then froze in horror.

Reese Carey was sitting in his leather desk chair, his back turned to her, staring into the Chicago night. He was holding a gun to his temple.

For a moment, Megan was paralyzed with panic. She wanted to scream, but she knew it might startle him into pulling the trigger. She held her breath for one heartbeat, for ten, then spoke very, very softly.

"Father?"

He whirled around in the chair, dropping the gun to the desk, and his usually red, cheery face was pale with strain. "Meg," he said hoarsely.

She closed the door behind her, stepping into the walnut-paneled office. "What in God's name is going on?" she said, fear making her usually warm voice strident. "Don't fob me off with excuses anymore, I'm not buying them. What's happening to you?"

For a moment he said nothing. Then he put his face in his hands, and his big shoulders heaved with sudden, noisy sobs. "I wouldn't have done it, baby. I wouldn't have done it to you. I would have waited...."

"Why were you going to kill yourself? Daddy, you're not sick, are you?"

He raised his head then, and the tears streaming down his face looked strange, unreal to her. Her father, who laughed and joked and bullied his way through life, shouldn't be crying. "I'm in trouble. Big, big trouble, and I can't see any way out of it."

"It can't be financial. I checked our accounts when you started acting so oddly. We've got plenty of money, plenty of contracts, prospects..."

"Not for long. Not if Ethan Winslowe has his way."

She sank down in the chair opposite him, a sudden foreboding making her cold inside. "What does Ethan Winslowe have to do with anything?"

"He's out to destroy me," Reese said, and for a moment, Meg almost laughed at the melodrama in his voice. Until she looked at the gun on the desk.

"Why would an architect want to destroy you? You've never even met him. The man's a full-blown eccentric who never leaves his house. What would he have against you? You've built dozens of his designs, you've helped give him the reputation he enjoys. Why would he want to hurt you?"

Reese shrugged. "God, I don't know. The man's crazy, we all know that. As far as I know, no one's even seen him. I've been told he's multiply handicapped, kept alive by machines. Other people say he's just agoraphobic. It doesn't matter—the bottom line is he's nuts and he's out to get me."

"You still haven't told me why. He must have some reason. If he didn't, how could he do you any harm? The man doesn't even have a telephone in the back of beyond or wherever he lives."

"Oak Grove," Reese said. "And he could do it, have no doubt about that. He's like a giant, evil spider spinning his web, and I'm well and truly trapped."

Even with the gun in sight, this was getting too farfetched for Megan. "Why?" she said again with some asperity.

Her father considered for a moment, and he got that look in his eye that she knew far too well, the look that meant he was trying to figure out how much of the truth he had to tell. "You remember the Springfield Arts Center?"

"How could I forget? The collapse of that roof killed two workers and injured a score of others. We're just lucky the investigation proved it wasn't the company's fault."

"Yes, that's what the investigation proved," Reese said glumly.

"Supposedly it was Winslowe's fault, wasn't it? Was he fined or something?"

"They could never prove anything."

"And Winslowe's holding it against you? Five years later, he's decided you railroaded him . . . ?"

"No," Reese said. "It just took him five years to find out that it really was my fault."

Megan took a sharp breath. "How could it have been? You followed the blueprints, you knew what you were doing."

"I was trying to cut costs. You've seen his plans—always the best of everything. A recluse like Winslowe has no sense of economy—he thinks money's like water. I didn't think those roof trusses needed to be that heavy gauge."

"So you changed the specifications?" She didn't want to hear this. The nightmare collapse of the arts center roof five years ago was something that none of them ever forgot. The one consolation had been that it hadn't been their fault.

"Your mother had just died!" Reese cried. "I wasn't thinking clearly. The business was going through a tough spell, and I thought we could come up with a little extra working cash if we just cut back on the reinforcements. I never thought it would have collapsed like that. If Winslowe only used normal design standards, it would have been fine."

"But that's what makes Winslowe so special, so sought after. He does things differently, and if you follow his specifications to the letter, it works. Father, how could you!" she cried.

"Don't you start in on me! There hasn't been a day when I haven't regretted it, haven't been eaten up with guilt. You know their families were well taken care of. You know nothing like that's ever happened again.''

''But Ethan Winslowe found out.''

''I don't know how he did. The man's uncanny, sitting out there in the middle of nowhere. And now he's going to destroy me.''

''Just calm down,'' Megan said, more to herself than to her father, as her fingers gripped the sides of her chair. ''Exactly what can he do?''

''He has proof, or so he says. He's going to turn it over to the federal investigators next week unless I can come up with a reason why he shouldn't.''

''That sounds like blackmail!''

''It wouldn't be money he wants. The man has more than he'll ever need. I don't know what he wants from me. It's hopeless, Meg. There's no way out.''

''Don't be ridiculous,'' she said flatly. ''You can't be a coward at this point in your life. So you made a mistake. A terrible, tragic mistake. But you've suffered for it, you've done your best to make amends. Who the hell does he think he is to pass judgment on you?''

''I don't imagine he's quite sane.''

''There must be something we can do.''

She'd known her father for her twenty-seven years. She knew that slightly speculative expression he could get in his faded blue eyes as he weighed possibilities. ''I'm supposed to present myself at his place in Oak Grove by Saturday. If he hasn't heard from me, he'll go ahead and destroy me.''

''Can't you call him . . . ?''

''He has no phone, you know that as well as I do. He won't answer my letters. And I know for damned sure that throwing myself on his mercy won't do me a spit of good. He's going to destroy me, Meg. There's no way out. Unless..."

"Unless?" *Here it comes,* she thought.

"Unless you were to go in my place. The man isn't thinking this through clearly. He doesn't realize that he's not just destroying a man, he's destroying a family, a company, thousands of lives...."

"Hundreds," Meg corrected with the ruthlessness she sometimes had to use to cut through her father's high-flown emotion. "Let me get this straight. You want me to go out to Oak Grove and plead your case for you?"

"He won't listen to me. All he wants is revenge. He'll listen to you, Meg. He'd have to be blind not to."

"What makes you so sure he isn't blind? Enough rumors have been spread about what kind of shape he's in...."

"He couldn't be blind. Not and design the buildings he's designed. Will you do it, Meg? Will you save me?"

She'd been trapped, quite neatly, by a master. There was no alternative, not and live with herself. "My airplane tickets—"

"Are for Tuesday. You could drive out to Oak Grove, spend one night and drive back to an airport in time to make connections."

"Why can't I fly to Oak Grove?"

"Meg, you can barely find it on a map. The nearest airport is five hours away. You'd have to rent a car and—"

"You've already got this all figured out," she said shrewdly.

Her father had the grace to flush. "I've been a desperate man, Meg. I've thought of every possibility. I'd never ask you—"

"You already have," she pointed out.

"Will you do it?"

She didn't even hesitate. She already knew she had no choice. "Of course," she said, trying to keep the stiffness out of her voice. "But I'll fly to the nearest airport and send my other stuff on to New York for my London flight. That is, if I can get tickets...."

"I've made a reservation for myself. You can use that one, and we'll just change the return flight to New York instead of Chicago." He got up from the desk, suddenly full of energy. "Let me go find the papers Winslowe sent. Oak Grove has to be the armpit of civilization, but I've got a fairly decent map..." His voice trailed off as he left the room.

Megan watched him go, her eyes narrowed at his sudden cheer. She'd seen him get what he wanted before, and she recognized all the signs. On impulse, she leaned over the desk and picked up the gun. Unloaded, of course, and her father knew guns well. The whole scene had been carefully staged for her benefit.

She ought to walk out and never come back. He'd managed to railroad her again, just as she was finally claiming her independence.

On the other hand, doing this one last thing for him would assuage her guilt. She would have earned her freedom if she talked Ethan Winslowe out of pressing charges. The man had to be reasonable, no matter how odd his reputation. She had a gift for negotiating, for making an opponent see the other side of matters, a gift her father had used often enough.

This time, she'd be using it for more than getting the best possible terms on a contract. This time, she was bargaining for her father's livelihood and her own life. If Ethan Winslowe held to his revenge, there'd be no way

she could leave Chicago. She'd need to stand by her
father in his disgrace.

No, it was her life she'd be fighting for, too. Setting
the gun back down on the desk, she leaned back in her
chair. It was going to be a hell of a weekend.

ENDLESS HOURS LATER, SHE was beyond stress, beyond
worry, beyond regret. The late flight out of Chicago had
been full of turbulence and grumpy flight attendants.
She had had to change planes twice, each one getting a
little smaller and a little choppier. By the time she arrived at a small municipal airport outside of Benning-
ton, Tennessee, she was feeling jarred, achy and angry.
And depressed, knowing she had a five-hour drive ahead
of her.

Oak Grove was a tiny, faceless town that nestled
somewhere between Kentucky, Arkansas and Missouri.
None of the states wanted to claim it, and it had the odd
distinction of having belonged to all three in the last one
hundred years. Currently, it belonged to Arkansas, but
that probably wouldn't last too long.

The only rental car was an aging Ford with no springs
whatsoever. As Megan drove through the long, empty
hours of early morning, she told herself things would
look better when the sun rose. If it ever bothered to.
There was a gloomy mist falling, and the late-spring
weather seemed bleak, timeless. Somewhere beyond the
side of the road, dogwoods must be blooming, azaleas
and forsythia and tulips and daffodils. All she could see
was gray.

The road narrowed as it climbed through twisty, dark
hills. She was still more than fifty miles away when the
road turned to gravel and the rain turned that gravel to
mud. She was forced to slow down to something slightly

faster than a crawl, and for a moment, she considered pulling off to the side of the road and trying to catch a little bit of sleep. She hadn't seen another car in three hours—no one would be likely to be traveling this god-forsaken road and find her sleeping.

But she couldn't do it. She wanted to get to Oak Grove with a need that bordered on desperation. The sooner she faced Ethan Winslowe, whatever there was of him to face, the sooner she could get away, back to that horrible little airport with its horrible little plane. Her flight to Europe left New York in less than seventy-two hours—she was already cutting it close.

Besides, when it came right down to it, she was afraid. Afraid of facing Ethan Winslowe, afraid of what she'd find. Afraid that all her pleas, all her reasonable explanations were going to fall on deaf ears, either literally or figuratively. Afraid this midnight trip from hell was going to be a miserable, agonizing waste of time.

She almost missed the town of Oak Grove when she came to it. The gray mist had lessened somewhat, the sun was making a vain effort to poke through the thick clouds, and it was just past eleven in the morning. The gas gauge on the Ford was heading toward empty when she passed a cluster of buildings that suggested civilization was near at hand. She drove straight through, looking, but things rapidly became uninhabited again. There'd been a rusty gas pump near what seemed to be an abandoned store five miles back. She had no choice but to turn around.

This time, she saw the sign. Covered by weeds, rusted so that it was almost unreadable, the once-white sign said Oak Grove, Founded 1835. Underneath, someone had scratched something with a knife. Slowing the car, she peered at it. Lost, 1902, it said.

A tiny shiver of fear ran across her backbone as she pulled up next to the gas pump. She didn't recognize the brand, and she could only hope there was even a trace of fuel in the old-fashioned pump. She sat there in her car, staring at the deserted street, and her hands came up to rub her chilled arms.

There was a church. Every speck of paint had peeled off, the front was a mass of weeds, but the windows were intact, and a sign listed services for almost every day of the week. Next to the church was a store with dingy, fly-specked windows full of old canned food and faded clothing. Oak Grove looked like a ghost town, she thought. The houses were dark and empty looking, the town deserted, eerie, a place no one in their right mind would want to live....

"Fill 'er up?"

She screamed, thoroughly spooked. "Yes, please," she said, pressing a hand to her racing heart. "I'm sorry, you startled me."

"Yeah," said the man. "I have a habit of doing that."

A fitting resident of a ghost town, Megan thought. He was ageless, the man who'd materialized beside her window, moving with a slow gait that seemed more sullen than elderly. She glanced back at the town and for the first time, realized that some of the blinds were being pulled back from the curtained windows. People were watching her covertly.

"No credit cards," the man said when he finished, appearing beside her just as abruptly. He watched with interest as she shuffled through her meager supply of cash. "You just passing through? We don't get people in these parts very often."

This sudden curiosity would have been disarming if Megan had been able to rid herself of the notion that he clearly wanted her gone. She handed him a twenty-dollar bill, waited while he laboriously counted the change, and then she flashed him her friendliest smile, the one guaranteed to melt Chicago bus drivers and postal workers everywhere. "As a matter of fact, I'm looking for someone."

He remained unmoved. "That so?"

She didn't let her smile falter. "A man by the name of Ethan Winslowe. He lives around here, doesn't he?"

If the man had seemed distant and unfriendly before, he now seemed positively icy. "Winslowe don't cotton much to visitors. You'd best keep on your way."

"I've come to see him," she said firmly. "I have an appointment."

The old man narrowed his eyes. "He's not going to want to see you. That man doesn't see nobody, and nobody wants to see him. They say the last person who looked him in the eyes turned stone blind."

Megan's mouth dropped open. "I beg your pardon?"

"And then there's old Mrs. MacInerny. She saw him one day when she was out walking and ain't been right in the head since. He's a son of the devil, he is, girly. No one's rightly sure whether he's real or not, whether he's dead or alive. Some say he's a phantom, haunting that crazy old place, but truth of the matter is no one wants to find out. You'd better get away from here before you run into anymore trouble."

"I'm not going anywhere but to Winslowe's house. I don't believe in such malarkey."

"Your funeral," the old man announced with an air of gloomy satisfaction. "Don't say I didn't warn you."

"You warned me, all right. You still haven't told me how I can find him."

"First left. Just keep driving—you'll come to the old Meredith place sooner than you'll ever want to."

It was lack of sleep, Megan decided there and then. It was sheer exhaustion, not to mention tension, that was making this odd old man sound so sinister. "Meredith place?"

"His granddaddy's. No one in their right mind would ever want to come back there to live, but then, Winslowe ain't in his right mind. Everyone around here knows it." And then the man disappeared back into the deserted-looking building, slamming the door shut behind him.

Just as well, she thought, starting up her car again. She might have been crazy enough to ask him another question. Considering the strange answers he'd already given her, she'd be better off waiting to see what she found at the end of her journey.

It took her half an hour to drive what couldn't have been more than five miles. The road turned into a rutted swamp, one the old Ford could barely negotiate. She was so busy dealing with the driving conditions that she didn't have any time to look ahead. When the road finally ended, she pulled to a stop, sitting there staring up in mingled awe and horror.

Chapter Two

The town should have prepared her for what she'd find when she reached the old Meredith place. Ethan Winslowe's designs should have prepared her. Meg had seen almost every one of the buildings he'd planned, those that had actually been built and those that were nothing more than prototypes, some so exotic, no one would ever live in them.

But the old Meredith place was beyond her wildest dreams—or nightmares. The facade was ordinary enough, a big Victorian mansion dating from just before the turn of the century, complete with gingerbread trim and wide porches. But spreading out on both sides was the strangest conglomeration of additions: wings, gables, gambrels and jutting peaks from every possible design period, from Greco-Roman to Country French to Bauhaus to modern. It looked like an architect gone totally mad, turning his own house into a crazy quilt of building styles, and for a moment, Meg panicked, looking for a place to turn the lumbering sedan around so she could get away from there.

The car was stuck, thoroughly and deeply embedded in the mud. The more she tried, the more the wheels spun. The house in front of her was still and silent;

whatever gremlins lived there were paying no attention to a lady in distress.

She had no choice finally but to climb out into the mud, cursing herself for wearing high heels, cursing the rain that was now soaking down, cursing the puddles beneath her. It was just before noon on Saturday. Reese's ultimatum was by five o'clock that day, and yet, no one seemed to be expected.

She trudged through the rain, up the front staircase to the door. There were lace curtains in the front windows facing the wide porch, politely in keeping with that style of the house. They also shielded whatever occupants lurked inside, peering out at her.

Meg gave herself a sensible little shake. She'd let the old man in the village spook her. There was nothing sinister around her, just a brilliant recluse who had business with her father. Business she planned to take care of quickly and efficiently, and then head back to light and civilization.

She heard the echo of the old-fashioned doorbell inside the house. It was late April, but the rain was cold and bone chilling up there in the mountains, and Megan shivered. If she had any choice at all, she'd turn and leave, she thought. But even her momentary cowardice had been defeated by the ruts in the driveway. She glanced back at her mired-in car. She wasn't going anywhere until someone was willing to get her out.

She was just about to ring the bell again when the door was jerked open. "Who are you and what do you want?" a man demanded abruptly, glowering at her, his huge bulk filling the doorway and blocking any view of the hallway.

She had no choice but to look at him. This wasn't Ethan Winslowe, of that one fact she was certain. He was a huge hulking giant of a man, well over six feet, with massive shoulders and forearms, grizzled gray hair and eyebrows and a sullen, swarthy face. She guessed he was somewhere in his late fifties or early sixties and just as friendly as the old codger in town.

It took all her self-control not to take a nervous step backward. "I'm looking for Ethan Winslowe."

"So's everybody else. Mr. Winslowe doesn't see visitors. Go away."

"I believe he'll see me. I'm Meg Carey. Reese Carey's daughter."

The man hesitated in the act of slamming the door. "Where's the old man?" he demanded, and it took a moment for her to realize he meant her father.

"In Chicago."

"Go back and tell him his time's up."

"I'd like Mr. Winslowe to tell me that. I've come a long way to see him—"

"You weren't invited. Go away." Once more, he tried to slam the door, but she had the presence of mind to put her foot in the way.

"Ask Mr. Winslowe if he'll see me," she said again with pleasant firmness.

The man in the doorway cackled then, an unpleasant sound that increased the chill sweeping through her body. "I'll ask him," he said finally. "For your sake, you better hope he says no." And to her surprise, he opened the door wider.

She wasn't quite sure what she was expecting. Something out of *The Addams Family*, perhaps, but the front hallway and living room were neat, pristine, almost period pieces of Victoriana. The man nodded in the direction of a stiff-looking sofa. "Stash yourself there. I'll see what he says. Just don't get too comfortable."

Not likely, Megan thought, watching him disappear. The room was dark, gloomy on such a rainy day, and her unwilling host hadn't bothered to turn on any lights. She glanced around her, looking for a lamp or a switch, anything to chase away some of the eerie shadows. There was none.

Disbelieving, she got up and began stalking around the room, looking behind the draped Victorian furniture for something as mundane as an electrical outlet. There weren't any.

"Looking for something?" That same rough voice interrupted her.

She straightened up, knowing her pale cheeks were stained with color. "An electrical outlet."

"Ain't any. Leastways, not in this part of the house. Which is where you'll be staying."

"Staying?" Megan echoed uncertainly.

"Yup. Ethan's said since your daddy's too big a coward to show up here, then you'll have to do. I'll show you to your room."

"I don't want to stay," she said, trying to push back the panic that was like a raven's wings beating behind her eyes. "I simply want to talk to Mr. Winslowe and then leave. Surely that can be arranged."

"Surely that can't," the older man mocked her. "For one thing, lady, your car is so far stuck that it'll take a backhoe to get it out, and there's no one here to drive one. Won't be till the workmen come back on Monday morning. For another, Ethan sees people on his own terms. After dark. So you just follow me and make yourself comfortable because you aren't going anywhere until he says you are."

A sense of utter disbelief washed over her. "I can't...."

"You will," the man said, his rough voice implacable. "And don't think you can try to find your way out of here without your car. There's no one within fifty miles who'd help you. And I'd make sure you wouldn't get even a tenth of that distance. Ethan says he'll see you, and see you he will. It's my job to take care of everything Ethan requires, and he's decided he requires you. So why don't you stop making such a fuss and I'll show you to your room? It's another five hours till dark, and even then, Ethan might not be ready. You look like you could do with a rest."

For a moment, she didn't say anything. Things were rapidly taking on a sense of unreality. Eighteen hours ago, she'd been enjoying her farewell party. Now she was trapped in a bizarre, unelectrified house in the middle of nowhere with a car mired in the mud and a bruiser determined to keep her there.

She considered running for it, but the man had already informed her it would be a waste of time. She believed him when he said no one in the town of Oak Grove would help her. She considered flinging herself on the turkey-red Oriental carpet and having a temper tantrum the likes of which she hadn't indulged in since she was five and a half years old. That wouldn't do her any good, either.

She took a deep breath, drawing herself up as tall as her five foot two inches plus high heels would let her. "That sounds like a good idea," she said. "I don't suppose this place comes equipped with running water so that I could wash up?"

"You'll have your own bathroom. Plumbing works fine, and there's more than enough hot water for the three of us. You got any bags in that car of yours?"

"No. I wasn't planning on staying," she said absently. "Three of us?"

"You. Ethan. And me, I'm Salvatore. I take care of things around here."

"That's all? What about a . . . nurse?"

Salvatore simply stared at her for a moment. "Who needs a nurse? I can do everything for Ethan that needs doing. For that matter, I'm a damned good cook. You got a problem with that?"

"Of course not."

"Then follow me. And watch your step. This place gets a little tricky in spots."

That was an understatement. As long as she followed his hulking form through the Victorian hallways, things were fine. It was when they started into the new sections that things got difficult. The gloomy day let little light into the twists and turns of the passageways. They went at right angles, left angles, up flights of stairs, down flights of stairs. Some of the hallways had electric light, most of them didn't, and within five minutes of this endless journey, Megan gave up trying to memorize her way. She didn't know whether Salvatore was deliberately leading her on a roundabout passageway to confuse her or whether the house was really such a maze. Remembering the strange patchwork exterior, she expected it was probably the latter.

Salvatore stopped suddenly in a narrow hallway that was made of stone. One narrow slit in the wall let in a mere thread of rainwashed light, and the heavy wooden door creaked as he opened it. "This was where your father was going to stay," he announced. "It's the only room in the house that's habitable."

That was a debatable point. While the design of that section of the rambling house resembled a medieval castle, the room he'd shown her to was closer to a dungeon. The mattress on the floor probably wasn't made of straw, but it wasn't a Posturepedic, either. There was a brown wool blanket folded up at one end, and judging by the icy temperature of the room, that wouldn't be enough. The one pillow was small and lumpy looking and covered with something that looked like burlap, there were no chairs, no tables, nothing but a bucket in the corner of the room.

She walked over to it, her high heels clacking noisily on the stone floor. "Is that my modern plumbing?" she asked in a deceptively calm voice.

Salvatore shrugged, then moved over to another door set deep in one of the walls. He withdrew a ring of keys worthy of a medieval chatelain, fitted one into the lock and opened the door. "Ethan said you could use the bathroom."

Meg didn't move. She could see beyond Salvatore's bulk to an impressive-looking bathroom—a huge marble tub and gleaming wall sconce set with unlit candles. "You were going to make my father use the bucket?"

"This wasn't a social visit, Miss Carey," Salvatore said. "You hungry? You need anything?"

I need to get out of here, she thought, but she kept it to herself, knowing it wouldn't do her any good. She wasn't leaving until Ethan Winslowe gave the word. "Nothing," she said, ignoring the emptiness in her stomach. She wasn't going to accept anything from this place; nothing but her freedom. "Unless you want to tell Mr. Winslowe I'd appreciate seeing him as soon as possible. I want to get away from here...."

"I told you, you aren't getting out until Monday. That car is stuck fast."

"You must have other vehicles here. You could give me a ride to the nearest town with a car-rental agency...."

Salvatore was shaking his head. "No cars, Miss Carey. Even if we did, I doubt Ethan would let me take you. No, you'll simply have to drop your big-city timetable and wait." He headed out the door.

She didn't want to be left alone in this dark, cold place. Already she was shivering, and even Salvatore's sullen presence might have been some comfort. A comfort she wasn't going to ask for. "I'll be fine. If I need anything, I'll come looking—"

"No, you won't. I'm afraid I'm going to have to lock you in. This place is too dangerous to let you wander around alone. I'll check back in a couple of hours."

She was stunned into silence, a silence that lasted as Salvatore closed the door behind him and turned the key in the lock. The darkness closed in around her, gloomy and suffocating. The windows were high set and barred, the casements letting in almost no light.

For a moment, she wanted to scream, to run to the heavy door and start beating against it. Only sheer willpower held her still, that and the knowledge that if she did give in to panic, it would only make things much, much worse.

She took a deep, calming breath, then another. She didn't cross the room to make certain the door was truly locked—Salvatore didn't make mistakes. And things weren't quite as bad as they could have been. He'd left her a box of matches and the wall-sconces had tall candles in them. Her shoulder purse had two slightly battered candy bars at the bottom and a half-finished science-fiction paperback she'd lost interest in. The situation wasn't nearly as dismal as she had first thought, particularly if she ignored the fact that she was locked in.

The bathroom was positively sybaritic compared to her dungeon. The towels were thick and white, and there was even a terry robe, the kind she'd found at better hotels, hung on the back of the door. The hot water was just as abundant as Salvatore had promised her, and there were even some hyacinth-scented bath crystals.

At one forty-five on a rainy Saturday afternoon, when she should have been well on her way to New York and then to Europe, she found herself locked in a dungeon, having a perfumed, candlelit bath and even enjoying herself.

The terry robe dragged on the floor as she wrapped it around her body. That was another advantage to this place, she thought, pushing her sheaf of dark blond hair back. There were no mirrors around to force reality home when she stepped out of the bathtub and confronted her naked self. She found her body a constant vexation—it remained stubbornly rounded and ten pounds overweight no matter how little she ate and how much she exercised.

The mattress on the floor was a little more comfortable than she had imagined. The softness of the terrycloth robe kept the wool blanket from being too itchy, and the pillow was made of feathers. She sat cross-legged and made a feast of her first candy bar, then stretched out with her novel.

Her taste in science fiction ran toward women-authored extraterrestrial romances. The hero in this particular one had been a little too bizarre, even for Meg's tastes. A tall, green lizard with tiny scales instead of skin, he'd metamorphosed into a jellylike glob halfway through the book, leaving the earthling heroine

frustrated and untouched, and Meg had stopped reading. Now she would have read romances about amoe-
bas—anything to take her mind off her current situation.
The only problem was, the vast green blob reminded her
a little of Ethan Winslowe. Somewhere in this huge
place, he was lurking, possibly tied up to life-support
systems, a huge, evil spider waiting to... to...

That didn't bear thinking about. Maybe he was simply an agoraphobic Howard Hughes-type. Maybe he was
Salvatore himself. Whoever and whatever he was, she'd
face him, calmly, bravely, and deal with him as he
needed to be dealt with. And then she'd get the hell out
of here.

With a resigned sigh, she turned her attention to the
romantic tribulations of Medora and X'n*d, squinting
in the candlelight. In no time at all, she was sound
asleep.

THE ROOM WAS VERY DARK, the only light the flickering
image of the television monitors. Salvatore opened the
door, shutting it behind him silently. He had good eyes
in the dark, cat's eyes. He didn't need bright sunlight to
see. A good thing. There was very little light in Ethan
Winslowe's house, even on the brightest day.

"What do you think of her?" he asked, leaning
against the door.

The man in the chair didn't move, didn't blink his
eyes. One might think he was made of stone, so still did
he sit. Salvatore knew better.

"What color is her hair?" Ethan's voice was slow,
deep, issuing from the depths of the chair.

Salvatore glanced at the black-and-white monitor.
Meg Carey was lying on the mattress, a paperback novel
had fallen from her hand, and the white bathrobe was

wrapped around her. "Blond," he said. "Dark blond, with streaks in it, like sunlight."

"Sunlight," Ethan echoed.

"Nice blue eyes. Friendly, big. Nice body, too, not too thin. But you can see that, can't you?"

The girl had shifted in her sleep, rolling over onto her back, and the bathrobe shifted with her, exposing the warm curve of her breast. In another second, the screen went blank, turned off by an imperceptible move on Ethan's part. The other screens remained lit, illuminating empty rooms, empty hallways. "Remind me, Salvatore. What do we know about Megan Carey?"

Salvatore breathed a tiny sigh of relief. "Twenty-seven years old. An only child, devoted to her father. Graduate of the University of Chicago, master's degree from Northwestern. Up until yesterday, she worked for Carey Enterprises. She'd quit to go traveling, or so word has it. I don't know whether she caught wind of what her father had been doing and wanted to get out before she got brought down, too—"

"Unlikely. If she was trying to escape, she wouldn't have come here. What about her personal history?"

"Two love affairs, one with a college student that lasted most of her junior year. Apparently they broke up over his drug use. The other was with an executive in the company. That ended a while ago when he got involved with someone else. She sees men on a casual basis but doesn't seem too serious. She reads science fiction and murder mysteries, likes Italian food and works out at a health club three times a week."

"Efficient as always," Ethan said. "You never cease to amaze me."

"I like a challenge," Salvatore said modestly. "She's had chicken pox, measles, a broken arm in a cycling accident and a benign heart murmur. No abortions, no pregnancies. Her doctor's computer is a piece of cake to break into.''

"Do you think she knows about her father?"

"From what I can gather, no. She's known for her sense of honor. If she'd even suspected what he was doing, she would have stopped him. Maybe not blown the whistle on him, but she would have stopped him.''

"Maybe," said Ethan. "Then again, maybe not. We'll have to see. She likes to read, does she?"

"Anything but horror novels. I guess she's gullible.''

Ethan's laugh was enough to send cold chills down anyone's spine but Salvatore's. "Make arrangements to move her to the tower room, Sally. Leave her a few more amenities, including a decent bed. Maybe you'd better see about finding her some more clothes. You must know what size she wears.''

"Size eight. Bra size, thirty-four C, shoe size, seven. I'll see what I can do. Anything special for the tower room?"

"Yes," Ethan said. "No books but Stephen King novels.''

Salvatore chuckled. "Anyone tell you you were evil, Ethan?"

"You have, many times. See to it, old friend.''

"It is done, O master," Salvatore said with a mocking flourish, closing the door behind him and plunging the room into darkness once more.

The man in the chair didn't move, his eyes surveying the empty screens. And then, with a minuscule movement, he turned the middle one on.

Meg Carey lay in the center of the pallet. The bathrobe had come undone enough to expose her shapely legs. Her hair was thick and slightly curly around her shoulders. The color of sunlight, Salvatore had said. An interesting recommendation to a man who avoided sunlight.

A stubborn chin, even in sleep, he thought, cataloging her. A soft mouth, slightly parted, a nose that was totally without character. He half wished she'd open her eyes.

He'd been enraged when Salvatore had first told him Reese Carey had sent his daughter in his place. But the moment Ethan had set eyes on her, he'd realized this made things a great deal more interesting. Justice or revenge, he wasn't quite sure which it was, was going to be far sweeter, and Reese Carey, in his blind cowardice, had sent the means directly into Ethan's hands.

Ethan Winslowe couldn't wait for night to fall—and the games to begin.

Chapter Three

The cold, stone room was more like a tomb than a dungeon when Meg awoke hours later. The meager candlelight wavered in darkness from some unseen breeze, and the shadows were tall around her. She lay very still, shivering beneath the scratchy blanket, and told herself she had no reason to be frightened. This was almost the twenty-first century. She wasn't being kept prisoner in a mausoleum of a mansion by a deformed madman and his swarthy henchman. Even if it seemed like it.

She sat up, shoving her hair away from her face, pulling the terry robe around her. If only it weren't so dark. If only she had clean clothes and something to eat. If only...

Thinking about it was a waste of time, something to send her into weak-minded tears. She needed to pull herself together if she was going to finally face Ethan Winslowe and bargain her way out of here with her undeserving father's reputation intact. What meager light had come from the casement windows was now gone—surely he'd deign to see her soon.

She was fully dressed again, sitting cross-legged on her pallet and trying to read her novel by candlelight when she heard the scrape of a key in the lock. She held her breath, her heart pounding noisily beneath her thin cotton sweater, as a huge, menacing shadow preceded her visitor into the room. When the candlelight revealed Salvatore's impassive bulk, she breathed a sigh of relief, then wondered at it. Wasn't she more than ready to see the infamous Ethan Winslowe? Wasn't she more than ready to give him a piece of her mind?

"Have a good rest?" Salvatore asked.

"No." She stretched her legs out in front of her in an attitude of deliberate ease. Not for anything would she let him see how spooked she was. "I presume his highness is ready to grant me an audience by now?"

"Don't assume nothing, girly. I'm moving you to different quarters."

She raised an eyebrow, hoping the effect wasn't lost in the dim light. "Don't tell me you have other dungeons?"

"This place has so many different rooms, you could spend months and never stay in the same bed twice."

"I'm not going to be staying months," she said, unable to keep the slight waver of panic out of her voice.

The smile beneath Salvatore's thick gray mustache was positively wicked. "That's up to Ethan. At least in your new room, you'll have a real bed. And books." He chuckled at some private joke.

Meg didn't like that chuckle. "I think I'll stay here."

"Girly, you don't have any say in the matter. If you don't think I could carry a little bitty thing like you, then you don't know diddly. You're going to get up and come with me or we're gonna have a real undignified struggle."

"Don't call me girly," she said. "My name is Meg. Miss Carey to you." She waited long enough to assuage her pride, then rose, tucking the novel into her purse.

"That's the ticket. You'll like your new room. There's a nice view of this godforsaken countryside. That is, when it isn't dark outside and raining."

"I'd rather have a view of Chicago. When do I get to see him?"

"When he says so. And not a moment sooner. I wouldn't be in any great rush if I were you." He started out the door, confident she'd follow. Which, indeed, she did, too nervous to remain behind. "Haven't you heard what the townspeople say about him?"

"Why should I have talked with anyone in the town?" she countered.

"You stopped for gas at Ferdy's place. I don't imagine that old reprobate would let you go without filling you full of stories."

"How did you know I stopped?"

Salvatore didn't bother to turn around, and she had no choice but to keep up with him. "I have my ways. Bet he told you the one about Mrs. MacInerny going mad when she saw Ethan. And did he tell you about the cows? What few cows were left in the area dried up when Ethan came back here. Or what about the children?"

"The children?" she asked, her voice shaky. *I won't believe this,* she thought. *He's only trying to frighten me.*

"There've been any number of young people who've come out here and never been seen again."

"You're making this up." She told herself she was breathless from all the twisting stairs they'd been climbing, even though she could run six miles without getting winded.

"That's the sort of story that people like Ferdy tell. And they believe it and worse."

"It sounds like something out of the Middle Ages. Why haven't they burned him at the stake?"

"Oh, they'd like to, missy. They would surely like to. They just can't catch him. He's like a phantom. No one sees him and lives to tell the tale."

"Stop it! You're making this up."

Salvatore chuckled, a reassuringly normal sound. "Most of it. Either me or them. One part of it's true, though." They had stopped outside another door, this one made of a different heavy wood, with different hardware. She didn't know how far they'd come; she'd again lost track of the staircases and the sloping passageways.

"What's that?"

He opened the door, illuminating the inky darkness beyond with his candle. "The children really do disappear."

If the other room had been a medieval dungeon, this was more like a castle. The huge bed in the center of the room was on a raised platform, and it dominated even the lofty proportions of the place. The casement windows were set lower in the stone walls, and this time, there were no bars on them. A tapestry chair and carved chest stood in one corner, and the bed hangings were sumptuous gold and crimson.

She cast a suspicious look at Salvatore as he moved about the room lighting the candelabra that stood at either end. "Are you certain you brought me to the right place?"

"Ethan's orders. He thought you deserved better treatment. That's because he hasn't met you yet. Once you start in on him, you'll be back in the dungeon." Salvatore chuckled, stepping back. "Bathroom's through there, basically the same as the other one. I've ordered you some clothes, but they won't arrive until tomorrow. In the meantime, there are some things in the chest that should help.''

''You ordered me some clothes? How? This place doesn't come equipped with a telephone, does it? And why should you bother? I'm only staying until my car can be pulled out.''

''You're staying as long as Ethan says you are. And we have a dedicated fax machine. Federal Express will make the delivery.''

''Then I can get a ride back with them....''

''Bring it up with Ethan.''

''I will if I just get a chance to see the man.''

''Now that's not likely to happen.''

Meg's frustration level was reaching mammoth proportions, overcoming even her nervousness. She stomped over and plopped herself down on the bed, ignoring its inviting comfort. ''What do you mean?''

''I mean Ethan doesn't like people looking at him, you should have figured that out by now. If and when he decides to talk to you, it will probably be in darkness.''

For a moment, she was speechless. ''If? What are the alternatives?''

''One, that you stay here until he changes his mind. Or two, he'll send you away and concentrate on crucifying your father. If I were you, I'd hope he chooses number one.''

''I hope he chooses to stop this melodrama and talk with me tonight.''

''That's also possible. I'll let you know when I bring you your supper.''

''I don't want any.''

''I'm bringing it anyway. Just relax, girly. At least you've got plenty of books to read.'' He gestured to the small bookcase she'd almost overlooked, stacked with paperback novels. The room was too dark for her to read the titles, but that was at least a minor comfort if she were forced to keep waiting.

"I'll be back." He'd already pulled out that heavy ring of keys as he headed to the door.

"You're not locking me in again," she said, her voice rising in panic.

"For your own safety, girly. This can be a dangerous place, and we don't want you wandering where you don't belong."

He'd already locked the door by the time she reached it, and the heavy wood muffled her cries, muffled the heavy tread of his footsteps as he walked away.

"SHE'S WORSE THAN THE townspeople," Salvatore announced in disgust when he stepped back into the darkened room.

Ethan Winslowe didn't move. "No one's worse than the townspeople."

"She's just as gullible."

"That's because we're going out of our way to frighten her. The good people of Oak Grove have come up with horror stories on their own. We're doing our best to frighten Meg Carey witless," Ethan observed dispassionately. "It's working very well, too." He glanced over at the monitor. The candlelit room was murky, but he could see her leaning against the door, for a moment looking abject. He didn't want to see her cowed. If she were beaten too easily, he'd have to let her go. And he was feeling more alive than he had in a long, long time. "Feed her," he said. "Then bring her to me at midnight. Make sure she knows what time it is. I'll see her in the computer room."

"She won't eat."

"We'll simply have to convince her."

"Ethan." Salvatore's voice was troubled. "Are you sure you ought to be doing this? I mean, she hasn't done anyone any harm as far as we know. Her father's a crook, but we don't know that she's anything more than a loving daughter."

"I don't imagine she is," Ethan said in his slow, almost dreamy voice. "Are you feeling sorry for her, old friend?"

"A little. I don't think she deserves to be frightened."

"I should let her go?" He asked the question very softly. "Say the word, Sally, and I'll release her."

Salvatore shook his head. "That's up to you. She came here for a reason—you might as well hear her out. But then you should let her go back home."

"And if I don't want to?"

"I don't understand why not."

Ethan moved his head a fraction, to stare at the television monitor. She'd moved from the door, across the room to stare out the casement windows. She was wearing the clothes she'd come in, a baggy pink cotton sweater, a long, loose skirt, mudsplattered highheeled shoes. He liked her better in the terry robe. He'd like her even better in nothing at all. "Let's just say I'm enjoying being a voyeur," he said.

"Ethan..."

"Don't worry about it. She'll be safe from my evil designs. In a week, she'll be back in Chicago, safe and sound."

"A week. You're planning to keep her here that long? We might run into trouble when the workmen arrive on Monday."

"The house is big enough. Don't worry so much, Sally. For now, I feel like playing with fire. I don't even mind if I get burned."

Salvatore shook his head, knowing the gesture was unseen in the darkened room where his old friend stared at the woman on the television monitor. "I'm not worried about singed fingers, Ethan. I'm worried about the place burning down around us."

"You worry too much. I promise you I won't hurt her. I probably won't even scare her as much as you have. I just need a little distraction. It's been a long time since Ruth."

"Ethan..."

"Bring her to me at midnight, Sally. Who knows, she might even be able to convince me to let her go." She turned from the window, pushing her hair back from her face, and he watched the nervous parting of her lips, the rise and fall of her breasts beneath the baggy sweater. "Maybe," he murmured.

IT HAD TAKEN ALL HER willpower to resist the tray Salvatore brought her. True to his word, he was a good cook, if she could judge by the devastating smells coming from the tray. Roast chicken and rice with baby peas, and something that looked and smelled like lemon cheesecake. He'd even brought her a glass of wine, something she would have killed for in her current strung-out state of mind.

She sat in the baronial-style chair and stared at the tray with mute antipathy. It made no sense, her refusal to accept food from their hands. It wasn't as if she suspected them of trying to poison her. After all, why should they? Drugged wine she wouldn't put past them, but that, too, was unlikely.

No, it wasn't from any fear of the ambrosial smells that had issued from the contents of the heavy silver tray before they cooled. It was an absurd fancy based on some Greek legend she'd read. Someone—was it Persephone?—had been kidnapped by the Lord of Darkness and stolen down to hell. She would have been just fine and dandy if she hadn't succumbed and eaten six pomegranate seeds. When someone finally showed up to rescue her, she'd already sealed her fate. For each pomegranate seed, she had to spend one month a year in the dark kingdom.

Of course, there were those who said the eating of pomegranate seeds was merely a sexual allusion. Persephone had given in to the powerful sexual lure of the Prince of Darkness, not her desire for pomegranates.

As for Meg Carey, she wasn't interested in either food or sex. Not that she envisaged the mysterious Ethan Winslowe as even remotely a sexual creature. Nevertheless, she was determined to keep her distance, to accept nothing from him she wasn't forced to accept, such as a bed for the night.

She fell asleep in her clothes as the night drew closer around her. She'd finished her book, then discovered that the only books the room held were Stephen King novels. She was already spooked enough—the last thing she needed was to read horror novels before she tried to sleep.

Even so, her dreams were bizarre, erotic and frightening. X'n*d, the lizard-blob hero of the book she'd finished, was a dead ringer for Ethan Winslowe. He was sitting in the middle of a muddy green pool, tubes and wires hooked up to him, keeping him alive, and he was beckoning to her. Sort of like Jabba the Hutt in one of those Star Wars movies, something huge and soft and evil that drew the unwitting heroine in.

And then he shifted, away from the amorphous mass into something leaner, more dangerous, with lizard scales that were surprisingly warm to the touch. And she was touching him, staring up into yellow eyes as she ran her fingers across the fine scales....

"Wake up, girly," a voice broke through. "He's ready to see you."

Meg didn't move. She'd slept so soundly, she hadn't heard Salvatore open the creaking door, slept so soundly that he was able to materialize beside her bed. "Go away," she said, pulling the heavy damask cover over her. "I'm not ready to see him."

"I'm glad you're enjoying our hospitality. It might be a hell of a long time before you get another chance."

She'd already accepted the fact that she had no choice in the matter. She pulled herself upright, pushing her hair out of her face, and glared at Salvatore. The candles around the room had burned down low, and several of them had guttered out. She felt rumpled and sleepy and bad tempered, and suddenly, oddly afraid. She no longer felt like some Greek maiden abducted into hell. She felt like someone approaching a Gorgon. One look, and she'd be turned to stone. Or, like the fabled Mrs. MacInerny, she'd go stark staring mad.

Ridiculous, she chided herself. The contents of the bookcase should have tipped her off. Salvatore and his employer clearly read too many Stephen King novels. She wasn't going to let them terrorize her, she simply wasn't.

"All right, I'm coming," she said grumpily, squinting at her watch. Her reliable Rolex, a present from her father on her twenty-fifth birthday, had inexplicably stopped working. All of a piece, she thought wearily. "What time is it, anyway?"

"Midnight," Salvatore said. He was holding a candlestick in one meaty hand, and his face looked shadowed and positively evil.

"What else? I'll be ready in a moment."

"He doesn't like to be kept waiting."

"I don't like to be kept prisoner," Meg shot back. "He can wait while I use the bathroom, can't he?"

"Maybe."

"He'll have to." She slammed the door behind her. For a moment, she leaned against the closed door whose hook held a terry robe that was a twin to the one in her dungeon. What was this place, the Gothic Hilton, she thought with a misplaced giggle.

Cool water didn't do much to help her wake up. Brushing her hair into a semblance of order didn't do much to restore her state of mind, and she wondered why she was doing it. Did she want to impress Ethan Winslowe? She wanted to murder Ethan Winslowe, and she had every intention of telling him just that. Maybe. Still, it didn't do a woman any harm to feel confident, she thought, pinching some color into her pale cheeks and wishing she'd brought her makeup with her. At least her lashes were naturally dark. Otherwise, she'd look like a ghost. A fitting resident for this house of horrors.

Salvatore was exactly where she'd left him, looking bored. His hangdog eyes surveyed her improvements and he smirked. Clearly he'd noticed everything she'd done, and she wished to heavens she'd left herself looking like something the cat dragged in. "Take me to your leader," she said flippantly.

She watched with sudden surprise as he unlocked the bedroom door. Why had he bothered to relock it in the first place? And the noise of the key in the lock, the sound of the door creaking open, was surprisingly loud in the room. How could she, normally a light sleeper, have slept through that? Unless he'd come in some other way.

She glanced over her shoulder as he stepped into the corridor. There were no other doors in the room besides the one leading to the bathroom. There was no way he could have gotten in. Was there?

"Don't fall behind," Salvatore warned. "I might have a hard time finding you."

She started after him, wishing she'd dared to leave her high heels behind. She needed every inch of support she could muster, but her ankles ached and her feet hurt, and if her two previous journeys were any example, she had a long hike ahead of her.

"Don't you believe in flashlights around here?" she questioned crossly, scurrying to keep up with him.

"Don't need 'em. I probably wouldn't even use a candle if you weren't with me. Rats don't bother me."

"Rats?" She didn't even care that her voice quaked.

"Every old place has 'em. As a matter of fact, I think Oak Grove and its environs have more than their share. Don't worry about it—they're more afraid of you than you are of them."

"I doubt that."

"Besides, Ethan keeps them well fed. Rats are only dangerous when they're starving."

"He keeps them well fed?" she shrieked, and her voice bounced off the stone walls and echoed down the dark passageway.

"Not so loud, girly. Ethan learned long ago that if you can't change something, get rid of something, then you accept it with good grace. It's a lesson you could learn."

"Sure. Next time I'm infested with rats, I'll buy rat food."

Salvatore only chuckled, turning a corner and heading into another part of the house. An electrified part. The wall sconces were dimly watted light bulbs, reassuring Meg that there were no rats keeping her company.

And then they were in darkness again, a darkness so thick that Salvatore's candle could barely penetrate it. "Watch your step," he muttered as they started down a steeply ramped passageway. Ramps again, she thought. Ethan Winslowe must be bound to a wheelchair.

"I can't see."

"Feel your way along the wall," Salvatore suggested irritably.

She did just that, almost afraid of what she might touch. But the walls were smooth there, plastered and solid, and she kept her left hand running along one side, needing the security.

At that point, she needed all the help she could get. She couldn't rid herself of the notion that someone, something was watching her in the dark. Salvatore's broad back was to her, so it couldn't be him. And no one could see in such inky blackness, could they? The only other resident of the house was Ethan Winslowe himself, and she expected to see him tied up to life support systems somewhere in the center of this monstrosity.

"How bad is Mr. Winslowe?" she asked suddenly, unable to stand the uncertainty any longer.

Salvatore stopped still in the hallway, an unwilling chuckle rumbling out of him. "Depends on what you mean," he replied, turning to look at her.

She was glad it was too dark to see her face flush. "I mean, how bad is his condition? Is it life threatening?"

"That's a matter of opinion. What do you think is wrong with him?"

"I'm asking you."

"Well," said Salvatore, "I ain't talking. You'll have to ask the man himself. If you dare." And he started onward at a faster clip than ever.

She hesitated a moment too long. He turned a corner ahead of her and she was momentarily plunged into darkness.

She bit down the scream that threatened to bubble up. He'd come back for her, he had to. If she just held very still . . .

It was like a soft breeze. A touch of warmth, of spring air, a breath, a caress. It ruffled through her hair, across her clothing, touching but not touching, more a promise of touching. The feel of warmth, insubstantial but real, and no threat at all. She closed her eyes in the darkness, trying to draw the odd feelings within her trembling body, and then as swiftly as it had come, it disappeared and she was alone in a dark, haunted, cold hallway.

The light from Salvatore's candle reappeared. "Are you just going to stand around in the darkness?" he demanded irritably. "Ethan doesn't like to be kept waiting."

"I—I think I'd rather go back to my room," Meg said in a weak voice. That brief, otherworldly encounter had left her more shaken than she would have imagined.

"Sorry, that's not an option. We're here."

"Where?"

"Around the corner. He's waiting."

He could damned well wait, for all she cared, Meg thought. She wanted to get out of there, away from the suffocating darkness, away from rats and danger and deformed creatures of the night. Though she wouldn't have minded feeling that almost-supernatural caress once more.

"I'm coming," she said between gritted teeth, following the light.

A door stood open in the next corridor. A pale blue light was emanating from beyond, and she could hear the unmistakable noise of machinery. Computers, perhaps. Life-support systems. Oxygen tents? Just how bad was Ethan Winslowe?

Salvatore moved out of the way, and Megan paused in the doorway, for one moment afraid to go on. The room beyond was dark, warm, with a myriad of tiny lights blinking from various machines. In the center of the room was a tall chair, almost a throne, and in that chair, in the darkness, was a motionless, shadowy figure.

"Come into my parlor," she muttered beneath her breath.

Whatever Ethan Winslowe's physical limitations, they didn't involve deafness. "Said the spider to the fly," a slow, deep, rich voice issued from that chair. Unwillingly, she stepped into the room. And Salvatore closed the door behind her, plunging her into darkness.

Chapter Four

I am not afraid, Meg told herself fiercely, not moving into the darkness. The door was solid behind her back, and she didn't bother reaching out to see whether it was locked or not. She'd already learned that Ethan Winslowe and his henchman were damnably thorough.

"Are you afraid of me, Ms. Carey?" the deep, rich voice mocked. "Why don't you come closer?"

That was enough to straighten Meg's backbone. "I'm not afraid of anyone," she said, sounding more confident than she felt.

"Then why don't you come and sit down? Salvatore's brought you another tray of food since you didn't touch the earlier one. Why don't you eat something, and we can discuss why you're here."

"I'm not hungry," she said, taking a step into the darkness. "And you know perfectly well why I'm here."

"Sit down, Ms. Carey." He didn't raise his voice, but suddenly Meg decided it might be better if she did as he ordered. She moved forward, hand outstretched until it encountered a straight-backed chair in front of a wide table. She could smell the food and her stomach cramped in longing as she sat, pushing the plate away from her.

"I'm not hungry," she said again, peering at him in the darkness. She couldn't see much at all. Ethan Winslowe was sitting in some sort of chair that seemed to resemble a throne. He was in darkness, a shadowy, menacing figure, and she heard the faint, gulping sound that probably came from a respirator.

"It wouldn't do you any good to starve yourself," he said in a more agreeable voice. "How do you expect to escape if you haven't got any stamina?"

"I'm not going to have to escape. You're going to be reasonable and call me a rental car so that I can drive out of this godforsaken countryside."

"Godforsaken it is. But I don't have a telephone."

"Then you can fax me a rental car," she said somewhat desperately. Suddenly she felt very hot. All day long, she'd been shivering in one stone-clad room and another, but this cocoon of darkness was like a steam bath. Invalids needed heat, didn't they? If only he'd let her open a window. Though this dark room probably didn't even have windows. Didn't Salvatore say Winslowe hated sunlight?

"You aren't leaving until I say you can go, Ms. Carey," he said, very gently. "And I'm not ready to let you."

Maybe if she ate something she'd feel better, she thought. She was feeling light-headed and dizzy, probably from disorientation and lack of sleep. She certainly wasn't going to pass out in front of this dark nemesis, but she didn't feel capable of making the long trek back up to her room without something in her stomach. At least she had the dubious security of knowing that a wheelchair couldn't maneuver the long, winding stairs to her turret room. Once she was up there, she'd be safe from the man in front of her.

She took a bite of chicken, eating slowly, stalling for time. "What do you want from me, Mr. Winslowe?"

"Call me Ethan. And I believe I'll call you Meg. After all, we're going to be together for a while."

She ignored the taunt. "What do you want from me?" she asked again.

"Isn't it more a question of what you want from me? I wasn't the one who showed up uninvited. Where's your father? Cowering back in Chicago, hoping you'll pull his fat from the fire?"

"My father made a mistake. People do that, you know. People who don't sit in the middle of some crazy mansion passing judgment."

"I have a reason to sit in the middle of my crazy mansion."

"I'm sure you do." She refused to let herself feel guilty. The man in the shadows in front of her might be a poor invalid, but he was also a brilliant, vindictive man who was, for all intents and purposes, holding her prisoner. "But what right do you have to pass judgment?"

"The right of a man whose reputation was damaged by your father. The right of the injured party for revenge."

"I would have thought that the men who were killed were the injured parties."

"He told you that much, did he? What else did he tell you?"

Meg ate another bite of chicken. What had smelled so fiendishly delicious earlier now tasted like paper. And why was her head pounding so abominally; why did her throat feel raw? She reached blindly for the glass beside her plate and took too large a gulp of wine. "He told me he made a mistake. He was worried and upset and not thinking clearly." The rawness in her throat reached into her voice, and she realized she was pleading. "For God's sake, my mother had just died. Can't you make allowances for human frailty? Don't you realize how guilty he feels? How much he's suffered?"

"I know just how guilty he feels. How much he's suffered." Ethan Winslowe's voice was icy cold in the overheated room. Meg could feel the sweat forming at her temples, between her breasts, and yet she was shivering.

"Then why can't you leave him alone?"

"I will leave him alone."

For a moment, she couldn't believe she'd heard him correctly. She shook her head, a useless physical gesture to try to drive the fogginess away. "What?"

"I said I'll leave him alone. As long as you stay."

This time she knew she'd understood him. "You can't be serious."

"Completely. As long as you stay here, I'll leave your father in peace. The moment you leave or the moment I tire of you, then I'll destroy him."

The silence filled the inky black room. Once more she heard the watery gurgle that had to come from his respirator and the tiny little blips and beeps from the machines that were probably keeping him alive. If she only had the determination, the sheer cold-blooded courage, she could probably knock him over and rip out his life-support systems before Salvatore could return. And then Winslowe would be no threat at all.

But she could scarcely kill in cold blood, even someone who was clearly deranged and dangerous. "Then you give me no choice," she said in a deceptively calm voice.

"No choice at all."

She steeled herself, wondering exactly how far she was going to have to go to save her father. To save the company that so many people depended on. "And exactly what will my duties entail?"

Dead silence met her question, and then he laughed, a dry, eerie sound. "Don't tell me you're imagining I expect you to be my bed partner? You do have strange fantasies, Ms. Carey. You strike me as someone far too young and far too inexperienced to be able to deal with someone in my...condition. I don't want sexual acrobatics. I want...companionship." There was an odd note in his voice, one Meg was too angry to define.

"I don't feel very companionable."

"Perhaps that was the wrong word. I want distraction. Your hatred and distrust is probably far more entertaining than an effort to please me. I'll make a bargain with you. You can try to escape, and if, by any unbelievable set of circumstances, you manage to get away, I'll leave your father alone."

Again that ominous gurgle. "It's a bargain, then," she said faintly, wishing she felt stronger, angrier. "I'll despise you, insult you and do my damnedest to escape. And you'll leave my father alone."

"A bargain," he agreed, and she was feeling ill enough to imagine the distant trace of concern in his voice. "Are you feeling all right?"

"Of course not!" she snapped, rising on unsteady feet. She couldn't eat another bite—she knew she'd throw up if she tried. "I'm being held hostage by a madman who's intent on destroying my father. It's enough to put a girl off her feed."

Again he laughed, that dry, rusty little sound. "Salvatore will take you back to your tower. He could probably manage to come up with something to help you sleep. He has all sorts of interesting abilities."

"An aspirin will do me just fine," she said.

"Why?"

"Why?" she echoed, furious. "Because I have a headache. This place is either too damned hot or too damned cold, and I want..." She let the words trail off. She was about to say, in a miserable little girl's voice, that she wanted to go home. But she wasn't going to show weakness to this vast, unseen creature of the night. She wasn't going to show vulnerability to anyone.

"The rooms are climate controlled." Ethan Winslowe's voice came out of the dark. "Ask Salvatore to adjust the temperature for you. What else was it you were going to say? What else did you want?"

Maybe if she asked him, begged him, he'd let her go. Maybe if she cried...

"You aren't going to be tiresome are you?" he continued before she could decide. "I do hate weeping women. I warned you—I need to be kept amused if I'm going to let your father alone. The moment you begin to bore me, I'll go after him and bring him down."

"You're a monster," she said, her voice low and raw and furious. "A sick, evil creature, and if I have to spend another moment in this hothouse mausoleum with you, I'm going to throw up, probably all over your wheelchair. Call Salvatore and let me go back to your room."

"Not bad for a beginning. You'll have to come up with some better epithets, though, if you're going to be here for a while." The door opened behind her, sending a dim pool of light into the darkened room, one that didn't even begin to reach the man in the middle of the room. "Salvatore, give Ms. Carey whatever drug she desires and check the climate control of the turret room. She seems to be feeling a bit feverish. And give her the key so that she can lock herself in.''

"At least I don't have to worry about you bothering me," she snapped.

"Why ever not?" He sounded genuinely curious.

"There's no way a wheelchair could make it up those long steps, and I know construction well enough to know there's no elevator in that tower."

"True enough. Your sexual fantasies will have to wait to be fulfilled." Again that gurgle of sound.

"I'll jump out of the tower first." She wouldn't do any such thing, but in her dazed condition, it sounded reasonably dramatic.

"There are bars on the windows, Megan," he said very gently. "Don't worry about it. I've told you, you're safe."

She headed out the door without bothering to say another word, almost faint with relief at leaving him. Until she heard his soft, rich voice follow her into the dimly lit hallway.

"You're safe," he said again. "For now."

ETHAN WINSLOWE SAT VERY still, watching Megan stumble away behind Salvatore's hulking figure, and his eyes were narrowed in his beloved darkness, filled with a rare feeling of compunction. She was right. Who the hell was he to play God, to sit in judgment? Particularly since he was lying to her. He had no intention of sparing her father, not if she presented herself to him wrapped in nothing more than a satin ribbon.

He found himself smiling wryly at that enticing image. And then he moved, bringing his glass of whiskey and water to his mouth and draining the final drops, the faint watery sound carrying in the darkness. He'd sat and drank and watched her, his night-attuned eyes able to see far more clearly than hers could. He could see the whiteness of her face, the slightly desperate softness around her mouth, the anger in her eyes. She was strong and tough, willing to fight him on every level. He was looking forward to it, to keeping her fully busy and involved with him while he brought her father to his knees.

She hadn't looked well, but he assumed it was simply nerves and exhaustion. However, she didn't look the nervous type, and he'd known from his steady, unblinking perusal of the monitor that she'd slept away most of the afternoon and evening.

And the room was, if anything, cool, not the hothouse she accused it of being. He certainly didn't fancy having a sick female on his hands. She wouldn't be nearly as entertaining.

The door opened and Salvatore filled it. "She's settled for the night, Ethan. But she doesn't look well."

Ethan turned to the bank of monitors, switching them on. Meg Carey had collapsed across the high bed, kicking off her shoes but leaving her clothes on. Her eyes were shut, her breathing seemed labored, and even on the black-and-white monitor, he could see the flush mantling her cheeks. "Hell and damnation," Ethan said, staring. "She does look sick. How inconvenient."

"Then why don't you let her go? You certainly aren't going to let her father off the hook, are you?"

Ethan stared at him. "How long have you known me?"

Salvatore nodded. "Point taken. So I'll ask you again. Why don't you let her go?"

"Because I don't feel like it." With an abrupt motion, Ethan rose, towering over Salvatore's impressive bulk. "Any more questions?"

"What if she needs a doctor?"

"Then we get good Dr. Bailey out here. He should be able to manage without killing her. In the meantime, you can get me another drink."

He could feel Salvatore watching him in the darkness. He'd grown so accustomed to the shadows, he felt more comfortable there, but Sal's compassionate eyes didn't bother him. It was Megan Carey's eyes that bothered him, looking at him clearly through the darkness he trusted she couldn't pierce.

If she was sick, it was an inconvenience, a delay, and nothing else. He'd simply have to be patient. He had plans for her, fascinating plans. He wanted to see the anger in her eyes, he wanted her hatred and fascination.

And he wanted to see what happened when he finally took her.

MEGAN DREAMED AGAIN. Strange, terrible dreams that filled her head with silent screams, filled her heart with terror and pain, filled her body with longings she'd never felt. She kept waking up in the darkness of the tower room, the candles flickering in some obscure draft. She could hear the distant thunder, the steady beat of the rain against the walls of the turret. She lay back, staring up into the darkness, and thought about Ethan Winslowe.

He'd told her if she escaped, he'd leave Reese alone. It was clearly her only option. If only she didn't feel so wretched. Her throat felt swollen, her chest burned, and she alternated between bone chattering cold and a burning fever. Salvatore might have poisoned her food—

she wouldn't have put it past him, except that she had been feeling strange before she'd even touched a morsel.

One thing was clear, she couldn't stay there. She couldn't entrust her safety to the good graces of a maniac. She had to get out of there, and fast. If Winslowe broke his promise and went after her father, Reese would have to fend for himself. She'd done her best for him and gotten into the worst mess of her life. She needed to get out of it as quickly as possible.

She couldn't find her shoes in the candlelit darkness. She couldn't see clearly at all, with her head pounding, her breath rasping in her throat, her chest aching. It didn't matter. It was spring, even in this wretched part of the country. She could go barefoot, she could walk out that long, twisting road. She believed Salvatore when he said nothing but a backhoe would get her car out of the mud. It had been raining off and on since she arrived, and the mud would have only gotten deeper. She'd walk, and keep on walking until she found someone who could help her.

Surely someone in that benighted little nontown of Oak Grove would help her. They hated Ethan Winslowe enough that they should be glad to do him a disservice.

If not, she'd just keep on walking. Not the way she'd come—there hadn't been any sign of civilization along those back roads for hours. But surely up ahead, life must take on some semblance of normalcy. And once she reached a tiny pocket of sanity, she'd never look back.

She vaguely remembered that deep, disembodied voice telling Salvatore to leave the key. It was in the lock, on her side of the thick oak door, and for a moment, she just stared at it, blinking, not quite believing it was going to be so easy.

The turret was deserted, lit by an eerie light that just might possibly be gaslight. She started down, her labored breathing echoing in the darkness, and she had the sudden morbid thought that she might slip and fall, tumbling to her death on these stone stairs. No one would ever find her. Salvatore would get rid of her body, and her father, coward that he was, would probably pretend he had no idea where she'd gone. He'd simply assume Winslowe wouldn't dare turn him in, and everything would be status quo.

It wasn't until she reached the bottom step that she realized how bizarre that particular fantasy was. That her father would countenance her death simply for his own well-being, was beyond being strange. And yet, even if her brain was clear and cool, she wouldn't put it past him.

Once at the bottom of the turret, she hadn't the faintest idea where to go. She'd been taken on too many roundabout journeys to have the faintest sense of direction. She vaguely remembered that Salvatore had taken her to the left when she'd had her audience with the local phantom. She'd head toward the right, toward the sound of rain. As soon as she found a door, or failing that, a window, she'd head out into the night. The sooner she escaped from this bizarre mansion, the better off she'd be.

She almost gave up hope of finding a way out. She must have stumbled for hours in the blinding dark, groping along walls that changed from stone to plaster to wood paneling. The sound of the rain, not far beyond the maze of hallways, was maddening, promising a freedom that seemed unattainable. She found she was weeping, and when her hands touched cool glass, she almost didn't recognize it.

She sank her head against it for a moment, peering into the darkness beyond, into the rain. She had to get out as quickly as possible, the pain in her chest was growing unbearable, the heat was smothering her. She needed the cool rain or she'd die.

She tried to smash her fist against the pane of glass, but it simply bounced off, too weak to shatter it. And then she realized she hadn't stumbled against a window. It was a French door with an ornate latch. A latch that was unlocked.

She fell outside, into the rain, stumbling a few steps before collapsing on some sort of slate terrace. In the inky, water-soaked darkness, she could smell fresh earth and spring flowers. Someone was out there with her, someone was moving across the garden toward her, but she wasn't afraid. It wasn't a wheelchair carrying some vast form of evil, and it wasn't the hulking, villainous Salvatore. The man approaching her was tall, thin and old, moving toward her through the rain oblivious of the downpour.

He knelt beside her and she blinked up at him, into a lined, ancient face and the kindest eyes she'd ever seen. She reached out a hand toward him and tried to say something, but the only sound that came from her throat was a helpless little croak, and her hand touched nothingness.

"Don't try to talk," the old man said, his voice soft and soothing. "I'll go for help."

"Don't leave me," she choked. "Don't let them find me."

"They won't hurt you. I promise, I won't let them hurt you."

What could a frail old man do against the combined forces of evil, she thought wearily. And yet, she believed him. She knew she should get to her feet, but her muscles refused to obey her command. With an almost imperceptible nod, she dropped her head back to the cool, wet slate and closed her eyes.

"ETHAN, SHE'S GONE!" Sal's voice broke through the fitful dozing that gave Ethan what little sleep he enjoyed. He sat up, staring at the bank of monitors in front of him. The turret room was empty, the door left open, her shoes still resting on the floor beside the bed.

He kept himself firmly in check. "She escaped faster than we thought. That fever must have been feigned. She's as adept a liar as her father ever was."

"I don't think so," Salvatore said doubtfully.

"Don't you? I'd think you'd be relieved at this turn of events. You didn't really approve of me keeping her here. And you were right—it wasn't a particularly prudent idea. But since when have I been prudent? It doesn't matter now. We can concentrate on Reese Carey without having his daughter distract me."

"I don't think she was faking it, Ethan. And I don't think we can simply assume she'll make it out of here safely. It's raining cats and dogs, the temperature's below fifty and she's not wearing any shoes or sweater. Not to mention the fact that I think she was sick to begin with."

Ethan stared at him. "What do you expect me to do, ask the townspeople to help?"

Salvatore snorted. "Fat lot of help they'd be. I'm going to go look for her. If I find her, I'll drive her to the airport and get her away from here."

"You won't do any such thing. If she's still here, she's staying."

"Ethan . . ."

He rose, a tall, lean figure in the murky darkness. "I'll find her. You take the Jeep and get Dr. Bailey. If he's drunk, sober him up. If he refuses to come, use your gun. But bring him and whatever medicine he might need."

"You know where she is?"

"Let's say I have a fairly good idea. I also know this place better than anyone, even you. I have a better chance of finding her faster. Go ahead, Sally. If she's as sick as you think she is, we don't have time to waste."

It had been a long time since he'd seen Sally move that quickly. He didn't move for a moment, wondering what he had gotten himself into. He'd taken one look at Meg Carey in one of the ubiquitous television monitors and thrown good sense to the wind.

Salvatore was right; he should let her go. He should make sure Doc Bailey didn't kill her with one of his quack cures, keep out of sight, and the moment she was able to travel, send her on her way. And maybe there was a chance in hell he'd do just that.

He'd been alone for too long, had his own way for too long. He'd started thinking he was some sort of god, some invulnerable ruler of his twisted kingdom. He needed a dose of reality.

But first, he needed to find where Meg Carey had disappeared to. And the very first place he was going to check was Joseph's garden.

THE MAN WHO CAME TO HER IN the darkness wasn't the same man. In the driving rain, she couldn't see his face, but he was younger, stronger. He picked her up in his arms with an effortlessness that made her grimace and curse her extra ten pounds. She opened her mouth to apologize, but the faint croaking sound didn't carry above the wind and rain.

She had no idea who was carrying her into the pitch black house, finding his way with the surefootedness of a night-stalking animal. It wasn't Salvatore—this man was leaner, with deft hands tucking her shivering body against him. Hadn't Salvatore said there were only the two of them in the house? Who, then, was the old man she'd met in the garden? Who was the man carrying her through the inky darkness?

And who the hell cared? She'd never hurt so much in her life. She didn't care if he was Jack the Ripper on his way to fling her from the turret. If it stopped the raging pain in her chest, it would be worth it. All she wanted was peace and safety. And for some odd reason, in the dark stranger's arms, she felt just those feelings. And with an absurd flash of trust, she closed her eyes and surrendered to the darkness that surrounded her.

Chapter Five

Ethan stood in the corner of the turret room, out of range of the candelabra Salvatore had carried up to light old Doc Bailey's way. Doc kept his head turned carefully from the man he knew was watching him. The old drunk knew well enough that he wouldn't go blind or crazy from looking at Ethan Winslowe. He'd been forced to face him enough times to know he'd survive. But like most people, he didn't look forward to the prospect and avoided it at all cost.

Which suited Ethan just fine, he thought with the faintest trace of humor. The fewer people who wanted to intrude on his privacy, on his physical space, the better.

Except for the woman who lay on that high bed, her breathing labored, her color, even in the candlelight, ghastly. She'd intruded, unannounced, unwelcome, and he was damned if he was going to let her go easily. Even in death.

"She's got pneumonia," Doc said, and it was lucky for him his voice wasn't slurred. "Expect we got it in time, but she ought to have a chest X-ray."

"She's staying here," Ethan said, and Bailey didn't turn in his direction. He wasn't a man to put up an argument. He'd made a desultory request for Ethan to leave when he'd examined his patient, but Ethan had flatly refused. He'd stood in his corner, watching, as the old man thumped her chest, listened to her heartbeat through the lacy peach-colored bra.

"Penicillin works best in cases like these. Problem is, I don't have the adult dose with me."

"I thought Sal warned you . . ."

"He did, he did." Bailey managed to sneak a sheepish glance in the general direction of Ethan's feet. "But I didn't have any on hand. Whole town's been going through the flu."

"Damn the whole town."

"I brought some kid's stuff. She'll have to drink half a bottle at a time, and it tastes like some sort of candy, but it should do the trick."

"It better, old man," Ethan said.

Bailey looked up for a moment, then veered his eyes away in shame and horror. "I haven't made a mistake in a long time."

"No. I've made sure of that. But when you do, it's a real killer, isn't it?"

Bailey didn't say another word. With Salvatore's help, he tipped half a bottle of thick pink medicine down Meg's throat, then set her back against the pillows. She opened her eyes for a moment, trying to focus them, but she didn't look at the two men hovering over her bed. Instead, her gaze went directly to the figure standing tall in the shadows.

It was too dark to see his face from the bed; he'd made sure of that. And even if she could, she'd probably only remember as a fever-induced nightmare. She shut her eyes again, drifting off.

"She needs to get out of those wet clothes," Bailey announced then, keeping his head down. "And she's going to need some nursing. I could send someone out—"

"I'll take care of it." Ethan's voice was low and implacable, and Doc Bailey nodded nervously.

"Maybe later. I know someone—"

"I'll take care of it. Take the doctor home, Sal."

Bailey practically ran from the room without a backward glance at his patient. Ethan found himself half hoping the man would take a tumble down the twisting stone steps and break his miserable neck. Only the inconvenience of having to explain kept him from moving forward and giving the doctor a little push.

"You'll be all right?" Salvatore paused in the doorway.

Ethan glanced over at the woman on the bed. "We'll be fine."

"Ethan . . ."

He didn't take his gaze from Meg's pale, pale face. "Yes?"

There was a pause. "Nothing," said Sal. And a moment later, they were alone.

MEG COULDN'T REMEMBER when the fear and anger faded. Maybe when the pain in her chest got so bad she didn't have room for anything else. Maybe when the two men found her, the old, gentle one going for help, the younger, stronger one keeping her safe in the darkened turret.

Night shifted into day, the rainy shadows filling the room. Strong, deft hands were caring for her, sponging off her fevered body, smoothing away her sweat-drenched hair, pouring that sickly sweet medicine down her throat until she thought she'd gag. She'd tried to open her eyes, but the darkness in the room made focusing close to impossible. She knew he was there, sitting beside the bed, standing at the window, pacing the floor as she struggled for breath. She knew he was there and she was at peace.

She didn't wonder about the monster downstairs in the bowels of the poisonous old building. She didn't wonder about Salvatore or her father or her trip to Europe and freedom. For the time being, she was content to drift in a fevered haze, knowing that the dark stranger would watch over her.

There was a time, when the room darkened into a thick, smothering cocoon of blackness, when she knew she was going to die. It was a strange thought, to die in such an odd place, away from all who loved and cared for her. But she wasn't alone. Even through the all-encompassing darkness, she could see him, sitting by her bed, as insubstantial as a shadow, watching over her.

The old man came, too, when the other was asleep. He seemed to drift through walls, ghostlike and ethereal. Between the two of them, it was surprising she'd survived this far. But there was nothing insubstantial about the dark stranger's hands on her body, holding her as she coughed and choked, pouring that sickly sweet medicine down her throat.

She lay in the bed, so hot she could scarcely bear it, her chest on fire, as she listened to the thunder and lightning outside the turret windows. She was neither awake nor asleep, and she could feel herself floating toward death. Except that she wasn't floating, she was being carried along by a rip tide that she fought against, struggled against, kicking at the covers that were smothering her, kicking at the thickness of the air that couldn't penetrate her lungs.

She felt her body being scooped up, and for a moment, she fought, afraid that death had come to claim her.

"Be still," his voice hissed in her ear, and she knew she was safe. It was her caretaker, her savior, holding her trembling body high against his hard chest as he carried her to the casement window.

He kicked it open, and for a brief moment, she wondered whether he planned to throw her out onto the slate terrace far below. No, he wouldn't do that. He'd jump with her, she thought hazily.

The cool rain whipped through the open window, bedewing her face, the chilly breeze was like needles, icing its way into her body. But it was reaching her lungs, desperately needed breath, and she gulped it in greedily.

Another streak of lightning sliced the darkness in front of her and she looked up at the man holding her as he was illuminated for one brief moment, and he looked like a phantom from hell. In that short flash, she saw only one side of his face, and that was possessed of a beauty that was positively unearthly, a fallen angel gone to rule in hell. He seemed to have no other half to his face at all.

And then the room was pitch dark, the wet wind from the open window guttering the candles that had provided the only illumination. She was alone in the darkness with a monster, and she should have been screaming and struggling in panic.

It took all her limited strength, but she lifted her hand, touching the loose white shirt he wore, clinging to it as she sank her head back against his shoulder. That small gesture of trust, of acceptance, was all she could make, but it was enough. She could feel the faint lessening of the tension that wired his body.

He managed to drag a chair over to the window, sinking into it as he tucked her in his lap. "You need another dose of this stuff," he said in his low, beautiful voice, a seductive voice to match the seductive beauty of his half face. He tipped the thick medicine down her throat and she swallowed obediently, leaning back against him.

"Tastes like bubble gum," she croaked, and he bent his head closer. He had long, silky hair, and it brushed against her mouth.

"What did you say?" he asked, his low voice urgent.

"I said the medicine tastes like bubble gum," she repeated patiently, every word a painful struggle, one she was determined to make.

"I've never tasted bubble gum," the dark stranger murmured. "What does it taste like?"

She could no longer see anything but his vague outline in the darkness, feel the strength of him beneath her weak body. "Try it," she suggested, meaning the bottle of medicine.

He could see her clearly in the blackness, she knew that. His eyes were accustomed to the darkness, and he could see every nuance of expression. "I think I will," he said softly. And he put his mouth on hers.

If she'd expected anything at all, it was a light, paternal feathering of her lips. But she hadn't expected it, and his mouth didn't brush hers. It covered hers, opening her soft, dry lips against his as he kissed her with a leisurely thoroughness, as if he had the whole night, the whole of his life, to learn her mouth.

The burning in her chest was fading, replaced by a burning lower, in the pit of her stomach, a crazy longing that was as ridiculous as this entire situation. Common sense didn't help. She was being seduced by the night, by the man, by her own sickness, and if she had an ounce of strength, she would have kissed him back.

He lifted his head, inches away from hers, and she could have sworn he was smiling. ''That's what bubble gum tastes like?''

She couldn't answer. She wanted him to kiss her again. She was so hot—she wanted him to strip off her clothes and lay her down on that high, soft bed. She wanted him to lie beside her. He was so strong, so invincible that not even the darkness troubled him. But she couldn't tell him that. She could do nothing but lean against him, pressing her face against the soft white shirt and the bone and muscle beneath it.

''You're going to live,'' he said, his voice fierce. ''You're not going to leave me. I'm not going to let you go.''

She'd heard those words before, and knew that somehow Ethan Winslowe was holding her. Ethan Winslowe had kissed her. Ethan Winslowe was keeping her alive. ''I'm going to live,'' she agreed, her voice no more than a thread of sound, as an unutterable weariness began to wash away the last remnants of consciousness. ''I'm not going to leave you,'' she whispered. And then the darkness closed in completely, as she gave in.

ETHAN DIDN'T BOTHER trying to relight the candles after he set Megan's frail body down on the bed. He didn't need them to see her, and the wind would just blow them out. He stood over her, watching carefully. Her skin was cooler now, her temperature dropping. It had dropped before, and risen higher again, but somehow he knew that this time it was finally on its way down for good. She'd passed the crisis. Despite everything, she was going to make it.

I'm not going to leave you, she'd said. Words spoken in fever, in sickness, in gratitude. She hadn't known what she was saying. And she most certainly hadn't known to whom, to what, she was saying them. She hadn't known he had every intention of holding her to that promise.

No one had ever said that to him before. He'd never wanted it, not since he'd been seven years old and finally accepted his mother's unwillingness to look at his face.

But he wanted it this time. Wanted it so much, with such a fierce possessiveness that nothing was going to stop him. Nothing was going to take Meg Carey away from him.

Ethan wondered for one brief moment whether he'd finally gone over the edge. Whether the lifetime of isolation had finally turned him into the madman the townspeople believed him to be. One look at a woman and he was ready to risk his safety, privacy, everything, just to keep her with him.

He didn't know her, had scarcely talked with her. While pretty enough, she was no ravishing beauty to obsess him so. And yet, he could hardly force himself to leave her side. And the thought of her leaving his house at all was a torment he couldn't have imagined.

His obsession made no sense, but it existed. He needed her, more than he'd ever needed anyone, and he wasn't about to be noble or self-sacrificing. He needed her, he wanted her and he was going to have her. And no one and nothing was going to get her away from him until he was ready to release her.

He heard Sal's heavy approach. He knew the disapproval that was radiating from his old friend, and he told himself he should care, should try to explain. But how could he explain when he didn't even understand it himself?

"How's she doing?" Sal asked, coming up beside the bed and staring down in the darkness at the pale figure lying there.

Sal's night vision wasn't nearly as good as Ethan's, but even so, Ethan leaned over and flipped the sheet over her lightly-dressed body. He didn't want anyone else looking at her, even in total darkness. "She's better," he said. "I think her fever's finally coming down."

"Ethan . . ."

"Don't ask it, Sally. Don't even hint it."

"Do you know what you're doing?" his friend asked finally. "Do you know everything you're risking?"

"Yes."

"Then there's nothing more to be said."

"Nothing more," Ethan agreed, staring down at Meg's faintly parted lips. They were slightly bruised looking from his kiss. He hadn't realized he'd kissed her that hard. "Do me a favor, Sal," he said in a meditative voice.

"Anything."

"Get me some bubble gum."

MEG DIDN'T KNOW HOW MUCH later she finally awakened. Hours or days or weeks. Sometime during the darkness, the men had left her, the old man who guarded her, the younger man who wanted her. When she finally awoke, the turret room was flooded with sunlight and she was alone. Or so she thought.

"You're looking better," a woman's voice said, and the sound was so unexpected that Meg could do nothing but stare. The woman who approached the bed was middle-aged, a plump, pretty woman with a maternal air about her that radiated comfort. "Doc Bailey thought you might be surfacing about now, but it seemed to take forever. How are you feeling?"

Meg didn't say a word for a moment, considering first her chest, where the tight burning had faded to a dull ache, then her aching joints and terrible headache. "Ghastly," she said finally in her croaking voice. "I must be getting better."

The woman grinned. "That's the ticket. Let me ring Salvatore and he'll bring you some broth. Doc said you could try to get some food down, if you felt like it."

"Who are you?"

The woman whirled around. "Didn't I introduce myself? My name's Ruth Wilkins. I've been brought in to nurse you back to health."

"Where is he?"

"Who?"

"The man who was here?"

For a moment, Ruth's face creased in confusion. "Doc Bailey? Salvatore?"

"No. Him." Meg didn't know whether she was imagining the wary expression on Ruth's face.

"You don't mean Mr. Winslowe, do you?" Ruth asked carefully. "He wouldn't come up here."

Meg shook her head, more as an effort to clear it than as a negation. "I don't mean him. I mean the dark man."

Ruth's expression closed off completely. "Must have been a fever dream, dearie. The only people who've been here are Salvatore and Doc Bailey, and Doc's only been here twice. No one else lives here. I'm just a day worker myself, brought in to help take care of you...."

"What about the old man?"

Ruth's expression of uneasiness grew even more marked. "There are no old men around here."

"There's a gardener. At least, I think he was..."

"Don't talk about it," Ruth said firmly, shoving a thermometer into Meg's mouth. "It was just a fever dream. Trust me, there are no young dark men, no old men wandering around in the garden. Just Winslowe and Salvatore. Now you just lie back and rest, let the thermometer do its work, and I'll find you something to put in your stomach. It's been five days since you've eaten anything."

The thermometer dropped from Meg's mouth, rolled off the bed and shattered on the stone floor. "Five days? I've been sick for five days? What's the date?"

"Thursday, April 28. Why?"

Her plane had left for Europe three days ago, left without her. "No reason," Meg mumbled.

"Well," Ruth said briskly, "you've had a close call, make no mistake about that. You're lucky, that's what. The nearest hospital's over ninety miles away, and it's not much of a facility to begin with. You were better off here, where you could be properly looked after."

"Were you looking after me?" Meg asked, sinking back against the pillows. She already knew the answer. This woman hadn't been bustling around her darkened room, filling it with energy and bright chatter.

To her credit the woman didn't lie. "Only recently, as you've begun to come out of it. Let me get you your medicine, and then I'll see about some food." She produced a bottle of bright pink medicine, poured half of it into a glass and handed it to Meg. "Drink it all down, dearie. This stuff may taste like candy, but it saved your life."

"Bubble gum," Meg whispered.

"Beg pardon?"

"It tastes like bubble gum." She remembered now, remembered his mouth on hers, tasting the medicine. Remembered his hands on her body, holding her when she shook from chills, soothing her when she was burning up. "When you come back, you can answer some questions."

Ruth paused at the door. "I don't think so."

"Why not?"

"Because I don't really know anything. I don't know why you're here or how long you'll be staying."

"I don't want to know about me. I want to know about him."

"No one talks about Ethan Winslowe."

"Why not?"

Ruth looked nonplussed for a moment. "We simply don't. Most people are too afraid of what he might do if he heard they were gossiping about him."

"You aren't most people. You aren't afraid of him," Meg said with sudden shrewdness.

"Then let's just say he has little enough in this life. The one thing that matters to him is his privacy, and I'm going to leave him that."

"I'll be glad to leave him his privacy, too. I just want to get out of here. Go home." It was an almost automatic plea. Why did it suddenly feel like a betrayal on her part? Why was she no longer certain that was what she wanted?

It didn't matter, since Ruth Wilkins was clearly not going to help her escape. "There's nothing I can do to help you. I'm sorry. Can't you just be patient? He's not going to hurt you, you know."

"You don't even know why I'm here. Why he's keeping me a prisoner." Meg had hoped to shock Ruth, but apparently nothing Ethan Winslowe did could shock her.

"He must have his reasons. I trust him enough to not interfere."

"You know him that well? I thought he kept out of the way of townspeople."

A pale pink stained Ruth's plump cheeks. "I knew him that well," she said. And disappeared down the turret stairs.

Meg sat very still, listening to the sound of Ruth's footsteps disappearing on the stone stairs. The burning was back, but this was another, insane kind of burning.

It was repulsion, she told herself. The thought of plump, motherly Ruth making love with ... no, having sex with the monster that dwelled below was stomach turning. He'd hinted that it would be, that it would take a talented, sophisticated woman to deal with someone in his condition. So why was her horror at the very idea tinged with curiosity and something that absolutely couldn't, wouldn't be jealousy?

And why did she persist in thinking Ethan was a monster? The people in town clearly thought so. Winslowe himself had told her that was what he was. But was he? She'd always considered herself a compassionate person. If the man below was hideously deformed, it could hardly be his fault. He'd spent his life hiding away from society, it was no wonder he'd grown dangerously antisocial. Why should she condemn him so heartlessly?

Because he was trying to destroy her father. Because he was holding her prisoner in his strange mansion. Because he was a mocking, dangerous creature who clearly meant her harm.

He wasn't a monster because of his physical challenges. He was a monster because of the darkness of his soul.

And suddenly she remembered the dark man who'd held her and rocked her and soothed her and kissed her.

God help her, there was no way the two men could be one. Was there?

Chapter Six

It was another three days before Meg began to feel a
semblance of normalcy. Three days of lying in bed, sip-
ping at chicken broth and lemonade, listening to herself
cough. Three days of Ruth's relentlessly cheerful com-
panionship and Salvatore's occasional, glowering presence. Three days of Stephen King novels in the day and
nightmares at night. Three days without seeing anyone
else, not the dark stranger, not Ethan Winslowe, not the
mysterious old man from the garden. Three days to go
quietly mad.

They moved her to another room, this one on one of
the lower levels. It was equipped with oil lamps, a step
up from the flickering candlelight of the tower room,
and the style of the room was cozy Victorian, almost
New England, with sash windows that let in the drizzly
daylight. Her clothes had disappeared, down to her underwear, and she was dressed in a flowing white gown
that looked as though it belonged to Ethan Winslowe's
great-grandmother. It didn't matter. The cotton was so
old and fine that it was whisper soft. It was also whisper thin, illuminating her body if she happened to wander around. Fortunately, she was too weak to wander
much farther than the bathroom.

The nights were the hardest. She managed to sleep through the days, her weakened body helping her change her usual patterns. By midnight she was awake, burningly awake, and alone in the fussy Victorian room with its four-poster bed, with no one but Stephen King for company.

She woke with her scream echoing through the pitch-dark room. The rain was still falling outside, it must have been falling for weeks, and no trace of light entered the uncurtained windows. The oil lamps had been extinguished, leaving her in total darkness, and she reached in desperation for the matches she'd left on the bedside table, the old oil lamp she'd been fool enough to blow out.

Her arm encountered glass, and it went smashing to the floor, filling the room with the pungent scent of lamp oil. She uttered a quiet little moan of panic, sinking back against the pillow, when she heard his silken voice out of the blackness.

"Don't move."

She didn't question how he got there. She'd half known, when she'd been pulled from sleep by a nightmare she couldn't even remember, that he had to be there, waiting.

"It's too dark," she said.

"You climb out of bed and you'll cut your feet to ribbons. Salvatore will clean it up tomorrow."

"It's too dark," she said again.

"You'll get used to it." He was closer than before, moving silently, like a cat. An electric wheelchair would have made some sort of humming noise, wouldn't it? Therefore, he had to be walking, didn't he? Or floating?

She shook her head, banishing the eerie fancy. He was only a man, more or less. Not a ghost. Not a phantom of the night.

"You could even grow to like it," he said, his voice low and sinuous, snaking through the darkness like a ribbon of sound. "Everything's better in the night. Secrets are kept, ugliness is glossed over. Candlelight makes everyone beautiful. Surely you've enough vanity to realize that."

"Actually, I'm not a terribly vain person."

His laugh was low and bitter. "Aren't you? I'm afraid I am, more's the pity. I haven't much to be vain about."

There was no answer she could make to that. He was close, dangerously close, hovering just at the far corner of her bed. And she knew without question that he was the dark stranger who'd watched over her during her illness. The man who'd kissed the taste of bubble gum from her mouth. Ethan Winslowe. And she shivered in the darkness.

"When are you going to let me go?" she asked, keeping her voice even and steady.

"Are we back to that again? I thought you weren't going to be boring."

"Would you have let me die? Out here, miles and miles from decent medical care? How would you have explained my disappearance? How would you have gotten rid of the body?"

"I don't make explanations to anyone," he said. "I don't have to. And I don't imagine I'd have any trouble disposing of a corpse if it came right down to it. Don't underestimate my power, Megan. There's no one within miles of this place but the forty-some residents of Oak Grove, and they'll do anything I tell them to."

"They're afraid of you."

"Yes. But I provide their only income, as well. So if they balk at one of my commands, they run the risk of not only having their livelihood cut off, but turning blind or mad, or both."

"You know what they say about you." Somehow the knowledge that she'd listened to their gossip embarrassed her.

"I know everything I need to know. For instance, I know you're scared to death after reading Stephen King."

"Don't you have anything a little more cheerful to read?" she asked, not bothering to deny it. She believed that disembodied voice when he said that he knew everything he needed to know.

"I left them on purpose."

"You wanted to scare me?" Why should the notion surprise her? He'd been trying to scare her since she arrived. The only wonder was that she wasn't frightened right now, alone in the inky darkness with a man she considered a monster. A man who kissed like an angel.

"Of course. But don't panic. You've been reading *Christine*. Take it from me, you won't be going anywhere near an automobile for ages."

"Somehow, I don't find that reassuring."

"It wasn't meant to be." He was closer still. She wished that the time when she had been so sick hadn't blurred her memory. She couldn't reconcile the notion of Ethan Winslowe, the deformed creature who lived in the bowels of the old Meredith place, with the man who'd found her in the garden and carried her upstairs, the man who'd rocked her and held her and kissed her. She thought for a moment that she might have seen his face, but if she had, that memory was gone along with her bone-shaking fever.

"Would you have let me die?" she persisted.

"What do you think?" he countered, and she wished her smashed oil lamp was still at hand instead of filling the room with a musky scent. She'd throw it at him.

She'd probably miss in the darkness. "I don't think you would have," she said finally. "I think you would have found a car or gotten an ambulance or a helicopter, and gotten me to a decent hospital."

"Your innocent faith is one of your many charming qualities. If I sent you to a hospital, there'd be a lot of unpleasant questions. And you'd have escaped. Do you think I would have allowed that?"

"So you would have let me die?" She couldn't, wouldn't believe it of him.

"You'll never have to find out, will you? All I'm suggesting is that you not be so trusting in people's eventual decency. There's very little decency around here, and very little decency in me. I'm used to having my own way, and be damned to the consequences."

She didn't believe him. He'd gone so far to tell her he was a monster that she was finally beginning to doubt. "Could you light one of the lamps?"

He laughed. "You don't need to see my face. You've been frightened enough for one night. Go back to sleep, Megan. You need to get your strength back."

"So I can leave here?"

She couldn't even see his shadow, but somehow she knew he shrugged. "So you can try to escape, perhaps. It doesn't matter. First you need to get well. Then we can argue."

He was closer still, achingly close, his voice low and beguiling. "Lie down and go to sleep," he said. "There are no monsters here to trouble you. No demons and phantoms to fill your dreams. Only me. Go to sleep and I'll watch over you."

He was going to touch her. Put his hands on her shoulders and push her down on the bed. And then would he release her? Or would he follow her down while she was half sick, half asleep, wholly drugged with the night and his presence and his low, insinuating voice.

She slid down on the bed, pulling the fine linen sheet over her. He laughed then, a light, amused sound only faintly tinged with bitterness. "Don't worry, little one. You look too much like a Victorian virgin in that night-gown for me to touch you."

"Women who are barely five foot two don't like being called 'little one,'" she said in a frosty voice. "And I'll have you know that I'm far removed from a Victorian virgin. I've had lots and lots of experience."

How could she sense a smile on a face she'd never seen? "Two brief affairs scarcely constitute lots of experience."

She didn't ask him how he knew. She was already beginning to accept that he knew everything, that she couldn't lie to him, couldn't hide anything from a man who could see as clearly in the dark as most people saw in broad daylight.

"Just tell me one thing," she said, snuggling down in the soft bed with surprising ease. "Has anyone asked about me? Anybody tried to find out where I am? I've been gone more than a week, I've missed a flight to Europe, and I haven't been in touch with anyone. Has anyone been asking about me?"

She didn't know what his brief hesitation meant; whether he was thinking up a lie, or whether he was simply debating how much to tell her. "No one's been asking," he said finally. "You've known your father all

your life. Surely you should realize a devout coward as
he is will simply ignore your disappearance and hope for
the best. You have no one to turn to, no one to help you,
Megan. No one but me.''

"And you're going to help me?" Her voice was
skeptical.

He was so close. She could feel a faint breeze dust
across her face, and she almost arched upward, into it,
reaching for his touch. Instead, she used all her limited
control to lie very still.

"Go to sleep, Megan," he said instead of answering
her plaintive question. "By tomorrow, you'll be
stronger, ready to plot revenge."

"Revenge is your thing, not mine," she murmured.
Why was she suddenly so sleepy? Why was the scent of
spilled lamp oil soothing and vaguely, irresistibly erotic?
Or was it the voice of the man in the darkness, the creature of the night she'd never actually seen?

Tomorrow, she promised herself. Tomorrow she'd be
strong enough to go searching for him in the merciless
light of day. Whatever deformities he was hiding
couldn't be that awful that he needed to spend his life
hidden away. Could they?

"Sleep," he said, his voice low, soothing, almost a
physical presence dancing across her skin. "You can
worry about tomorrow when it comes."

Had he read her mind? Had she spoken out loud? It
didn't matter. "Sleep," he said again in his hypnotic
voice. And she slept.

"I WANT TO KNOW HOW I could have eaten nothing but
chicken broth for a week and not lost a pound," Meg
demanded later the next morning as she tugged her ancient, most comfortable jeans up around her hips. Sal-

vatore had grudgingly brought her suitcase from wherever it was he'd stashed it, and she'd finally gotten rid of her trailing Victorian virgin's gown. The memory of Ethan Winslowe's gentle taunt was too unsettling. The memory, the thought of Ethan in general was too unsettling.

When she'd awoken, just after dawn, the broken glass had disappeared, a new oil lamp stood on the table by her bed, and only the faint scent of fragrant lamp oil still clinging in the air convinced her that she hadn't dreamed last night's visitor. She'd decided she'd been too easily seduced by the darkness and the otherworldly air of her host. A pair of jeans and a loose cotton shirt would bring reality back. How could one have erotic fantasies wearing bright red Reeboks?

She peered out the window into the murky light. The rain seemed to have stopped, at least for now, and it even seemed as if the sun might struggle past the clouds for a bit. The thought of being out in the fresh air was so intoxicating, she almost made a run for it.

The window of her current bedroom was on one of the middle floors of the bizarre old house, overlooking a formal rose garden complete with trellises and an ornate gazebo. It was too early for roses, particularly in such a rain-soaked area, but the leaves that covered the gazebo were thick and glossy, obviously well tended. She could see the figure of a man in the distance, through the curtain of greenery, and she pressed her forehead against the windowpane, staring, wondering if Ethan Winslowe had left his midnight lair.

The man moved too slowly, too carefully for her nocturnal visitor. She could see stooped shoulders, a shock of white hair, and knew she'd finally found the other man she'd been seeking, the old gardener.

"Come and tell me who this is, Ruth?" she requested, not taking her eyes off the man.

Ruth ignored the request, bustling through Meg's suitcase, hanging up clothes with a muttered tsk of disapproval.

"Don't bother with that. I won't be staying here that long," Meg said impatiently, turning to look at her. "Come and tell me who this man is."

Slowly, reluctantly, Ruth moved to the window. "What man?"

"The one..." He'd disappeared. "Hell and damnation. He was over by the gazebo. The old man I told you about, the one who found me when I collapsed."

"I've told you before, there are no old men living here. Only Ethan and Salvatore."

Meg turned her back to the window, giving up her quest. For now. "How old is he?" she asked.

"Salvatore's somewhere in his late fifties."

"I can see how old Salvatore is. How old is Ethan Winslowe?"

Once more, that shuttered expression came over Ruth's face. "It's hard to say."

"You can manage to guess. Fifties? Nineties? Twenties?"

"He's ageless."

"No one's ageless but Dick Clark."

"Who's Dick Clark?"

Meg stared at her in fascination. "Don't you have television in Arkansas?"

"Not in Oak Grove. It's considered sinful."

"And have you lived all your life in Oak Grove?"

"Too much of it. I try to keep away from the village nowadays, but there was a time when I was trapped. Same as most of the young ones, until..."

"Until . . . ?"

"I've been talking too much. I've got to get home to my family."

"Family?"

The wariness finally left Ruth's face, and Megan could see how very pretty she once was. "My husband and my two kids. Jason and Brian are fourteen and sixteen, and taller than I am. And there's my husband, Burt."

"Somehow, I didn't think anyone around here had anything as normal as a family," Meg confessed.

"Most don't. I'm just luckier. I've had two good men. My first husband, John, was killed in a mining accident when the boys were babies. I married Burt five years ago, and we couldn't be happier. As long as we keep away from Oak Grove."

"I would have thought keeping away from here would be even more important."

"I don't spend much time here. Not unless I'm needed. But if I am, you can bet your life I'll be here, come hell or high water. You shouldn't believe everything you hear, Meg. Things aren't as black-and-white as they seem, and the bad guys are quite often the good guys, and vice versa."

Ruth was gone before Meg could question her further. She took one last, longing look out the window, but the old man had disappeared. Sinking back down on the bed, she thought about what Ruth had said. As far as Meg could tell, there weren't any good guys at all in this place. Everyone was a villain, with the possible exception of the mysterious old man and Ruth herself. Did that mean that in reality there were nothing but good guys? She'd be wise not to trust anyone but herself.

She was halfway through *The Shining,* unable to put it down, when Salvatore knocked at her open door. He had his customary expression of disapproval on his swarthy face, and his glance at her casual clothes was disdainful. "You've got a visitor."

Meg just stared at him for a moment. "A visitor? My father...?"

"You think Ethan would just let your father walk in? Don't count on it, sweetheart. It's the local padre. Pastor Lincoln, to be exact. Come to offer you succor."

Meg looked at him warily. "You think a minister is going to countenance Winslowe's keeping me prisoner here?"

"Not likely. Lincoln thinks Ethan is the spawn of the devil. I'm sure he'll offer you a way out."

"Does Ethan know you're letting me see him?" She still didn't move from the bed, not trusting her sudden good fortune.

"Ethan knows everything," Sal said, echoing his own words. "As a matter of fact, it was his idea."

"Even though he'll give me a chance to escape?"

Salvatore's smile wasn't the faintest bit reassuring. "It's up to you whether you want to take it."

The trip through the hallways was long and torturous, following Salvatore's broad back. Nothing looked familiar, and if Megan had traveled that particular pathway before, she didn't remember it. She had to stop several times to catch her breath, to fight the lingering spasm of coughing that was pneumonia's legacy. It wasn't until they reached the front hallway that she recognized anything, and the knowledge that they'd reached it from the opposite direction was depressing. The house was so impossibly vast that she could get lost in it for days. No wonder Salvatore no longer bothered to lock her in.

She headed for the parlor, but Sal's meaty hand on her arm stopped her. "He's on the front porch. He doesn't want to set foot under the devil's rooftop."

Megan looked up, trying to discern whether Sal was kidding. Sal wasn't a man for jokes.

Still, all the better. If Pastor Lincoln was convinced that Winslowe was evil incarnate, he wouldn't have any qualms about getting her out of there.

Salvatore opened the front door for her, keeping out of her way as she stepped into the fitful sunlight. Her first view of the pastor wasn't encouraging.

He was a tall man, thin, with a prominent Adam's apple. Dressed appropriately enough in black, he had thinning gray hair and surprisingly cherubic pink cheeks. He also had the faintly bulging eyes of a fanatic.

"Sister," he cried when he saw her. "God has sent me to deliver you from this house of evil, to bring you to the bosom of the Holy One and wash away your sins. Give me your hand and I will lead you from this unclean place."

"Actually, the house is spotless," Meg couldn't resist remarking. She'd grown up in a nice, liberal, Protestant church, and fanaticism always made her uncomfortable. At his sudden frown, she realized how foolish she was being, throwing away her best chance of rescue because she didn't happen to like the man's style, and she quickly managed to look demure. "I would appreciate a ride out of here. My car..." She looked to the driveway where her rental Ford had last been seen mired in the mud. In its place was the pastor's form of transportation, a rusting old mini school bus with the legend God

Sees All, Judges All, Punishes All on the side. It didn't look promising.

"That evil spawn of Satan has destroyed it with a thunderbolt," Pastor Lincoln announced. "Come away with me, now, before he turns you into one of his unholy ones."

She almost wanted to refuse, which would have been madness of the highest order. "You can give me a ride to the nearest town?"

"Of course, my child. To Oak Grove."

"But I need to get back to Chicago, to my family...."

"Your only family is God's!" he declaimed. "We'll do all we can, but first we must purify you...."

She started backing away at that. "What denomination are you, Pastor Lincoln? I'm United Church of Christ myself, and—"

"Those sects are all unknowing," he said loftily. "I follow the true way, like my father and grandfather before me."

"But you must have been trained—"

"Don't need training, sister, when you have a calling." He clamped a hand down on her arm, and she was surprised by the steely strength in those skinny fingers. "Come with me, child. We'll teach you about the real God."

"No, thanks," she said hastily, pulling away. He was too surprised to hold on, otherwise she might have had difficulty escaping. "I think I'll stay here for now. But thanks for the offer."

"Evil!" Pastor Lincoln screeched, pointing his finger at her. His entire body was vibrating with outrage. "It's too late for you. He's taken you, made you one of his succubi...."

"One of his what?" she demanded, not knowing whether to be amused or outraged.

"There'll be no cleansing of your sins, short of fire. You're one with the evil, lost in the sins of the flesh, rioting in fatness and sensuality!" He ran down the steps to his school bus, still shrieking.

"Guess you made an enemy of that one," Salvatore said with a smirk.

"He made an enemy of me with that crack about fatness," Meg snapped back. "Is everyone around here loony tunes?"

"Just about," Sal said. "Ready to go back to your room?"

The enormity of what she'd just done hit her. She whirled around for one last wistful glance at the school bus as it jolted and jarred its way back down the road. Repent or Perish, it said on the back. Her only chance of escape and she'd thrown it away. So what if he'd wanted to purify her? It probably wouldn't have been any worse than what Ethan Winslowe had in mind for her.

She turned back to Salvatore, keeping her back straight. If one opportunity came, another would come. Ruth was her best chance so far—she had a good heart, even if it came with a misplaced loyalty to the Phantom of Oak Grove. Meg simply had to keep working on her.

"Ready," she said. "Unless..."

"Yeah?" he demanded impatiently.

"I'd really like to spend some time outside." She could hear the sounds of construction from the left side of the house. If Sal would just leave her alone on the porch, she could go in search of the workers. The day she couldn't talk to a construction crew and get them to do what she wanted would be the day she'd give up.

"They won't help you," Salvatore said, reading her very clearly. "They know where their paycheck is coming from."

She resisted the impulse to make a face at him. One person had her interests at heart, one person would help her, she knew it deep in her heart. "As a matter of fact, I'd like to spend some time in the rose garden I saw from my window. Got any problem with that?"

"I don't know. I'll have to check with Ethan...."

"Isn't he asleep in his coffin? Come on, Igor, take some responsibility on your own shoulders."

He glared at her. "He's not going to like your attitude."

"Tough. Let me go to the rose garden and I'll be docile."

There was a long pause. "Can't see the harm in it," Sal said finally, surprising her. "Just one word of warning."

"What's that?"

"Watch out for ghosts."

Chapter Seven

The rose garden was cooler than the front porch. The grass was wet and green beneath her sneakers, and the rich scent of spring earth was almost erotic in its intensity. Salvatore left her there, muttering something about returning in an hour, and she was alone.

The garden was lovingly tended, the roses very old and just beginning to bud. Ruth had told her the sullen townspeople of Oak Grove came in daily to take care of the house—one of them must have a green thumb to keep such ancient roses in such healthy shape.

But it wasn't a townsperson, she knew that instinctively. It was the old man who'd found her that night, the old man she'd glimpsed less than an hour ago from her window.

She turned and looked back at the house, shaking her head in amazement. From every angle, the building was a wonderment as one architectural style gave way to another, a crazy quilt of building styles that was both bizarre and oddly appealing. She could only guess which windows were hers. The turret rose above her, made of solid stone, and she knew with a pang that it must have been built exactly as the old castles of Europe had been built. The old castles she should have been visiting, instead of being trapped in a state like Arkansas. A place where nothing was as it seemed.

She crossed the damp grass and stepped up into the gazebo, sinking down on one of the wooden benches, hiding behind the greenery. Ever since she'd arrived at the Meredith place, she'd felt as if someone was watching her, following her every movement. She knew that no one could see behind the tangle of rose bushes. For a few minutes, she was going to sit back, alone, away from everyone, and try to figure out what in the world she was going to do to get away from there.

She wrapped her arms around her body. She should have worn something a little heavier than the soft cotton shirt she'd unearthed from her suitcase, but it hadn't seemed that chilly. She leaned back against a post, closing her eyes for a moment, and wondered whether she ought to shed a few tears of self-pity.

She decided against it. She was quickly regaining her health and no one had actually done her harm. Certainly she was trapped in this place against her will. She was also becoming more and more fascinated with its occupants, Ethan Winslowe in particular. If he were suddenly to capitulate, to let her father off the hook and set her free, her obvious reaction would be overjoyed relief. But it would be tinged with regret. Perhaps even disappointment. She had wanted to go to Europe for adventure. Whatever happened when she finally got there would probably appear tame after what she'd been through in the past week or so.

She opened her eyes and sat forward. A man was kneeling in the dirt on the far side of the gazebo, digging at the roots of one of the rose bushes, concentrating on his work. His hands were old and gnarled, stained with liver spots, and the white hair beneath his old cap was wispy. He must have felt her gaze on him for he looked up, and once more Meg looked into what must be the kindest, gentlest eyes she'd ever seen. Here was a man who was truly ageless—he looked at least ninety—and yet he was clearly spry and active if he kept this garden looking as it did. And she knew without a doubt that he did.

"I thought you might be asleep," he said, sitting back on his heels and brushing the dirt from his hands.

"I came looking for you."

He nodded. "I thought you might. Did you ask them about me?"

"No one will admit you exist."

His smile was peculiarly sweet. "I'm not surprised. Maybe I don't. Do you like my garden?"

"It's very beautiful."

"It's even prettier when the roses start blooming. By the middle of May, the place is a riot of color and scent. A perfect place for a wedding."

Meg was startled. "Is anyone getting married?"

"Not here," he said sadly. "The only one would be Ethan, and he never comes out into the daylight."

"Why not?"

"Ask Ethan."

"I'm asking you," she said stubbornly.

"Ask me something I can answer. You sent that crazy minister away, didn't you?"

Did everyone around here see everything? "'Crazy' is the word. I got the impression he'd dunk me in a vat of boiling water to cleanse the devil from me."

"I hadn't realized Ethan had gotten that far."

She sucked in her breath. It was one thing hearing Ethan referred to as evil by a crazed fanatic, another by this gentle old man. "You think he's the devil?"

He shook his head. "I know just who and what he is. If anyone's the devil around here, in my opinion it's Pastor Lincoln and his crazy followers. They run around saying everything's unclean and make life a living hell for the few people who don't believe exactly as they do. People like Burt and Ruth Wilkins. It doesn't help that Ethan does everything he can to goad them. If he'd leave them be, then they might let him alone, too."

"Do you really believe that?"

"No. Lincoln and his crew won't rest easy until they've destroyed Ethan. They're so convinced he's the epitome of evil that they can't use their limited brain power to think about anything else. Including how to get out of the mess their town has gotten into over the last century."

"It's a little hard to right the wrongs of a century, isn't it?" Meg observed.

"It depends whether they want to or not. The town of Oak Grove is doomed, evil. The best thing that could happen would be if one of those tornadoes came right through here and flattened everything."

Meg moved from the bench to the gazebo steps. The sunlight had faded into a misty afternoon fog, and the old man seemed faded, indistinct. "Isn't that a little extreme? What's wrong with the town? Just isolation?"

"They've chosen that isolation. It started around the turn of the century. It was a bad time for the people around here. Drought, year after year, wiped out their crops. Then came the windstorms, wiping out half the families. The only ones who survived were the ones who were too mean and bitter to die off. The ones who locked their neighbors out in the storms to face certain death rather than risk their own necks. And those mean, bitter people just keep inbreeding over the years, so now, there's no one but them left. The good ones leave any way they can manage it. The bad ones stay on, locked in their own miserable, bitter little lives.''

''I wouldn't have thought a whole town could be classified as rotten.''

''You haven't seen enough of this one. It's . . . evil. I hate to use Pastor Lincoln's word, but it fits.''

''Then why does Ethan stay here? Wouldn't that make him evil, too?''

The old man looked up at her out of indistinct, faded blue eyes. ''He stays here because he feels he belongs. He thinks all people are as cruel, as heartless, as intrinsically rotten as the people of Oak Grove. It reinforces his opinion of mankind.''

The weight in her chest grew, but this time she knew it wasn't from the lingering effects of the pneumonia. Her lungs were clearing. It was her heart that was heavy.

''Is there any way to help him?'' Her voice was very quiet in the stillness of the misty afternoon.

He looked at her with both surprise and compassion. ''Why should you want to? Hasn't he been keeping you a virtual prisoner here? Hasn't he threatened to destroy your father and everything you care about? Why would you want to help him?''

She didn't bother asking how he knew. Everyone around here seemed to know everything. Except for her. She knew absolutely nothing at all, and the longer she stayed around, the more confused she got.

''Maybe if I help him, he'll let me go,'' she suggested, knowing that was the least of her worries.

''I wouldn't count on it. Ethan's good at anything he sets his mind to, and tenacity is one of his dubious virtues. I should know. He blames Doc Bailey and the townspeople for his father's death more than fifteen years ago, and he's still working on the perfect revenge.''

"But why should he blame them?"

"Oh, they're to blame, all right. He had a heart attack out here in the gardens. Doc Bailey was too drunk to help, and the townspeople refused. Ferdy down at the gas station had the only working vehicle, and he wouldn't drive him to the hospital. Ethan's father might have died anyway, but the townspeople helped him along, and Ethan was an orphan before he was twenty.''

"That makes him about thirty-five," Meg quickly computed.

"How old did you think he was?"

"I don't know. I've never seen him. What happened to his mother?"

The old man snorted. "His mother was a worthless butterfly who couldn't stand the sight of her own son. She died in a car crash when he was twelve, and if you ask me, it was eleven years too late.''

"That's pretty harsh."

"She deserves it for what she did to him," the old man said, his voice calm and implacable. "He's not past saving, Meg, but his time's running out. Soon it'll be too late. I think you were sent for him. His last chance.''

The heaviness rose, threatening to choke her. "Last chance for what?"

"You'll have to figure that out for yourself," he said gently, his voice fading in the thickening fog. "Don't blame yourself if you can't save him. It may already be too late.''

"Save him from what?" She could no longer see the old man, only a faint outline in the swirling mist. A light drizzle had begun to fall and she retreated into the dubious shelter of the gazebo. "Save him from what? Don't go yet. You haven't explained—"

"I'll be here," his voice whispered from the distance. "When you need me, I'll be here."

"But who are you? What's your name? Where are you going? Who . . ."

"Joseph." She didn't know whether she actually heard him speak the name, or whether it somehow just echoed in her mind.

She called after him, but there was no answer. Only the thickening rain and mist, with her trapped on the gazebo island in the midst of it all.

"SHE CALLED ME IGOR," Salvatore said in an aggrieved voice.

Ethan laughed. "It's appropriate. After all, you really are the evil madman's faithful henchman. You don't have a hunchback or a cast in your eye, but we could do something with a costume."

"I didn't think it was funny. She said you slept in a coffin."

"I didn't know she was interested in where I slept. I'll have to enlighten her."

"Ethan . . ."

"I wish you'd stop doing that. Every time you say 'Ethan . . .' in that tone of voice you make me think of a schoolmarm. Next thing I know, you'll be rapping my knuckles with a ruler."

"Maybe you're acting like a schoolboy."

"Maybe. I wish I'd seen her send Lincoln on his way. It must have been amusing."

"It's what you expected, wasn't it?"

Ethan shrugged. "I don't count on anything. She might have been fool enough to go with him. It would have simplified matters."

"What are you going to do about her father?"

Ethan glanced at him. "Is there any hurry? I thought things could wait while I concentrated on his daughter."

"He's breaking ground for a civic center in Alabama next week. Nothing you designed, so you're off the hook if something happens. Maybe you don't need to do anything."

"Do you think I've gone after him because of my reputation?"

"No. But I don't think you've gone after him out of concern for your fellow man. I've known you too long, Ethan, to be fooled into thinking you've turned into a bleeding heart."

"True enough. I don't, however, enjoy knowing that people might die while a man I've helped makes money off them. Reese Carey wouldn't be where he is today if it weren't for my designs. Therefore I have a measure of responsibility."

"You also want a measure of revenge."

"Even more true, Sally. And I intend to get just that. His daughter's a good place to start. Where's our unwilling houseguest right now? Maybe it's time I told her a few home truths about her father."

"You don't think she's known all the time? That she's part of the cover-up?"

Ethan hesitated. "No."

"Good God," Salvatore breathed. "You've really fallen, haven't you?"

"Don't be ridiculous. Just because I think she's relatively innocent..."

"You don't believe anyone's innocent. Not until you've got proof, and all you've got with Meg Carey is gut instinct. Or is it something a little lower down than that?"

"I'm a man, Sally. I'm as capable of lust as the next man."

"I know that. I just didn't think you were capable of falling in love."

Ethan's reaction was absolute horror. "Give me a break, Sally. Falling in love is a euphemism for something a lot more biological."

"And your feelings for Meg Carey are biological?"

"Most definitely. And getting more overwhelming every day." Ethan leaned back in his chair, putting his fingertips together as he thought of Meg Carey's mouth. Of her surprisingly lush body beneath the thin cotton nightgown. He wanted to watch her again. Not touch her, not yet. He wanted to savor the anticipation. And he wanted her to savor it, too, even if she hadn't yet recognized that that was what it was.

"She's in the rose garden. Stuck in the gazebo while it rains."

"What the hell is she doing there?"

"Looking for Joseph."

"Do you think she found him?" Ethan kept his voice no more than idly curious, though he didn't know why he bothered. Sal knew him better than any human on this earth and he wouldn't be fooled for a moment.

"Not many people do. He came to her once, though, when she was lost in the rain. He might come again."

Ethan nodded. "He probably did. She has an amazing ability to draw people to her."

"It hasn't worked with me," Sal said righteously.

"Hasn't it? Why do you keep trying to get her away from my evil clutches, then?"

"Maybe because it's you I'm worried about. Not her. You can't just kidnap people, Ethan. You can't keep her prisoner here indefinitely. Sooner or later, they're going to come after you. Not that cowed bunch of fanatics in Oak Grove, but the state authorities. Maybe even the feds. You aren't going to get away with it for much longer."

"Who's going to send out a distress signal? Not the good people of Oak Grove. Not her cowardly father. She has no other attachments. Everyone else thinks she's gone to Europe. Reese Carey has probably convinced himself of the same thing."

"You're playing with fire, Ethan."

"I don't think it would matter much if I got burned, do you? I think I'm going to have to pay Meg a little visit tonight. Go and rescue her from the gazebo, Sal. This damp weather won't do her lungs any good. And you'd better make sure she has enough antibiotic to finish out the course. We don't want her having a relapse."

"Why not? That would force her to stay here longer."

"She's staying as long as I want her. Besides, I want her healthy. I have plans for her," Ethan said evenly.

"Ethan..."

"There you go again, schoolmarm. Go find her and get her safe and warm. Maybe it's time to move her again. Why don't you take her to the Roman section?"

"Which room?" Sal asked in a weary voice.

"I think it's time to up the ante. She's had enough Stephen King for now. Put her in the Pompeii room."

"So WHERE'S MY TOGA?" Meg demanded when Salvatore showed her into the dimly lit interior of her new rooms. She'd been hard-pressed to hide her gratitude when he'd showed up at the entrance to the gazebo with a huge gold umbrella to shield her from the rain. At least the precipitation had been accompanied by warmer temperatures. If that unnatural chill had stayed in the air, she would have probably been ready for a relapse.

The austere confines of her new rooms weren't precisely welcoming. At least there was a decent-size bed directly in the center of the room. This room was at least partway underground, and in the corner was a brazier with hot coals sending warmth into the air. The walls were covered with murals, ones she didn't bother to look at. For the time being, she wanted to change out of her damp clothes, get something to eat and figure how she was going to get out of here.

"Women didn't wear togas," Sal said repressively. "Bathroom's over there, and your clothes are in the closet. Be ready in half an hour."

"Ready for what? I planned to take a long hot bath. Romans were famous for baths, weren't they? I'm assuming this place comes equipped with a Roman-style swimming pool."

"You can use it later. Ethan wants you for dinner."

"To feed or to eat?"

Sal glowered. "Don't wear jeans. He doesn't like them."

That settled the question of what she'd wear to dinner. Obviously, jeans it would be. "I'll be ready in an hour," she said flatly.

The Roman section of the house even had a pillared portico with steps leading down into a courtyard complete with marble statues. Meg glanced out into the gathering gloom. For the first time, she'd have immediate access to the outdoors, unless, of course, Ethan decided to have her locked in again. Maybe if the rain cleared, she'd try to leave tonight.

Except that it was clear the town of Oak Grove wasn't going to provide any help. She might be able to find her rental car, but given the size and complexity of this old place, chances were slim. It was conceivable she could drive one of the construction vehicles she'd heard in the distance. At one point, she'd been moderately proficient at running a backhoe.

The problem with backhoes was that they only traveled about five miles an hour, maximum. She'd be better off on her own two feet. And better off waiting just a couple more days until her strength was back. It wouldn't do much good to take off and then collapse in a ditch a few miles away. And when it came right down to it, she wasn't sure who she'd rather have find her in those circumstances: the deranged Pastor Lincoln and his bunch, or Ethan Winslowe himself.

There was no hurry, was there? No one seemed to give a hoot that she'd disappeared off the face of the earth, up to and including her father. As long as she stayed put, Ethan had promised to leave Reese alone. Not that she was certain her father deserved any mercy, but certainly no man should be crucified for one shortsighted mistake. And then there was the company, with hundreds of jobs depending on it.

No, maybe she wouldn't wear the jeans, after all. Maybe she'd find her prettiest dress, follow Salvatore like the demure young lady she certainly wasn't and do her best to ameliorate Ethan Winslowe's uncertain temper. If she were just sweet and accommodating enough, he might be talked into dropping this whole crazy idea and letting her go.

And maybe pigs could fly. She wasn't about to use sex to get what she wanted from the man. That had too much possibility of backfiring right in her face. The baggiest, most wretched pair of jeans she'd brought with her, her loosest sweater and her grumpiest expression. Anything was worth a try.

There was only one minor problem with her current plan. When she stepped out of the bathroom wrapped in a voluminous towel, she found her damp pair of jeans missing from the mosaic floor of the room. Every pair of jeans she owned had been taken from her suitcase, and her Reeboks had disappeared. She was left with dresses, all of them too filmy or too clinging or too low cut.

Not that she usually considered her dresses provocative. They were all reasonably trendy, flattering fashions, ones she'd never thought twice about wearing.

She was thinking twice now. She didn't want Ethan Winslowe's unseen eyes traveling down the front of the clinging peach dress, dipping over the décolletage of the black knit, running along the curves of the blue sundress.

She had no real choice in the matter. The black knit had the longest hemline, the loosest cut, and if she just kept tugging at the neckline, there wouldn't even be a hint of cleavage. Hell and damnation, why hadn't she lost weight when she was sick? With her luck, she'd probably gained five pounds, all in the chest.

The ancient Romans apparently had no mirrors, so she could only guess what she looked like. Too pale, too defiant, too rounded. Target practice for Ethan Winslowe.

"You ready?" Salvatore hadn't bothered to knock. He'd swung the door open, standing there with a flashlight against the gathering gloom.

"Morituri te salutamus," she muttered under her breath, slipping on her highest heels for the modicum of moral support they gave her.

"What's that?"

"Just getting into the Roman spirit of things, Sal," she replied, shoving her hair back away from her too pale face and biting her lips. "We who are about to die salute you."

"I don't think it's going to go that far. Not if you're careful," Sal replied, absolutely seriously.

She looked at him in horror. "*Et tu, Brute?* I don't scare easily."

"I know you don't. More's the pity." Without a word, he took off down the darkened hallway, leaving her to follow him.

For a moment, she considered staying put. Not for a moment did she consider that she might really be in danger. Ethan had warned her about innocence and blind trust. The only person she hadn't trusted so far had been the minister. Certainly that wasn't a good omen for the future.

She wasn't going to improve her situation by cowering in her room, either. Chances were Ethan would come after her or send his hulking familiar. She'd lied to him. It didn't take much to scare her at all. At the moment, she was frankly terrified.

But staying in the darkened room didn't offer much of an alternative. Particularly when certain scenes of the last Stephen King novel she'd been desperate enough to read kept drifting into her memory, despite her efforts to banish them.

"Wait up, Igor," she called out after the rapidly disappearing light. And ignoring her panic, she took off after Sal into the darkness.

Chapter Eight

They were heading down, down, into the center of the house again, into darkness lit only by the occasional gaslight fixture. Meg stumbled after Salvatore, cursing her skimpy dress and her overactive imagination. Why couldn't the man dwell somewhere above the basements? She knew he could walk, knew he was strong enough to carry her one hundred and twenty-five pounds up the twisting tower steps. Why would he choose to dwell in the cellars?

When Salvatore ushered her through a wide doorway, she had her answer in the darkness of the room. He chose the basement for the lack of light. No shuttered windows to let in even a chink of daylight. Just the chill damp of the earth around them.

It was a different room from where Ethan had held his previous audience with her. There were no blinking lights in the background, but then, she knew now that he didn't need life-support systems to keep him going. She could make out a wide table covered in damask, set with crystal and bone china. Set for one. Candelabra stood on either side of the chair, but the pools of light didn't travel far into the room. He was somewhere beyond, watching her, watching as she moved forward and took the chair Salvatore held out for her. She could feel his gaze on her skin, as physical as a touch, running up her legs, her hips, her low-cut neckline. It took all her self-possession to keep from tugging at that neckline.

She sat very still as Salvatore placed food in front of her, filled her wineglass and then disappeared into the shadows. She knew he was gone, out of sight, out of hearing, as well as she knew Ethan Winslowe was there. In the darkness, she was learning to trust her other senses.

She glanced down at her plate. Boneless chicken in a delicate tarragon-scented sauce, wild rice, fresh white asparagus. The wine would be vintage, French and very dry. She sighed.

"You don't like the food?" Ethan's voice came out of the darkness. "Simply tell Salvatore what you'd like and he'll provide it."

"I'd kill for a Big Mac and fries," she said. "Washed down by a supersize Diet Coke."

"Sorry."

"What about takeout?" she suggested hopefully, picking up the heavy silver fork.

"The nearest McDonald's is one hundred and ten miles away. The food would be cold by the time Sal carried it back."

The chicken was almost sinfully wonderful. She could live without fast food for a little while longer. "I'm surprised you even know what a McDonald's is," she said, taking a sip of the wine. Exactly as she had guessed, and utterly delicious.

"I know. I just don't know what the food tastes like."

"You've never been inside one?"

"Hardly."

She leaned back in the chair, holding the wineglass. It was useless to stare into the dark in Ethan's direction; instead, she looked into the shimmering depths of the wine. "You're missing a great treat."

"I'll have to take your word for it. I expect I'll survive. What did you think of our local man of the cloth?"

"Pastor Lincoln? He's nutty as a fruitcake."

"He comes by it honestly. His father and grandfather were deranged fanatics before him. I gather you didn't want to avail yourself of his offer of help. Dare I hope you've grown attached to this place?"

"Hope all you want. In this case, it was a choice between the devil I could see and the devil I couldn't. I decided you might prove less dangerous in the long run."

"I don't know if I'm flattered or offended," he murmured.

"Let me know when you figure it out." She drained the wine, reached for the bottle and poured herself another glass. "What's a succubus?"

She heard his muffled explosion of laughter. "Is that what he called you?"

"Among other things. I've missed that term. What does it mean?"

"A female demon who has sexual relations with men in their sleep," he replied.

She considered the notion, hoping he couldn't see the faint stain of color in her cheeks. It was the wine, she told herself. "That doesn't sound like much fun," she said finally.

"It also includes the sexual partners of male demons," he added.

"I see."

"I imagine you do."

She set the wineglass on the table. She was too vulnerable to risk drinking even a moderate amount. Already she was growing hot, disturbed, uneasy. Aroused. Better to stick to water. Better to stick to an adversarial relationship.

"When are you going to let me go?"

"That again?" he demanded wearily. "You grow tiresome, Meg."

"Then send me home. Surely I've paid enough for my father's sins."

"Not really."

"One stupid mistake five years ago is not something to crucify a man over," she said with a trace of desperation.

"Not when people die? Not when he tries to foist the blame off on other people?"

"He's sorry. He told me so."

"And you think that, like a little boy who's broken a window or shoplifted a candy bar, all he has to do is say he's sorry and everything's all right?"

"What else can he do?"

"He could have the nerve to come here himself instead of sending you. And he could come up with something like, 'I'll never do it again.'" Ethan's voice was cold, implacable.

"But he..." A sudden, chilling thought came to her. "Would you believe him?"

"Of course not. But then, I have the advantage over you. I know he's still doing it."

"No!"

"Still using inferior materials, cutting corners, ignoring structural specifications in order to save money and line his own pockets. Risking life after life for his own greed, ignoring the blood that's already on his hands, and then sending his own daughter as a sacrifice to keep me from turning him in." Ethan's voice was savage in the darkness, the words like knives cutting into her.

"I don't believe you. He wouldn't...he couldn't..."

"You're not a blind fool, Meg, even though you try to be where your father's concerned. He's done the same thing with the Minneapolis Science Emporium and the Greenwich Art Center. Sooner or later, something's going to collapse, more people are going to die and you're going to be a willing accomplice to it all because of your idiotic loyalty."

"He can't be. He can't do it by himself."

"Of course he can't. He's got plenty of help from people like George Dubocek and Brian Donegal running the sites. And he's got help on the administration end. People like Mary Elder, and Phillip Zarain are working that end of it, covering up when cheaper quality support beams are ordered, when things are skimped. He'll get away with it until someone else dies, and then his house of cards will collapse as surely as the cheap buildings he's been erecting."

For a moment, Meg felt as if she were going to throw up. The taste of wine was like vinegar in her mouth, the delicate sauce like a pool of grease in the back of her throat. She wanted to scream at him, to throw the words back in his face, to tell him he was a liar. That her father wasn't the closest thing to a murderer. But the names he'd named made too much sense. Too many furtive looks, covered up deals, were beginning to become clear.

"And you were willing to let him get away with it? Let it continue, let people risk their lives as long as I stayed here and provided you with a little malicious amusement?" she managed to say, coming up with the only attack she could muster.

"No."

She jerked her head up. "What do you mean by that?"

"I mean no, I wasn't going to let it continue. I lied to you. The federal investigators have already been tipped off and given enough information that it will be relatively simple, even for bureaucrats, to find the smoking gun. Your father's destroyed, Meg. Ruined, disgraced and probably headed for jail."

"You were never going to save him at all."

"Never."

"I could have gone to him, made him stop—"

"There are buildings, public buildings, in dangerously weakened states. What would you have done about that?"

"You've kept me prisoner here promising me you'd leave him alone."

"I lied."

She felt cold, sick inside. "Why?"

He moved closer, and she imagined she could see his silhouette in the shadowed room. Tall, lean, dark. And dangerous. "Two reasons. One, you're a bright woman. You would have warned him, and he might have had time to cover his tracks. He's good at that sort of thing, and I don't have much faith in the federal investigators. They'd been fooled once, they could be fooled again."

"What's the other reason?" She felt a detached sort of control edge back.

"I wanted you here."

Baldly stated. She could feel the flush rise in her cheeks again and for something to do, she reached for her wineglass, draining it. "For revenge?" she asked.

"For a great many reasons. I'll leave it up to you to figure it out. But revenge wasn't one of them." He moved away again, and she was afraid he was going to leave her.

"What makes you think I wasn't in on this whole thing? Pocketing my share of the proceeds, turning a blind eye to my father's perfidy?"

"Your face."

"I beg your pardon?"

"You have a guileless face. I can see everything you're thinking in those huge blue eyes of yours, in that soft mouth. You'd be a lousy poker player, Meg. Everything is obvious on that pretty face of yours."

"Oh, God, I hope not." Belatedly she realized she had spoken out loud. She didn't want him to be able to read her fascination with him, her unwilling, demented attraction to a phantom she'd never even seen. She concentrated on the important things. "You trust me?"

He laughed. "Haven't I told you not to trust anyone? I believe your innocent face. But I believe the investigation I had done on you even more."

"Investigation?"

"Down to the names and durations of your two love affairs, your dental records and your bra size. Even the form of birth control you favor. I know everything about you, Megan Carey."

"No," she said. "You don't." She couldn't stand the thought that he'd pried into her life, rifled through her history like a pervert searching through her lingerie drawer. "You don't know my heart. My soul."

"Maybe not. But I'm learning."

That was the most frightening thing she'd heard since she'd arrived in the dark, haunted confines of Oak Grove, Arkansas. She pushed her chair back, knocking over the empty wineglass. "I think I want to go back to my room now."

"Is that all? I thought you'd be demanding I let you go home now."

"Would it do any good?"

She could feel his hesitation, knew his answer before his voice came out of the darkness. "No."

"Then my room will have to do."

"Sal's coming."

"Fine," she said, uncomfortable in her low-cut dress. She didn't want him looking at her, watching her. She didn't like the way it made her feel. Uneasy. And oddly, irresistibly excited.

"He'll bring you something to help you sleep."

"I won't need anything. The wine has been quite enough." Her voice was unnaturally polite.

"Tell me one thing before you go."

"Of course."

"Did you get to see Joseph this afternoon?" He sounded only idly curious.

"Yes. Why does it matter?"

"It doesn't. Not many people see him. He keeps a fairly low profile. He must approve of you." There was an odd note in Ethan's voice, one Megan couldn't begin to understand.

But at that point, she wasn't going to ask anything of him, even questions. Salvatore had reappeared, silent and impassive behind her, and she turned and followed him without even saying good-night.

That omission bothered her all the long way to her room. It bothered her after Salvatore left her, locking her in. It bothered her until she happened to glance over at the ancient Roman murals on the terra-cotta walls.

She heard the gasp of shock, knew that it came from her own throat. She couldn't believe what her eyes were telling her. Picking up the candelabrum Salvatore had left behind, she moved close to the walls, peering through the murky light at the murals.

She'd had three glasses of wine. Heaven only knew what Salvatore might have put in her food to drug her. Or maybe it was simply the stress of the situation that had addled her brain.

Or maybe it was Ethan Winslowe's twisted sense of humor. These weren't innocent murals of Roman daily life. These were graphic, highly erotic, even bordering on pornographic. Certainly Pastor Lincoln would consider them so, but then, he'd be the type to consider a romance novel porn. The paintings in front of her were shockingly explicit, yet not without a certain grace. And not without the ability to move her.

She backed away, plunging the paintings into darkness again. She felt hot all over, her skin damp and tingling. She wasn't a prude, she hadn't been sheltered, and she considered herself sophisticated enough in matters like these. So why did she feel so disturbed? So... aroused?

Maybe it was the result of finally feeling better. Maybe it was a normal state when one was recovering from pneumonia, but she somehow doubted it. Maybe it was the Stockholm Syndrome, that perverse state in which captives became attracted to their tormentors. Or maybe it was nothing more sinister than her overactive, over-romantic imagination, reliving the Beauty and the Beast legend.

Ethan Winslowe was a beast, all right, and there was nothing romantic about being held captive while he systematically destroyed her father.

A father who deserved whatever punishment was meted out, she reminded herself, a father who'd been ready to sacrifice her in his place. She was going to harden her heart, slam the door shut on any feelings that might linger, just as he'd slammed the door shut on any paternal responsibility....

It didn't help matters to stand abandoned in the middle of this room from another time, another place, and feel so mortally sorry for herself. She'd done her best not to have illusions about her father's feckless self-absorption. It shouldn't shock her, shouldn't hurt. But it did.

The bed in the center of the room might look Roman, but it was equipped with a thoroughly modern, well-sprung mattress. Salvatore, her keeper and lady's maid, had turned down the thick cotton sheets and laid a nightgown across the bed. A new one, made of thin, soft, white cotton. Another Victorian virgin, she thought with a forced smile. Except that the neckline was square and lowcut and the cotton was gossamer thin.

Throwing it over her arm, she headed for the adjoining bathroom and then stopped. Since her enforced residence in this strange old house, she'd made it a practice of changing in the various bathrooms. It had been instinct, and for the first time, she wondered why.

She glanced up at the ceiling, the walls, the corners of the room. Once she saw it, she was amazed she hadn't noticed before.

Of course, it might not be a video camera. It was small enough, disguised to look like part of a sprinkler system, and it might be the product of late-night paranoia. But she didn't think so. Somewhere, miles of corridors away from her, Ethan Winslowe was sitting in front of a bank of television monitors watching her.

He'd know she'd guessed by now. She stared up at the camera, shoulders back, hair pushed away from her face, and she considered making a rude gesture, then dismissed the notion. That sort of childish action wouldn't even make her feel better. She should simply continue on into the bathroom where she knew even a man like Winslowe would have the decency to leave her some privacy. There'd be no cameras in there, no microphones. She could even drag the mattress in there and sleep on the floor.

She still didn't move. Through the wavering candlelight, the murals seemed to dance in front of her, blatantly, healthily sexual. There was one in particular, with a generously built female stretched out on a bed very similar to the one Meg had been provided with. Instead of a healthy young man, she was being pleasured by some sort of mythic creature. Roman legend was full of them, half man, half beast, all endowed with amazing sexual powers. Satyrs, centaurs and other creatures she couldn't remember or had never known about. This particular apparition seemed dark and fascinating, and she could understand the obvious raptures the hapless female was enjoying. . . .

She must have had too much wine, Meg thought in horror. She must be going out of her mind.

But if Ethan Winslowe wanted to spy on her, then she might as well make it worth his while. With a slow, deliberate gesture, she reached behind her to the zipper that traveled up the back of the clinging black dress.

She pulled it down slowly, letting the dress fall around her shoulders. She looked away from the camera, toward the section of the mural she found so absorbing, and let the dress slide down her body, landing in a pool at her feet.

She could feel his eyes on her, like a physical presence, touching her skin. She'd worn black lace underwear, a strapless black bra, lace bikini panties and a black garter belt to hold up silk stockings. If Ethan knew so much about her, he'd know she was partial to racy underwear. He said he knew the black bra was thiry-four C. None of this should come as a shock to him.

She paused for a moment, stretching like a contented cat as she stepped out of her fallen dress. She felt sinful, sensual and deliciously evil as she stood there in her shocking underwear and her high, high heels. If he hadn't needed life-support systems before this little act, he would now.

Leaning over so that her hair fell in her face, she slowly unhooked one sheer black stocking. Sliding it down her leg, she stepped out of her shoes with a trace of regret. Men were supposed to find high heels unbearably erotic. She wanted Ethan Winslowe to suffer.

The next stocking followed. She unfastened the garter belt and tossed it in the corner beneath the video camera with all the aplomb of an elegant stripper tossing her clothing to a hungry crowd.

For the first time in her life, she didn't feel ten pounds overweight. She felt luscious.

She considered leaving him with that. Sauntering into the privacy of the bathroom, leaving him with the mystery still intact. But she'd gone this far, she was going to carry it through to the end.

Turning her back to the camera once more, she reached between her breasts and unfastened the front clasp, letting the bra drop to the floor. She could feel his eyes running up the long, clean lines of her back; she could hear his breathing, even though he was far, far away.

She turned back to him, clad only in the wisp of silk bikini panties, and in the warmth of the room, her nipples were hard. She could feel a flush across her face, a sexual arousal that stemmed from what she was doing to her unseen phantom, what she was doing to herself. Tilting her face toward the camera, she closed her eyes, breathing deeply. And sliding her fingers inside the waistband of her panties, she slid them down her legs, slowly, slowly, past her knees, past her calves, until she was completely, gloriously nude.

It was an odd, liberating feeling. An act of revenge, a reckless, heedless challenge. She opened her eyes again, staring up at the camera. And with a small, self-satisfied smile, she pulled the virginal nightgown over her head, leaned over and blew out the candlelight.

SALVATORE APPEARED BEHIND the bank of television monitors, unable to see what Ethan was witnessing. "She's settled for the night. Do you need anything else?"

Ethan didn't move. He couldn't. "Get the hell out of here, Sally. Now!"

"Is something wrong?" Salvatore started to move around the monitor screens.

"Get out!" Ethan said again in a strangled voice.

Salvatore was wise enough to stop. "You've got to let her go, Ethan. She's upsetting you—"

"She's upsetting me," Ethan agreed in a harsh rasp. "And she's not going anywhere. Leave me alone, Sally. Just leave me the hell alone."

The door closed silently behind Sal, leaving Ethan alone in the darkness once more. But he wasn't alone. In the murky shadows of screen number seven, Meg Carey lay stretched out on the bed in the center of the room, the white nightgown wrapped around a body that . . . a body that . . .

His own body felt ready to explode. He was shaking with reaction, and he knew he should be furious with her. That little striptease had been deliberate, a taunting reminder that she didn't really think he was a man.

But he was. And he was more in control than she realized. He'd seen the flush of color on her cheekbones, seen the tautness of her breasts, and known that in her deliberate and wholly successfully attempt to taunt and arouse him, she'd managed to arouse herself quite effectively.

For a moment, all he could think of was to head down the twisting corridors to her room, go to her in the darkness and take what she'd so mockingly offered. His body craved it; his soul craved it.

Ah, but his heart wanted something else. A heart he didn't think he'd owned. He wasn't going to go after her now, when he was half crazy with wanting her. The game wasn't ready to be played, not yet.

But soon. Very, very soon.

Chapter Nine

Meg dreamed again, but then, she dreamed every night. She told herself they were nightmares, but usually they were more of a mixture. Dark, threatening, intensely erotic, her dreams would wake her feeling restless, troubled, anxious and more determined than ever to escape.

When she awoke later that night, she lay very still, trying to sift through the dreams to find a trace of reality she could cling to. The room was very dark, with only a fitful light filtering in from the wall of windows that overlooked the garden. The bed beneath was solid, real. She could feel the thick cotton sheets beneath her, the warm air that surrounded her, the faint scent of fire in the air, the distant sound of chanting—

She sat bolt upright, pulling the sheet around her with sudden, instinctive modesty, shaking her head to banish the last traces of sleep-dazed fogginess. The smell of fire was stronger now, and the chanting louder.

Her first, wild thought was an extension of her nightmares. It was a horde of Satanists come to carry her off for a virgin sacrifice, and Ethan Winslowe was the devil incarnate.

Except that she was no virgin, and the only people who'd think Ethan Winslowe was the spawn of the devil were the shadowy townspeople. Things like that didn't really happen.

But the chanting was unmistakable, as was the smell of fire laced with gasoline. One thing was certain—she wasn't going to get any more sleep until she found out what the hell was going on.

She pulled an oversize shirt over her sleeveless cotton nightdress, not bothering to button it, and headed for the row of glass doors. Locked, all of them, and the garden beyond looked dark and deserted. Wherever the fire and chanting were coming from, it wasn't out there.

She never expected the hall door to be unlocked. She only tried it as a perfunctory gesture, and when it opened, she was too astonished to move for a moment.

The hall was pitch black. If she had any sense at all, she'd go back into her room, crawl back into bed and pull the covers over her head.

But, of course, she was going to do no such thing. If she couldn't see her way in the darkness, she could feel her way. Cowering in her room wasn't going to get her anywhere. If she ever expected to escape, she was going to have to do something about it herself.

In the end, it was easier without lights. She could concentrate on the sound of those chanting voices, on the smell of fire and gasoline, and not be distracted by logical choices as to which turn she should make. She tried to pay attention to her path. She had no serious hope of escaping tonight—if she had, she would have put on clothes and shoes. But every bit of information was a step closer to her goal.

She went up two flights of stairs, down one, across a rampway, turned a sharp left, turned a gradual right. And suddenly, there was light coming into the hallway. Granted, not much. Just a flickering glare from beyond a floor-to-ceiling window, but enough to draw her closer, closer to the flames and the sound of voices.

The window was open. It was also barred, though she wasn't absolutely certain it if was to keep people in or keep people out. Looking out into the night, she had a strong suspicion it might be the latter.

They were dressed in white. White sheets to be exact, with hoods, eye holes cut out, and there had to be at least thirty of them, of all shapes and sizes. Even children were there, if she could judge by the height of some of the sheeted figures, and that was the most disturbing thought of all. In front of them, providing illumination, was a burning cross.

She put her hands on the bars, leaning closer, trying to make out their muffled words. The voices were garbled, threatening pseudoreligious mumbo jumbo, but the message was clear. The inhabitants of the house were a scourge upon the land and they would be wiped out by the sword and by fire before long.

She shivered, absorbing the fanatical hatred. She knew the man in front by his high-pitched fury. Pastor Lincoln leading his flock. Some were carrying torches, and she wondered if tonight was the night to perish by the flame and the sword. Or whether the threats were just part and parcel of the mob's paranoia.

A gas can was flung from somewhere in the crowd, landing with a metallic clang and the breaking of glass. The sound was too far away for the can to have reached the house, but her increased foreboding proved justified when a torch followed, arcing across the inky dark sky and landing through the smashed windshield of her rented car.

It exploded into flame with a roar, and she stepped back, shocked and startled. Stepped back against a hard, warm figure.

"Don't turn around," Ethan Winslowe said, his hands coming up to clasp her shoulders.

She couldn't have if she wanted to. He seemed immensely strong, though the pressure on her shoulders was light enough. It was the psychological pressure that was holding her in place as surely as his hard, strong hands.

She stood very still, feeling the heat and pressure from the tall body behind her, feeling the heat from the flaming car outside. Small explosions echoed in the night over the chanting crowd, as the windows blew out, the gas tank exploded and the car was engulfed in flames.

The violence of the fire seemed to have temporarily sated the angry crowd. Meg watched as they began to back away, their threats no more than mumbled rhetoric now, the torchlit figures disappearing into the fields from which they had come. Meg found herself thinking odd thoughts. How did people get to a hate-filled rally? Did they drive or did they march? Did they dress in their sheets before they set off, or did they don them just before lighting their torches?

"They've had enough for tonight," Ethan murmured from behind her. "Each time they get a little more violent, a little more destructive. Sooner or later, they're going to try to burn down this entire building."

"Why?" It was the first time she'd spoken, and the question came out flat and prosaic.

"Didn't you listen to them?" His voice was low and beguiling. "They think I'm the devil incarnate, and anyone who chooses to stay here is as evil as I am."

"But I didn't—"

"Yes, you did," his voice overrode hers. "You spurned Pastor Lincoln's offer of haven and cleansing. Granted, you were between a rock and a hard place, but the good people of Oak Grove don't take that into account. They're a superstitious, narrow-minded bunch who try to wipe out anything that goes against what they think is right and proper."

"You could talk to them. Explain you aren't trying to hurt them or the town."

"I could. But why should I when it would be a lie? They know I'm out to torment them, and they're fighting back the only way they know how."

"Why?" she asked.

"I would have thought Joseph would have explained it all to you. They murdered my father."

"He explained. Your father died of a heart attack—"

"He died through their neglect," he said, interrupting her, his voice vibrating with rage. His hands were still on her shoulders, holding her in place, and she could feel the tension in them. And the faint tremor. "Besides, I'm not doing anything so very terrible to the citizens of Oak Grove. I'm providing them with a decent livelihood, and I don't show my face around town to turn people blind and crazy."

"What are you doing, then? Why are they so frightened and angry?"

"They're not frightened enough," he said, his fingers flexing gently on her shoulders. "I own most of this town. I'm deeding a large parcel of it to the Society for Psychic Research."

"They'd think you're importing Satan into this town," she said, wishing he'd release her. Wishing his fingers weren't soothing. Arousing through the oversize shirt she'd flung around her.

"How could I be when I'm already here?" he answered. "I'm just fulfilling their worst nightmares by bringing all my followers with me."

"It's not a joke. They really believe that," she tried to argue, but a strange lassitude had crept over her and she found herself drifting backward, leaning against him, her shoulders against his chest, her buttocks against his hips.

"I'm not responsible for their sick delusions. That comes from generations of isolation and inbreeding." His fingers slid beneath her loose shirt, pulling it gently over her shoulders and down her arms. "As a matter of fact, right now, I'm not worried about them at all. I don't even want to think about them. I want to think about you."

The people were gone, the sound of voices vanished, and even her destroyed car was nothing more than a smoldering shell. The scent of night air mixed with the faint smell of fire and a soft breeze wafted through the open window, ruffling her hair, tossing it back against the man standing so closely behind her. She leaned her head back slowly, so that it rested against his shoulder, and only for a brief moment did she wonder what was happening to her.

"That's it," he murmured in that deep, enchanting voice of his as his arm drew across her chest, holding her against him, gently, oh, so gently. He was much taller than she was, particularly when she was barefoot, and she felt tiny, vulnerable. She reached up to pull his arm away, but her fingers touched soft, flowing cotton and steely muscle beneath, and instead, she simply rested her hand against his arm as she closed her eyes in the darkness, no longer fighting it.

His other hand moved down her body, skimming it lightly, scarcely touching her, dancing over her skin beneath the filmy nightgown. "You shouldn't be afraid of me, you know," he whispered in her ear, his mouth brushing the sensitive skin beneath her ear. "I would never hurt you. Never." He kissed her there, his lips nibbling lightly at the burning skin, and she felt herself begin to tremble.

"Ethan," she said, her voice not much more than a strangled plea for help, and she reached up her other hand to touch him, to touch his face, but he caught it, pulling it downward with only the slightest force till it grazed the side of his thigh.

"Or is it the dark you're afraid of?" He released her hand, letting it rest against him, and drew his own up the loose front of her nightgown, brushing against the soft cloth. "You could learn to love the darkness, my angel. You could find that's the only time when you can be truly alive, with the soft, velvet blackness all around you, holding you, caressing you, bringing you a release you never guessed existed...." Her heart was pounding almost painfully against her chest, her skin felt prickly, and behind her, she could hear his heart beating just as quickly, feel the unmistakable hardness of his reaction to her.

"Ethan," she said again, a plea or a surrender, she no longer knew. All she knew was that if he didn't touch her, she'd go mad. "Please..."

"What are you asking for?" he whispered, his mouth brushing her temple beneath her tumble of hair. "Do you want to leave me, go back into the sunlight? It's harsh out there, and burning far too brightly. Stay here in the darkness, angel. Stay with me. Give yourself to me."

Never had she wanted anything more in her life. She felt as if she were suffocating with longing, trying to drag the breath into her lungs. She wanted to be absorbed into his very skin, to sink back into him and never surface, she wanted things she couldn't even begin to imagine, things his body promised, his words promised, his soft, enticing voice promised. How could she fall in love with a voice? How could she want...

"Stop fighting me, angel," he whispered, and his hand brushed her skin, the soft, sensitized flesh of her stomach. The row of tiny buttons had disappeared and her nightgown was open to the night air. "Stop fighting yourself. Give yourself to me." And his hand moved between her legs and touched her.

What strength she had in her legs vanished and she sagged against him. It happened with shocking speed, scarcely had his long, deft fingers found her than she dissolved, lost in a darkness of sensation and despair. She opened her mouth to say something, but nothing came out but a strangled gasp of surprise, of release, of an astonished pleasure so intense that what little existed of reality vanished, and her last, amazed thought was that, for the first time in her life, she was going to faint.

Ethan caught her as she collapsed, lifting her high in his arms. She was so very small, so very fragile. He could see her clearly in the inky darkness, the pale, blue-veined lids closed down over her huge eyes, her mouth pale and soft.

He hadn't had a chance to kiss that mouth. He did so now, feeling strangely guilty, but not enough to stop. He ran his tongue across her dry lips, dampening them, and then he kissed her, hard, with the full force of his passion set free while she was too insensate to be frightened by it.

Even unconscious, she responded, her mouth clinging to his, her body arching against him. He groaned deep in his throat as he reluctantly drew back. If he kept up with that, there'd be no way he'd be able to control himself. As it was, he wanted to lay her down on the polished floor beneath them and bury himself in her body. He was trembling with need, and it took every bit of his formidable self-control to keep himself from doing just that.

He wasn't going to take her tonight, much as his body craved it. He could have her, he knew. All he had to do was carry her back to her room, strip the rest of the nightgown off her and continue what he was doing. By the time she regained consciousness, she'd be too far gone to want to stop.

But that was almost too easy. Too soon. Anticipation was a major part of the delight, and his longing, his anticipation of her was more overwhelming than any of his previous sexual experiences. He was going to have her, but the time would be perfect, the pleasure so intense that it would be worth it. Worth what would have to come next.

Worth letting her go.

DREAMS, MEG THOUGHT AS she opened her eyes to the murky daylight. They simply got weirder and weirder. It was no wonder she'd had such a strange, erotic one last night. She'd been a fool and a half to do that little striptease in front of the video camera. She'd wanted to taunt and torment the unseen man who watched her. She wanted to punish him. Instead, she'd taunted and tormented and punished herself.

She turned over in the bed, pulling the heavy cotton sheet around her. Her first sight was the mural, the half beast ravishing the willing maiden. Quickly, she averted her gaze. That too, had added to her peculiar dreams. She could remember most of it very clearly, from the smell of smoke to the feel of Ethan's body against hers. . . .

She could feel her cheeks heat up, and she put her hand against one, feeling the flush. The dream had been so realistic, she could almost fancy she could smell the smoke.

She sat up in bed, suddenly, shockingly awake. It wasn't her imagination. The smell of wet smoke clung in the air, laced with gasoline. She hadn't dreamed the fire last night.

The warm air danced across her skin, and she looked down at her body. She was still wearing the nightgown, but twenty tiny buttons had been unfastened down the front of it. Quickly, she yanked it together, and then she saw the ring.

It was much too big for her small hands, a man's ring. Someone had placed it on her hand. On her left hand, on the fourth finger, where it still hung loosely. It was heavy, dull and, unless she was mistaken, solid gold. It felt warm, not from her own flesh, but from his.

She stared at the design, unmoving. She knew enough of Roman mythology to recognize the image of the god imprinted on it. Pastor Lincoln would have a fit if he saw it. Janus, the god with two faces, the god of beginnings, of sunrise and sunset.

She was shaking. Sitting in that bed in the middle of the room, her skin flushed and feverish, her body icy cold, she was shaking. It hadn't been a dream. None of it. Ethan had come up behind her in the darkness and—

She wouldn't think about it. She couldn't think about it. Salvatore must have drugged her. Or maybe, despite all evidence to the contrary, she had dreamed it. Either way, she couldn't allow herself to dwell on it. If she did, she'd go mad.

She pulled the ring off her hand and flung it across the room. It ricocheted, rolled across the floor, and came to a stop beneath the panel of the mural that Megan found most disturbing. For a moment, she didn't move, suddenly as mindlessly superstitious as those idiots from Oak Grove.

And then she shook herself. She'd had enough. Enough of being frightened, of being coerced, of being seduced by a voice and a mysterious phantomlike presence she'd never even seen.

She was going to see him. It didn't matter if he looked like Freddy Krueger, the hunchback of Notre Dame and something out of *Night of the Living Dead* combined. She'd track him down in this ridiculous mausoleum of a house and take a good, hard look at his shocking deformities. And then maybe her enchantment would begin to fade.

An odd word for it, she had to admit as she pulled her nightgown back around her and headed for the bathroom, away from Ethan's prying video camera. Not that he was watching her. He'd be asleep in the unfriendly daylight. She'd know, as surely as she could see him herself, when he'd be watching her.

It felt like an enchantment, though, she thought as she ducked under a shower where she first scalded then froze her body. Deliberately. An evil enchantment by a wicked troll. Like Rumpelstiltskin. And the only way she'd escape was to face the monster. Learn his face, instead of his name, and then his power would vanish.

She dressed in the bathroom, just in case Ethan happened to wake up and decide to watch a little closed circuit TV. Her jeans had reappeared, thank heavens, and she pulled on a soft, faded pair and topped it with a cotton sweater. Something loose, enveloping, covering a body that felt sensitized, dangerously alive and not the slightest bit violated.

She almost screamed when she stepped back into her room, before she realized it was Ruth Wilkins standing there, an odd expression on her face.

"I suppose you've been looking at the murals," Meg said, pleased at the briskness in her voice. "Pretty kinky, aren't they?"

"I've seen the room before," Ruth said, dismissing it as something of little interest. "I found this on the floor." She held out the ring, and her pretty face was troubled.

For some reason, Meg didn't want Ruth holding it. Didn't want anyone holding it. She took it from her, enfolding it in her hand. "It's mine," she said.

"He gave it to you."

Meg didn't deny it. "How did you know it was Ethan's?"

"He always wore it. Always. I can't imagine why..." Ruth's voice trailed off and her expression went beyond troubled to deeply worried.

"I can't imagine why, either," Meg said honestly. "I just woke up and found it on my hand."

"Did you sleep with him last night?"

Meg whirled around, shocked. "Don't be disgusting."

"It's not disgusting. I was his mistress for five years."

There was no chair for Meg to sink into in shock. She could only stare at Ruth, at normal, comfortable looking, middle-aged Ruth, and tell herself the emotion sweeping through her was surprise, not a raging jealousy. "I thought you were married. I thought..."

"I was a widow with two little ones to raise. No one in that rotten town would help me, give me a job, give me a hand. My kids were going hungry, we had no heat, we had no hope. Until Ethan suggested...an arrangement."

"An arrangement you accepted?"

Ruth nodded. "I had no choice at first. I had to take care of my babies, and Ethan was the only one who'd help me."

"In return for sex."

Ruth shook her head stubbornly. "I think he would have helped me anyway. But I couldn't just take from him, even for my babies' sake. It was a fair trade. More than fair. He had his needs met, and I had mine. Oh, yes, indeed, I had mine."

There was no longer any use in denying the jealousy that was washing over Meg. "And you never saw his face?"

"Of course, I did. He wouldn't let me agree to it until I saw him. It made no difference. He was offering to help me, and deep down, he's a good man."

"What—"

"I'm not going to tell you." Ruth forestalled the inevitable question. "If he wants you to see him, he'll show you. In the meantime, he deserves whatever privacy he wants."

Meg could have disputed that, but it would have been a waste of time. She had her own determination to breach Ethan Winslowe's privacy. "What ended your... relationship?" She'd almost said "business arrangement," but realized that would have been out of pique.

"I met Burt and we fell in love. I didn't even have to tell Ethan. He knew, and he let me go with his blessing. He saved my life, he saved my babies, and then he let me go when I had to. I'd do anything for that man. Anything." Ruth's voice was as fiercely protective as it would be for her two grown babies.

"Is that why you work in the house when no one else will?"

"The town thinks I'm the worst kind of whore. Maybe I am. All I know is that Ethan never made me feel like one. When he made love to me, I felt . . . cherished."

Meg held so tightly to the ring that her hand began to ache. "But now you're happily married."

"Very happily married. I wouldn't trade Burt and my life with him for anything. But I'll tell you one thing, Megan. Ethan's a very different sort of man. Everything he does, he does better. And that includes loving. I'm in love with Burt, I'm completely satisfied with Burt. But he's nothing like Ethan."

For a moment, Meg felt herself drawn into the notion Ruth's words were conjuring, and it took everything she had to fight it. "Is this your day for procuring, Ruth?" she asked coolly.

Ruth recoiled as if she'd been slapped. And then she managed a wry smile. "I don't want him hurt, Meg. If he gave you that ring, it means something, something I can't even begin to imagine. I don't want his heart broken."

"He doesn't have one."

"Oh, yes, he does. He most certainly does. And if you hurt him, you'll have me to answer to."

"You're imagining things. I no more have the power to hurt him than I have the power to fly to the moon."

"Maybe not," Ruth said. "And I don't suppose it's up to me to stop it. If you'll give me a minute, I'll get your things packed."

Sheer panic swept through Meg. "He's letting me go?" Why did the thought terrify her when it was what she wanted most in the world?

Ruth shook her head. "He's just moving you. He sent word that it was too noisy here for you. I guess Pastor Lincoln and his bunch of crazies were up to their weekly tricks. Ethan wants you someplace more protected. Nearer his own rooms."

That would dovetail well with her plan, Meg thought with only a trace of compunction. "Let me help," she said, crossing the room.

But Ruth had already finished packing Meg's clothes. "All done. Just follow me. It's a bit of a hike." She headed out the door without waiting to see whether Megan would follow her.

Megan stood there for a moment, and then walked to the mural that disturbed and fascinated her. She stretched out her hand, letting her fingertips brush the terra-cotta wall with its erotic etchings, brush the pleasure-suffused face of the young woman, the face of the demon. And then she dropped her hand, stepping away as if burned.

The ring was still in her hand. Moving over, she set it in the middle of her unmade bed, then turned to follow Ruth.

She got as far as the door. "Damn it," she muttered under her breath. And without thinking, she turned back, grabbed the ring and then raced after Ruth. As she went, she slipped the ring back on her hand. Left hand, fourth finger. And held it tightly in place.

Chapter Ten

Megan began to lose count of the different rooms she'd spent the night in. Except for the tower room, when she was so ill, she hadn't spent more than one night in any of the rooms Ethan had her moved to. The next three days were no exception. Ruth took her to a Southwestern-style room, complete with exposed beams and corner fireplace, a room simple and beautiful enough to make Meg temporarily resigned to being a prisoner. She even made it through the endless afternoon, evening and night alone, no company but Salvatore's dour presence when he brought her dinner and returned to take the dishes. He absolutely refused to talk to her, glowering at her instead under his heavy eyebrows, and his huge, hulking body vibrated with disapproval.

He was the one to move her the next morning. Ignoring her questions about Ethan, he took her to a room that looked like nothing more than a Park Avenue apartment. Except that there was no view of skyscrapers—just the edge of the woods beyond the windows of the fourth-floor rooms.

Still Ethan didn't call for her. Still he didn't come, even in her dreams. Each room had a video camera, but she simply ignored them, changing in the bathroom, keeping out of range of those vigilant eyes. Not that Ethan was necessarily watching her, she reminded herself in what she was certain wasn't pique. He seemed to have forgotten her existence. She could have carried her denied anger one step further and decided that now that he'd gotten what he wanted from her, he was ready to dismiss her.

Except he hadn't gotten a thing from that strange encounter in the darkened hallway. Unless pleasuring someone else was the only way he got his pleasure. Maybe he simply wanted her surrender. Not to take her, just to know that he could have her if he wanted her.

Well, he couldn't, she told herself self-righteously, striding around the parquet flooring of the apartment-style room. She'd had a moment of weakness, a moment of something bordering on insanity. She'd had plenty of time since then to regain the use of her brain, and she wasn't going to succumb to a beguiling voice and seductive hands again.

By the third day, Salvatore had moved her into a room so starkly modern that she thought she might scream. Glaring white walls, abstract paintings, a queen-size mattress on the floor, and chairs she couldn't even figure how to sit on comprised the furnishings. There were no Stephen King novels in the pure white bookcase that looked like a tulip. There were books on trigonometry, something she found even more terrifying than the undead.

"How long am I going to be here?" she demanded when Salvatore brought her lunch. The food was in keeping with the room—nouvelle cuisine, with more attention paid to the presentation than to the taste. Not to mention the paucity of the serving. She was a woman who liked to eat, and she didn't consider three curls of parsnip that resembled a snake to be much of a vegetable.

Salvatore shrugged. "You'll have to ask Ethan."

"I would, if I ever saw him. Scratch that—I know I'm not going to see him. I mean, if he ever decides to grant me an audience again."

"Can't say."

"Won't say, you mean." She glared at Sal. "I want to know what's happening with my father."

"I'll ask Ethan."

"Don't you know? I thought you were his dogsbody, his gatherer of information, his faithful manservant and all that jazz."

"I know. I just have to ask him whether I can tell you."

There were no words more calculated to put her into a flaming temper. She wasn't used to having her emotions rage so out of control. Her life in Chicago had been relatively calm and ordered. Too much so, which was why she'd been intent on escaping, on finding adventure. She'd found it, all right, in spades.

She took a deep, calming breath, determined to keep herself from screaming at Sal in rage. "Salvatore, you care about Ethan, don't you? Like Ruth."

She almost thought she saw a trace of amusement in Salvatore's sullen dark eyes. "Not quite like Ruth. But yes, I'd do anything for him."

"Then can't you see that he's making a big mistake keeping me here? He's just asking for trouble. If my father gets arrested, he'll have nothing to gain by keeping quiet about me. He'll send the police out looking, and even Ethan Winslowe couldn't keep them at bay."

Salvatore's expression didn't change. "What are you asking me to do?"

For a moment, Megan was nonplussed. "Let me go?"

Salvatore didn't move. "What if I did?"

She didn't believe it. Didn't believe the glimmer of hope he'd offered her. "I'd run. I'd get as far away as fast as I could. And I wouldn't say anything. Not about this place, not about Ethan, not to anyone."

"Your father's going to stand trial, and Ethan provided most of the evidence. Aren't you going to want revenge?"

"If what Ethan said is true, then my father deserves whatever happens to him. I was on my way to Europe when I came here. I promise, if you help me get away, I'll head straight to New York and take the next plane to England. My father can fend for himself." She swallowed her own momentary compunction. She pitied her father, she truly did. But she couldn't save him from the results of his own greed, and she wasn't going to try.

Sal actually appeared to be considering the proposition. "I'll think about it."

"Salvatore..."

"I said I'll think about it," he snapped.

"All right. In the meantime, do you suppose I might be able to get some fresh air? I think the rain has let up, at least for now. I'd like—"

"The doors are open to the garden." He gestured to the wall of what she'd simply assumed were windows. "You can go out there." He headed for the door and she felt a moment's compunction for the obvious torment she'd put him through.

"And you'll consider what I asked?"

"I'll consider it. In the meantime, do me a favor."

"Anything."

"Don't take off your clothes in front of the camera again."

She almost fainted. She could feel her skin pale in shock. She'd been so certain it had been Ethan watching her. The thought that Salvatore had been a witness to her ill-advised striptease was horrifying.

Too horrifying to be believed, she realized with a sudden wave of relief. Ethan wouldn't have let him watch. "Ethan tell you to say that?" she asked, pulling herself together.

She wasn't imagining the glint of amusement in Salvatore's eyes. "I'll say one thing for you, you're smart," he acknowledged. "I'll be bringing your supper early. I have to go into town."

"Would you . . . ?"

"I told you I'd think about it. In the meantime, you stay put and keep quiet. Ethan doesn't need any distractions from the likes of you."

"Then why won't he let me go?"

Salvatore refused to say another word, slamming and locking the white steel door behind him, and for a moment, Meg worried that she might have pushed him too far, too fast. There seemed a very real possibility that he might help her escape. She had no illusions that he was doing it for her. He was obviously worried about his employer, if that was what Ethan was. He knew full well that her continued presence in the huge old monstrosity of a house was a danger to everyone, particularly to Ethan's seclusion.

She glanced down at her hands, at the ring she was twisting around her finger with an unaccustomed nervous gesture. It was odd—she didn't seem capable of leaving it behind. Every time she took it off, she felt edgy and incomplete. She'd ended up wrapping a piece of purple yarn through it to keep it in place. Logical or not, she knew that if she lost it, she'd be devastated.

She glanced out the bank of windows. The day was relatively clear for a change, and she could see the rose bushes beginning to bud. Joseph, she thought. She needed to find Joseph, to sit in the sunlight and talk to him about things no one else would talk about. And she needed to make plans.

With Salvatore gone that night, it would be the perfect time to make her move. The problem was, she had two choices. One, try to escape. Her car was gone now, demolished in flames, and how the hell she was going to explain that to the rental agency in Tennessee was something she didn't care to think about. How do you tell the bored, gum-chewing employees of Cheap-O Rent-A-Car that you've been held prisoner by a deformed madman and your car was destroyed by a white-sheeted, torch-carrying mob?

The other choice was not a wise one, however. Her other choice was not to escape, but to go in search of Ethan Winslowe. Beard the monster in his den, find the phantom and face her fantasies, her nightmares, her terrors. Prove to herself that he was real, human, someone to be pitied, not to be frightened of.

And then she could leave. Salvatore would help her, she knew that. But if she left without seeing Ethan, without facing him fully, then he'd haunt her for the rest of her life.

The choice was made, and it had really been no choice at all. In the meantime, she had to figure out how she was going to get out of this room once Salvatore left for the evening.

It took her a few minutes to figure out how to work the sliding door to the garden, something that didn't augur well for her success in tracking down Ethan that night. When she stepped into the fitful sunlight, she was shocked by the blanket of humid heat that swept over her. After days of cold, chilly rain, the sudden warmth was a shock to her system, and no sooner did she take a deep gulp of the hot, damp air than her skin began to prickle with an odd chilliness.

"There you are," Joseph's soft voice floated over to her. He was at the end of the walled garden, on his knees in the dirt, his cap pulled low over his wispy gray hair, his gnarled hands digging deep in the loam. She moved toward him, rubbing her arms briskly, stopping a few feet away. "I wondered when you'd come to see me again."

She sank down onto the thick grass, sitting cross-legged. For some reason, she didn't move closer. It was as if Joseph had an invisible shield around him, one that kept people at a safe distance. Besides, now that she'd grown accustomed to the humid weather, she was discovering it wasn't as warm as she'd first thought. As a matter of fact, it was downright chilly.

"They keep moving me around. This is the first time I've been near an outside door in days."

Joseph nodded, looking up at her to smile with that sweet, otherworldly smile of his. "So, Megan, have you decided?"

"Decided what?"

"Whether you'll leave him? Or save him?"

The gentle question was like a fireball in the pit of her stomach. "How could I save him?"

Joseph sat back on his heels and shrugged. "I don't know if I could tell you. He's been abandoned by the women in his life. By his own mother, who was so horrified by the sight of him that she kept him a virtual prisoner in this house, surrounded by a few servants and his weak-willed father. By Jean Marshall, who went back to her university and turned her back on him. By Ruth.''

''He wasn't in love with Ruth,'' Meg protested, unsure how she knew that.

But Joseph nodded. ''You're right, he wasn't. But he cared about her, protected her. By that time, he was almost beyond falling in love. It was the only way he could let her go so easily.''

''Who was Jean Marshall?'' *I'm not jealous,* she told herself firmly. *I've never even seen the man, he frightens me. I'm simply curious. The more I know about him, the better my chances of escape are.*

''A physics professor at Princeton.''

''What?''

''How do you think Ethan survived most of a lifetime in this place, never going anywhere, seeing anyone? His family imported the best tutors and paid them enough, supported their research projects, to ensure that they kept their mouths shut about what they did or didn't see. It worked fine until Jean Marshall showed up. Ethan was in his early twenties then, and he fell head-over-heels in love with her.''

I'm not jealous. ''What happened?''

''Well, to give her her due, she fell in love with him, too. But she was a young, ambitious woman, used to city lights and lots of people. She wasn't ready to bury herself out here, and Ethan couldn't face people. When she found out she was pregnant, she had an abortion and left him with nothing but a note.''

''Oh, God.''

''She was afraid her child would carry Ethan's burden...'' Joseph let the words trail. ''Ethan understood her fears. He never blamed her, and I think he would have felt better if he had. Instead, he just drew himself in more firmly here. He made an arrangement with Ruth when she was in need, but there was honest caring on both sides. He just wouldn't let himself care too much. And since she married, there's been no one for him. No one at all."

"And you think I'm that someone?" Meg demanded, summoning up an anger to squash down other less-acceptable emotions.

"I couldn't say. You're here, aren't you?"

"I want to leave."

He simply looked at her out of eyes wise and ancient, and then he shook his head. "When Salvatore leaves tonight, you could go."

She didn't bother to ask how he knew. "I want to see Ethan first."

"Not wise. Once you see him, it will be harder for you to escape."

"Why?" she asked. "Is he so afraid of having his deformities viewed that he would keep me here . . . ?"

"It's not that simple. Not at all. You're already tied to him. You know it, even as you struggle against the bonds. If you see him, those bonds will only grow stronger, and before long, you'll never be able to break free."

"The others did."

"Ah, yes. But if you left him, he would die," Joseph said simply.

Meg shivered in the cool air, rubbing her hands along her upper arms. "Don't be ridiculous. People don't just die like that."

" 'Men have died from time to time, and worms have eaten them, but not for love,' " Joseph quoted. "Maybe not. But if you get any closer to him, if you don't leave now, I wouldn't count on anything. Ethan isn't like other men. His life has been entirely different, his emotions, his power are unlike those of other men. If you're going to leave him, leave now.''

"I'm not ready to go," she said stubbornly.

Joseph closed his eyes for a moment, weary. "Then it'll be on your head. Choose wisely, Megan. His life will rest in your hands." Joseph rose, backing away from her. The sun had gone behind a cloud, casting the garden in shadows, and a light, misting rain had begun to fall.

"But Joseph . . ."

"My faith is in you, child. If you want to find him, keep turning left. If you want to leave, turn right."

"I don't understand."

"Turn left, child. Always left." And he vanished into the billowing mists, leaving her alone in the garden, shivering.

MEG HAD NO WATCH, AND THE ever-changing weather beyond the wall of glass could give her little clue as to the time of day. Salvatore brought her a tray of cold meats and salad, thumping it down on the white lacquer table, and one look at his dour face warned Meg not to ask again. He was obviously wrestling with what was best for Ethan. She might or might not take that decision out of his hands.

She waited for his footsteps to die away, then tried the steel knob on the white door. Firmly locked. She'd have no choice but to go through the gardens, find a way over the wall.

But she'd wait until darkness fell. She wasn't quite sure why—Ethan could see more clearly in the dark than she could. The fitful daylight would only hinder him if he tried to stop her.

But still she waited, picking at her food, pacing her room, ignoring the video camera that watched her with its unblinking eye. They'd taken her sneakers, taken her jeans, taken anything of comfort that might aid her escape. She had no choice but to make do in bare feet and one of those filmy caftan-type things Ruth had hung in her closet.

She slept fitfully, tossing about on the mattress that lay on the polished black floor, and when she awoke, the room was in darkness. She reached out in search of a light, and then thought better of it. Her eyes could grow accustomed to the darkness—the quarter moon let in a faint glow through the bank of windows. Enough for her to make her way through the room, not enough to let Ethan watch her, if he was so inclined.

She didn't think he was. Ever since her crazy moment in front of the camera three days ago, she sensed that he'd kept away from his monitors. He probably hadn't really thought of himself as a voyeur. Until she'd turned him into one deliberately.

Well, she'd paid for that mistake, paid dearly. If she made it out safely, her body would remember forever.

The sliding glass door was locked. It took her a ridiculously long amount of time to come to that conclusion, but there was no moving it. Sometime while she slept, someone had come and locked it securely, keeping her prisoner once more.

She pounded against it, frustration and despair washing over her. Her fist simply bounced back. The glass was steel strong, one of the new forms used in construction. Of course, Ethan would use something like that in this patchwork of building styles that seemed to be his personal hobby.

She wasn't going to be defeated so easily, she thought, summoning her anger to wash away the despair. She glanced around the room, looking for something she could throw through the window, but all the furniture was soft and modular. Nothing that could make a dent in tempered glass. The hardest thing in the room was her high-heeled shoe, and she didn't even bother wasting her time trying it.

That left the other door. She might have more luck trying to pick the lock. After all, Ethan would have no reason to have fancy locks on all the doors, not unless he made a habit of abducting young women.

She stopped dead still at the sudden horrifying thought. What if she weren't the first? What if she were simply one in a long line of prisoners kept here for Ethan's enjoyment...?

It really was time for her to escape, she thought, shaking her head. Once her delusions got that extreme, there was no hope for her. Even Ethan's worst enemies, the people of Oak Grove, hadn't accused him of abducting young women. And she believed every word Joseph told her, though she couldn't say why. If he said Ethan had only been involved with two women in his life, then that surely must be the case.

She was the first, the last, the only young woman to be imprisoned in this strange, rambling house. And she was about to make her move toward freedom, and the hell with Joseph's warnings.

Finding something with which to work on the lock was a different matter. She wasn't a Victorian virgin with hairpins; she wasn't a television detective with her own set of lockpicks. For lack of anything better, she picked up the fork and began jabbing it at the keyhole.

The door opened at her touch, swinging wide. Whoever had locked the garden doors had unlocked this one, leaving the entrance to the darkened hall clear.

For a moment, Megan didn't move. Her eyes were used to the darkness, and she could see the hallway stretching to either side. Left and right. What had Joseph said? Left if she wanted to escape, right if she wanted to find Ethan?

Or was it the other way around?

For the life of her, she couldn't remember. Just as well, too, because she couldn't decide. She was torn in two, half of her wanting to get the hell out of the house, out of Oak Grove, out of Arkansas, away from phantoms who captured and then bewitched stray travelers. Back to the hard edges of reality where she'd never long for adventure again. Maybe she'd find some safe, boring executive, settle down and be a housewife—raise children, join the PTA and forget all about this lost moment in her life.

"Lead me, Joseph," she said softly, closing her eyes for a moment. She knew where he'd lead her. She opened her eyes again and slowly, deliberately turned to the left.

She walked forever through the darkness, always turning left. She went up ramps and down them, up stairs and down them. She was moving deeper and deeper into the house, and she knew she wasn't going to end up in the night air in freedom and safety. She was going to face the phantom.

The last passage ended. The door was set deep in the stone wall. She could feel the chilly air around her, and she knew she was in the massive cellars of the old place. Ethan would be beyond that door.

She could turn around and head back. Keeping to the right, always to the right, she could make her escape and never have to hear that low, bewitching voice again, feel his breath against her skin, his hands dance across her flesh. She'd be free.

She reached out her hand and turned the knob, opening the door into the room.

The door was more brightly lit than she'd expected. Candles were burning in wall sconces, throwing fitful shadows around the large, cavernous room, and it took her eyes a moment to adjust after her long journey through the darkened hallways.

He was standing at a table, his back to the door. "You're back early, Sal," he said, without turning.

He was tall, but she knew that. A lean, strong back, with black hair growing long, to his shoulders. He was wearing black, tight-fitting pants and a loose-flowing white shirt, and as the silence grew, she saw the tension sweep through his body, the knowledge that it wasn't Sal who'd opened the door.

And then there was a resignation in his strong shoulders, mixed with anger. And slowly, deliberately, he turned to face her.

Chapter Eleven

Meg wasn't sure what she'd expected. Lon Chaney with his skeletal face in *The Phantom of the Opera*. Freddy Krueger, dripping blood. As Ethan Winslowe turned slowly to face her, she was ready to see almost anything. Except what she did see.

The left half of his face came into view, and she drew a deep, shocked breath. He was astonishingly, almost unnaturally beautiful. White-gold skin, his eye dark and mesmerizing, his mouth wide and delicate, yet still masculine, his cheekbone high and well defined against the sweep of long black hair. It was the face she'd seen illuminated by lightning, one she'd thought was part of a fever dream, the stuff dreams were made of. And then he turned the rest of the way, and she could see the other half of his face. The nightmare side.

The mark bisected his face, spreading down his neck, disappearing into his loose white shirt, a livid purple-and-red stain that covered him. His other eyelid drooped slightly over his eye, and his mouth pulled upward, giving him a faintly satanic expression. It was a face to scare little children, and the contrast between the beauty of the other side of his face made it even more devastating.

There was no expression whatsoever on either side of his face. He simply watched her, waiting for her reaction, and for a moment, she wondered whether his face was capable of showing emotion.

She was absolutely terrified. Not of his face, not of his anger. She was afraid that she might say or do the wrong thing.

She cleared her throat, the noise loud and grating in the absolute stillness of the cavernous room, and then she squared her shoulders. "So what am I supposed to do?" she asked in her most matter-of-fact voice. "Scream and faint?"

There was just the faintest glint in his eye. He took a step toward her, the movement slow, graceful and threatening. Definitely threatening.

"Others have," he said.

She held her ground, determined not to back away from him. "I don't see why. You have a birthmark—"

"Is that what you'd call it?" he interrupted, a savage note in his deep voice. "Why don't you come up with all sorts of helpful advice? Tell me about the wonders of laser surgery. Or tell me I shouldn't be so vain. Why don't you—" he was very close now "—tell me how much worse off other people are and that I should pull myself together and ignore it." There was real rage in him, an anger that was both ancient and new. An anger directed at her.

She stared up into his face with helpless fascination, caught and transfixed by the contrast, the unearthly beauty, the sorrow and pain in his eyes. "I wouldn't do that," she said. "I wouldn't lie to you."

He was so close, too close, not close enough. "You're supposed to focus on a point past my left shoulder," he said bitterly. "You're not supposed to look at my face."

"So I won't go mad or blind?" She wanted to touch him. God help her, she wanted to reach up and touch his face, soothe the anger and helpless pain. She wanted to kiss his mouth now that she could see it.

"Don't try to convince me you're not disgusted by my face. You're trembling."

"You have that effect on me."

The tension running through him was at fever pitch—she could feel it thrumming in the still air—and he wouldn't listen to her, couldn't see that she was neither horrified nor disgusted.

"You're lying," he said bitterly. "I know revulsion when I see it."

"Do you?" She stopped thinking. He was tall; she was barefoot and tiny. She reached up, cupping his face with her hands, both sides of his face, and pulled him down to her, kissing him full on the mouth.

For a moment, he froze, and she could feel the shock trembling through his body. Stillness washed over them, a silent eternity.

And then he pulled her against him, hard, slanting his mouth across hers, kissing her back with a passion that was devouring, frightening, filled with such longing that she felt as if she were going to be sucked up into a vortex of emotion.

And the worst part of it was, she wanted it. She wanted to melt into him, to lose herself in the darkness and delight he promised her. Except that if she did, there'd be nothing left of her. She'd simply cease to exist, and the thought terrified her.

She wrenched herself away, falling back, away from him, and his face reflected the uncontrolled savagery of his kiss. He'd done it on purpose, she realized dizzily.

Let loose the tight rein he kept on himself in an effort to frighten her. To test her.

"You see," he said with a mirthless laugh. "You're scared to death of me."

She shook her head, her silken hair falling in her face. "No," she said. "I'm scared of myself."

And then she ran.

She half expected him to follow her out into the darkened hallway, but there was no sound of pursuit. She crashed into a wall in her headlong pace, having temporarily lost her night vision, and then she started moving again, her breath coming in strangled rasps, as if she'd been running for miles, her skin hot and cold and shivery, her nerves screaming out. She'd taken left turns to find him in the center of his spider's web, she'd have to take right turns to escape.

It seemed hours that she struggled in the darkness, and then suddenly, she was back at her own corridor. Light poured out of her open door, a light she hadn't turned on when she left, and she paused in the doorway, staring.

She could keep going. Except that she could barely walk another step. The small light at the far end of the room provided just enough light to keep monsters at bay. Except that Ethan Winslowe was no monster, no monster at all.

She closed the door behind her, glancing up at the camera. Moving over, she sank down in the corner beneath it, well out of range of its vigilant eye. She drew her knees up, wrapped her arms around them and sank her face down. And slowly, achingly, she began to cry.

THIS TIME WHEN ETHAN heard the door open, he knew without a doubt that it was Salvatore. He was sitting in the computer room, tipped back in a chair, his feet up on the wide teak counter, his eyes shut. There was nothing to see. The television monitors were all blank, turned off. The few candles that lit the room were sporadically placed and already guttering.

"What's wrong?" Sal demanded immediately, and Ethan found himself smiling in the darkness, a small, wry smile. Sal knew him too well, could read the very air around him.

He opened his eyes and sat up, turning the chair to look at his old friend. "She found me."

"Hell and damnation. I locked the witch in—"

"Don't call her that."

Sal took a deep breath. "All right. I locked *her* in, I made doubly sure of it. She was asking me to help her escape—I would have thought if she'd been able to get out, she would have headed outside."

"Maybe she got lost. This place isn't designed for easy access." Ethan knew he sounded no more than casually interested. He also knew that Sal wasn't fooled.

"Maybe," Sal said. "So what happened?"

"You mean did she scream and faint? Not exactly." He leaned back again, remembering her expression. Wary, startled. But not revolted, even though he'd looked for that reaction. If anything, she'd looked momentarily...entranced.

He shook his head, cursing his suddenly romantic nature. "She's a strong-minded woman, you know that," he said. "She just took it in her stride." Again, not the truth. He remembered the sudden, shocking feel of her hands on his face, her mouth pressed against his with something akin to desperation. He'd let his iron control slip then, just to see how far he could push her. It wasn't until that moment that he'd really frightened her. And he suspected that if he'd caught her again, kissed her again, she would have lost that momentary terror.

"You need to let her go," Sal said, the stubborn plaint almost boring by its repetition.

"Perhaps," Ethan said. "But I need to keep her here even more."

"She's going to bring you down. The police will start looking for her sooner or later, and Reese Carey will send them straight to you. It's only been a question of luck that he hasn't put them on to you. He's going to want some revenge, and he has nothing to gain by keeping quiet."

"The moment he starts asking where his daughter is, he'll lose his only ace in the hole. He has nothing else, no cards left to play. I've got the majority of the evidence against him, and he knows it. He also knows that I haven't given everything to the district attorney. He'll keep his mouth shut for a while longer."

"Even though his daughter's missing?"

Ethan's smile wasn't pleasant. "Have we ever had the delusion that Reese Carey was a decent man? He'll look after himself first and gladly sacrifice his daughter to do so. He's probably got himself convinced that I'm some sort of reclusive Prince Charming and the two of us are having a passionate affair."

"Are you?"

Ethan jerked his head around. "I didn't think there was anything wrong with your eyesight, Sally."

"Let her go, Ethan. We could go back to the island. We've been happy there, you know we have. You have friends, people who accept you as you are. You can live a normal life there, away from this sick, crazy town.

Away from her. She'll break your heart, Ethan. She'll destroy you.''

"Don't you think I'm too tough for that?"

"No," Sal said flatly. "I think she'll kill you. Let her go."

He considered it for one brief moment. Considered the safety of his seclusion, the safety she was tearing down with her huge blue eyes and soft mouth, with her irresistible body and fierce spirit. "Not yet," he said.

"It'll be too late, Ethan."

"Not yet, Sal," he said again. Even though he knew that Sal was absolutely right.

THE DOOR TO HER ROOM slammed open, bouncing against the wall. Megan lifted her head from the softness of the mattress, staring up blearily across the sunlit room. "You got a visitor," Sal announced in a hostile voice.

For a moment, Megan simply stared blankly. It had been a long time before she slept, before she could muster the energy to crawl from her spot in the corner and collapse onto the mattress. For hours, she lay there awake, staring into the darkness, but when sleep had finally come, it had come with a heavy, drugged vengeance, with no dreams to haunt her mind or torment her body.

She struggled to a sitting position, blinking. "What?"

"You heard me. You've got a visitor. You want to see him or not?"

He knows I found Ethan, she thought. *And he's furious.* "Him?" she said aloud. "I don't think I care to go another round with Pastor Lincoln. The man's insane."

"I won't argue with that. But it's not the good pastor. It's an old friend of yours. Says his name is Robert Palmer."

"Rob? Rob's here?" Her mind couldn't comprehend it. For five weeks last summer, she'd thought she was madly in love with Rob Palmer. It had been a foolish mistake brought about by her twenty-seventh birthday and a handsome man's lies, and she'd ended it the moment she found she wasn't the only recipient of his attentions. Still, they'd managed to keep on being friends as well as co-workers, despite his occasional attempts to rekindle their abortive affair.

"So he says. You want to see him?"

"You mean you'll let me?"

"Yes," said Sal.

"Does Ethan know?"

"Ethan knows everything."

This must be a trap, a trick. "What does he want?"

"I imagine he wants to rescue you," Sal said, his voice clearly bored.

"And I imagine I'm not going to be allowed to go."

"Imagine all you want. I think it'll be up to you."

"Give me a minute to change."

"Don't you want to pack?" Sal asked.

Meg halted by the closet. "But . . ."

"Even if he hasn't come to take you back, he's bound to if you ask him. You want me to pack your things?"

"Is this a trick?" she asked, wary.

"Nope. If you want to leave with your ex-lover, then Ethan says you can go."

She glared at him. Of course, he knew Rob had briefly been her lover. It wasn't only Ethan who knew everything. Salvatore probably found the information for him in the first place.

"I'll be ready in five minutes."

"Take your time," Salvatore said with his first touch of real affability. "He'll wait."

Salvatore had put Robert in the front parlor with its staid Victorian decor. He looked just as he'd looked the last time Meg had seen him at her going-away party, with one of the junior vice presidents draped over him. Well dressed, handsome and at ease, even under these peculiar circumstances. He turned when he heard her approach, ignored Salvatore and gathered her into his arms, kissing her fully on her unsuspecting mouth.

She pushed him away, controlling her instinctive, irrational shudder of distaste, distaste for the bland mouth, the bland face. "Rob," she said, her voice full of wary relief.

"You look wonderful, Meggie. We were worried about you. First you disappeared, then your father was arrested and there was no word from you. We were afraid something had happened."

"Who's we? How did you find out where I was?" God, he was handsome, she thought dispassionately. Perfect features, perfect teeth, perfect hair.

"We?" he echoed. "The company. Madeleine, for one, and the board of directors. Granted, so far they've only been a figurehead, but with Reese in jail, they've had to do some hard work, make some hard choices."

She settled on the most important information. "Reese is in jail?"

"Actually, he's out on bail now, but he can't leave the state. That's why he sent me to find you. You don't know what it's been like, Meggie. An absolute madhouse, reporters everywhere, all the records impounded. Not that they'll be able to crack the computer code I used for your father's special projects. It would take more than a police computer specialist to get past all my safeguards.''

Megan looked at him, doing her best to disguise her horror. "You knew what he was doing?"

"Of course I did, just as you did. Reese Carey knows more about construction than some crippled recluse. Sure he took chances, but he had years of knowledge behind him. One mistake, and they're making a federal case out of it.''

"I didn't know," she said, her voice faint as she surveyed the corporate shark in front of her. He was as bad as her father, willing to endanger innocent lives in pursuit of more and more money.

"Didn't you?" Rob shrugged. "Reese told me you did, but I don't suppose it matters. Have you been able to make any progress with Winslowe?"

"Progress?"

Rob allowed his irritation to surface briefly. "To get him to back off. The government doesn't have much of a case without Winslowe's assistance. He can still make or break your father. Surely after all this time you have some influence.''

"None at all.''

Rob looked as if he was going to argue the point, then thought better of it. "Then I'd better take you home. We have work to do.''

"We do?"

"Don't be dense, Meggie. We can still effect a coverup. Discredit Winslowe. He won't take the stand, of course, and we can poke holes in his so-called evidence. Make it seem like he's just trying to foist the blame onto Reese. After all, why would he want to be a one-man vigilante? What business is it of his how Reese builds his buildings?" Rob took her hand, exerting his considerable charm. "Come on, baby, together we can do anything. We were good together, you know that. We can whip this company back into shape, send Reese on a nice long honeymoon and when he comes back, no one will remember the stink that Winslowe made. We'll talk him into an early retirement and—"

"What's this 'we'?" she asked, calmly detaching her hand from his.

"They've named you temporary president, Meggie. We need you back to mount a fight. Without you, my hands are tied."

She smiled faintly. "I'm not coming back."

He looked as if he'd been slapped. "Don't be ridiculous. You can't leave your father in the lurch like this. If we don't do something, he's going to be looking at massive fines. Maybe even a prison term."

"Good."

"Baby..."

"Don't call me baby. I never liked it. Carey Enterprises can go belly-up for all I care. The people who work for the company can find other jobs. More honorable ones. My father can pay his debt, either out of his pocket or with a few years of his life. I'm not going to bail him out with lies. I'm not going to discredit Ethan Winslowe to do it."

"What the hell's been going on here?" Rob growled.

"What do you think? I've been gone two weeks, and I haven't been spending them alone."

"You're sleeping with him? With that monster?" Rob demanded, aghast.

"That's none of your business. And what's between Ethan and my father is none of mine. Go away, Rob. I'll be just fine here."

He shook his head in disgust. "Just like that? You want to stay in this godforsaken place, surrounded by a town of genetic throwbacks?"

"Let's just say I don't want to go anywhere with you. When I'm ready to leave, I'll leave on my own."

"You're crazy."

"Goodbye, Rob. Give my father my love."

"Yeah. Sure." He started toward the door, then turned, ready to give it one last try.

She wasn't prepared for his move. One moment, she was watching him leave, struggling with her own mixed feelings about once more dismissing deliverance, the next, she was wrapped in his arms, his wet mouth devouring hers, his hips grinding against her, his hands on her rear, yanking her up against him.

She fought against him. Somewhere in the distant recesses of her mind, she thought she heard a roar of rage, but it had to be her imagination. A moment later, Rob was plucked off her, sent spinning against the door by Salvatore's efficient strength.

"I wouldn't do that if I were you," Sal said in a friendly tone. "Mr. Winslowe doesn't take kindly to people manhandling his guests. Particularly Miss Carey."

Rob stared at the two of them, and his breath was coming in rapid puffs. "What the hell is going on between you and Winslowe?" he demanded again, running a hand through his hair. He looked disheveled, far different from the corporate yuppie she'd been so briefly involved with.

"Goodbye, Rob."

He opened his mouth to make another demand, but not a sound came out, since Salvatore had picked him up by the seat of his pants and started him toward the door.

A moment later, she heard him go flying, then the slam of the door behind him.

Salvatore reappeared, rubbing his hands together briskly. "I can't say much for your taste in men."

"Go to hell," she snapped.

"So you want to stay after all?"

She was immediately wary. "I didn't say that. I just didn't want to go with him."

"Picky, aren't you?" Sal murmured. "I'll take you to your new rooms."

"New rooms?" she moaned. "Can't I spend more than one night in the same room?"

"Nope. Not according to Ethan. Besides, we don't want you making any more nocturnal visits, now do we? Mr. Winslowe cherishes his privacy." Sal started down one of the hallways, a different one from the two she'd taken so far, and she hesitated for a moment, wondering whether she ought to placate Rob long enough to get a ride to the nearest airport.

No, she couldn't do that. Not when she remembered his soft hands and blubbery mouth. And his sleazy justification for her father's criminal negligence.

Not when she remembered Ethan Winslowe, the two disparate sides of his face, the unearthly beauty and harsh disfigurement. Not when she remembered his mouth, his hands, his strength, his need.

She looked down at the ring on her finger. Now the god with two faces made sense to her.

For the time being, she wasn't going anywhere. Not anywhere at all.

Chapter Twelve

The cold, rainy weather of April turned to May, swamping the deserted little corner of Arkansas with a blast of heat. The flowers burst forth into sensuous blossoms, lilacs and irises and roses and peonies, and Megan left the windows open in the various rooms she was put in, left the windows open to welcome in the warm air, the scent of spring. Left them open to Ethan.

She knew he came sometimes while she slept. She would dream that a hand brushed across her face, drifting down her throat gently, a caress as light as the wind. She knew he watched her, watched her on the video monitors, came and stood by her while she slept. She always knew the nights he came to her. When she awoke, her skin would feel flushed, sensitive, tingling with life. But ten days passed without her even seeing his shadow in the moonlight.

Ten days of moving from room to room with only Salvatore's dour presence for company, with the occasional relief of Ruth's determined friendliness. Ten days of solitude, of an odd sort of serenity as she waited. Waited for the inevitable. Waited for him to come to her.

She had no doubt that he would. She could feel him all around her, feel his wanting, feel his need. At times, she wondered whether it was only her own, confused need that she was projecting onto him. Those were the dark times, the anxious times that sent her prowling the gardens, looking for solace, looking for Joseph and his remote wisdom.

But he was missing, too. Occasionally, she'd glimpse him in the distance, but by the time she reached the spot where she'd seen him, he'd be gone without a trace, only the scent of freshly-tended flowers reminding her that he'd been there.

Ten days. There were times when she awoke in the middle of the night, alone and frightened in the darkness. Those were the nights when Ethan hadn't come, hadn't watched her, hadn't touched her, she knew that without question. Those nights were the hardest.

Reality intruded into her dreamlike existence on those nights. She'd think of Reese, alone, under indictment, facing disgrace, facing jail, with his own child turned against him, missing from the face of the earth. Except that he knew exactly where she was, had sent her there, sacrificed her in a last-ditch effort to save his own hide.

She'd think of her apartment, of going to the movies, going out to dinner, reading the latest historical romance, eating yogurt and ice cream and drinking Diet Coke. Here she seemed to exist on hummingbird's tongues, food arcane and elegant enough to be an art form in itself. Every now and then, she'd struggle into the tightest pair of jeans she'd brought with her, certain that she had to be fading away like a good Gothic heroine. They were still as tight as ever across her hips.

She took to wearing the long, flowing garments Ruth had brought her, wispy things that drifted around her body in a flow of what she knew had to be silk. She wouldn't have worn them, except they were so comfortable, she told herself as she floated from room to room, wondering where Ethan was, wondering when he'd reappear. And nothing she did brought her any peace.

Sometimes, she thought she could hear him, his words, soft, drawing her deeper and deeper into the spider's web of enchantment he'd spun around her, and her dreams would turn sharply, deeply erotic. She was being bewitched, she knew it full well. Hypnotized, caught up in a spell that, sooner or later, she'd have to break. But for now, she felt strangely powerless, content to drift on a tide of lazy sensuality, her every whim catered to. Except her need for him.

ETHAN FOUGHT HIS NEED for her. For ten endless days, he wrestled with it, determined to keep his distance. Determined to push his longing for her, his aching need, to the level of a minor annoyance.

It was a losing battle. Maybe if he'd been able to keep away from her. Turn off the video monitors, turn off his desire for her. Maybe if he'd been able to keep to his underground lair, away from her.

But the temptation was impossible to resist. He would see her in the grainy, black-and-white monitor, watch her as she slept and know that he had to get closer. To breathe the same air. To smell the flowery scent that seemed to surround her. To touch her gilded hair. Salvatore was wrong—her hair wasn't the color of sunlight. Sunlight was harsh, glaring.

No, her shoulder-length blond waves were the exact shade of moonlight on a white rose blossom. A dreamy midnight color, silken to his gently questing fingers.

He had to send her away. He kept telling himself that he had to. The situation in town was escalating to intolerable levels, and he was giving it far too little attention as long as he was distracted by his unwilling guest. If he sent her away without touching her, he could concentrate on his lengthy plans for revenge.

But if he sent her away without touching her, it might just kill him. His body vibrated with longing for her; his soul ached for her. And he was half afraid he was going mad.

Just one more night, he promised himself. One last time. He turned off the monitor, secure in the knowledge that Sal was somewhere in the town of Oak Grove. Not that he didn't know exactly where Ethan disappeared to at night. But for this last night, Ethan didn't want a witness.

She slept lightly, fitfully, but he had the ability to move in complete silence. He stood over her as she lay on the bed, the white muslin curtains billowing around her, and he reached out his hand to touch the gentle swell of her breast.

But that would wake her and precipitate everything he'd been resisting. He pulled his hand back as if scorched, and a spasm of rage swept over him. It had been years since he'd railed against the unfairness of life. He'd accepted it with a certain grudging cynicism.

But tonight he wasn't in the mood to accept anything. He wanted to take and take and take. And he knew if he stood there for one minute more, he'd do exactly that.

He moved out into the garden, stopping by the shallow pool, staring blindly at the reflection of the moon. The longing was so intense, it shook his body, and in full, aching silence, he tilted back his head and called to her, not with his voice, but with his heart. Called for her to come to him, to break the impasse that was tearing him apart.

To come to him when he wouldn't let himself go to her. To come to him. To love him. Now.

MEGAN AWOKE ABRUPTLY, pulled from her sleep by an inexorable force. She lay there against the feather pillows, her eyes open in the darkness, trying to remember where she was. Slowly it came to her, inevitably.

They'd moved her to a new room the day before, a huge, airy room painted in white, with yards of white muslin curtains at every window, including the French doors that led into the garden. The bed was mammoth, bigger than a king-size one, and set on a low dais. The sheets were white, too, the softest Egyptian cotton, and the few pieces of furniture, the table, the one comfortable chair, were all white. The only trace of color in the room had been the flowers, a small vase of something she didn't recognize. They were a deep bloodred, with perfectly formed blossoms and a hypnotic scent that filled the room, filled her senses.

The small walled garden matched the room. Every flower in the garden was white—white roses, white peonies, white irises, white lilacs. She had no doubt at all that when the later flowers bloomed, they, too, would be white.

There was a shallow pool in the center of the garden, the pathways with their white crushed stone leading to it, and the clear blue of the water echoed the blue of the sky. The place was perfect, serenely beautiful and yet oddly, subtly unsettling.

She sat up in bed, in the darkness, the pervasive scent of the flowers filling the air. She pushed back the covers, reaching for the light, and then pulled her hand back. The moon was full that night, she could see the bright reflection of the garden through the billowing curtains. A breeze had come up, filling the room with life, and for a moment, she didn't move.

She should lie down and pull the covers around her, she told herself. She should close her eyes, close her heart, keep safe from the phantoms of the night.

But he was calling to her. She could hear him, in her heart. She could feel him, nearby at last, waiting for her, calling for her. And she could no more ignore that call than she could stop her heart from beating.

She slid from the bed, pushing aside the filmy curtains. The room was a shifting mass of shadows, but she knew without question he wasn't there. He'd been there, watching her again. And then he'd left, for what reason she couldn't fathom. He'd left without touching her, without waking her, but deep within his tortured soul, he was calling to her.

And she was answering that call with a kind of dazed certainty. Time had lost all meaning. All that mattered was Ethan, calling to her to come to him. At last.

She moved through the room blindly, her long white robe trailing after her, out past the billowing white curtains, through the open door into the garden.

The landscape was bathed in moonlight, the white flowers glowing faintly. In the shallow pool she could see the reflection of the moon, round and full and pearly white like the flowers of the garden. And she could see the reflection of Ethan, dressed in black, his body tall and lithe, his face turned away from her so that all she could see was the fall of black hair.

"Come to me," he said, and she didn't know whether the words were spoken aloud or directly to her heart. It didn't matter. She moved toward him through the garden, her bare feet silent on the sharp white gravel, knowing she no longer had any choice in the matter. Her heart had taken away that choice. She was his completely, and he'd barely touched her.

She stopped in front of him, afraid to reach out her hand. He would have to make the first move. His face was in shadows, only the beautiful side remotely visible through the fall of hair, the shifting of the moon shadows through the garden. She tried to look up at him, but she was afraid, and instead, she closed her eyes, shivering lightly in the warm night air.

He touched her then, his hand sliding along her neck, beneath her heavy blond hair, tilting her head back to face him without pulling her closer. "Open your eyes, angel," he said in a voice silken and beguiling. "Look at me."

She had no choice but to do whatever that voice told her. She opened her eyes, looking up at him fearlessly. In the moonlit garden, the dark side of his face seemed to disappear, leaving only the unearthly beauty of his profile. It didn't matter. It was more than his face that drew her to him.

His hand slid down her neck to the base of her throat, to the ornate clasp that held the dress together. His long deft fingers released it even as his eyes held hers, and the gown parted, falling loosely about her.

His other hand came up to push the gown from her shoulders, and it landed in a flow of silk at her bare feet, leaving her naked by the clear blue pool, gilded in moonlight.

He didn't lower his eyes to look at her body. Instead, he was intent on her face, her eyes, her expression. "You stayed," he said, and tension ripped the sweetness from his voice. "You could have gone with Palmer. If you'd asked again, Salvatore would have let you go."

"I didn't want to go."

"I live in darkness," he said, still not touching her, his voice low and urgent. "In the shadows, in the warmth and safety of the night. If you come to me, you'll live in shadows, too."

She lifted her head to look around, and her hair rippled down her bare back. "The moonlight is bright enough for me," she said quietly.

He reached out then, his hands cupping her face, his thumbs caressing her cheeks. "I must be mad," he whispered. "You'll destroy me."

"I'll love you," she said, but the words were silent.

"You'll destroy me," he said again, closing his eyes in sudden despair. And then he kissed her.

She had one coherent thought after his mouth met hers. That this was the way it was supposed to be. This was what people chased after all their lives. This was why a wedding ended with a kiss. This was something that sealed, that changed her life, that took her soul to a place strange and new and terrifying. This time she wouldn't run.

She pressed herself against him, needing the feel of his body against her, needing something to hold on to. He was lean and hard and muscular, and his soft black clothes pressed against her skin, arousing her with the very incongruity of cloth against nakedness. Her vulnerability should have added to her fright, but instead, it made her only more determined. Her mouth opened beneath his, accepting whatever he wanted to give her.

His arms slid around her back, arching her against him, and his mouth trailed down the side of her neck, to touch the wildly beating pulse at the base of her throat. And then, with sudden strength, he picked her up in his arms, holding her tight against him, adding to her sense of frailty, she, who'd never felt frail or vulnerable in her life.

She leaned her face against his shoulder, giving up the last ounce of fight. She was his to do whatever he wanted with, and if she felt passive, it was an oddly, intensely erotic passivity. He moved through the billowing curtains into the darkened room with only the white-shrouded furniture marking the way, and then he set her down on the bed, standing over her, watching her as he'd watched her so many nights before.

She looked up at him, silent, questioning, wanting him more than she'd ever wanted anything in her life. He was only a shadow in the darkness, a silhouette dressed in black, a phantom lover come to her bedside, and she knew a sudden longing for sunlight. She wanted to see him, to touch him, to know him.

But instinct told her to take him on his terms. So she lay back against the pillows, eyes half closed in the shadowy darkness, and waited.

She could hear the rustle of clothing, and she knew he was stripping off his clothes. She wanted to rise up on her knees, to reach out for him in the darkness, but she couldn't move, mesmerized but his unspoken command in the inky blackness. She was trembling, not with cold, not with fear, but with her need for him. She wanted him so badly, she thought she might die of it.

And then he was on the bed with her, his hands on her shoulders, pulling her to him, and his skin was hard and hot and damp against her. "Ethan," she whispered, a small cry of passion, of need, of surrender as his hands moved down her body, dancing across her sensitive skin, arousing her without touching anything but her waist, the outer sides of her thighs, her knees.

He lay back against the mound of pillows, pulling her with him, his mouth against hers, kissing her with a devastating thoroughness that was bringing her perilously close to madness. She couldn't come with just his mouth on hers, his hands on her waist, and yet she was astonishingly close to it. His hands moved upward, sliding against her midriff, and she felt the slight, arousing roughness of his skin as it danced along her softness, moving closer and closer to her aching breasts. If he didn't touch her, she'd die. She knew it even as he tore his mouth away from hers, breathing heavily as he trailed kisses down the side of her neck.

Slipping away from her, he pushed her back on the bed, flat against the mattress. She reached for him, wanting to pull him against her, but he caught her wrists, holding them down beside her body. The touch of his mouth against her breast brought a reaction so intense, it was almost painful. She tried to arch off the bed, but he was holding her still with his hands on her wrists as he slowly circled one breast with his tongue, then tugged it gently into his mouth, suckling on it, nipping lightly with his teeth before turning his attention to her other breast.

She moaned, her breath coming in strangled gasps, and she struggled against his imprisoning grip. She wanted to touch him, to pull him over her, into her. Her body was twisting, desperate with longing. She needed him, needed him now. And yet she couldn't tell him. All she could do was writhe on the bed, trying to reach for him.

His hands released her wrists and for a moment, she was almost too dazed to react as he reached up and cupped her breasts, his thumbs caressing the dampened flesh. And then he moved his mouth downward, across her flat belly to the apex of her thighs, and she couldn't make a sound of protest. He kissed her in the downy thatch of golden curls, and then lower still, his mouth finding her with devastating effect. This time she struggled for a moment, her hands finding his head and trying to pull him away as his large, strong hands cradled her hips, holding her still. And then she wasn't tugging at him, she was threading her hands through his thick, long hair, holding him against her, arching against the devastating invasion of his mouth and tongue.

The darkness closed around her, the thick velvet night where no light penetrated, as the sensations swirled around her. It made no sense. Normally, she didn't even like what he was doing to her, had always found it vastly overrated. And yet now she was being turned into a quivering, mindless mass of female flesh in response to his mouth, his hands, his sheer intensity. She didn't want it; she wanted to give to him, not take, and yet he was giving her no choice.

He knew how to judge her reactions perfectly, the shift, the restlessness, the ripple of reaction, the strangled breathing. He knew when she was just on the edge of explosion, and he knew how to expand that edge, to draw her over it, willingly, tumbling to her doom with no more than a strangled cry. He knew how to prolong it so that she was clawing at his shoulders, sobbing frantically, certain her body could take no more until he showed her, with inexorable determination, that it could.

And yet it wasn't enough. She convulsed against his mouth, her body going rigid in reaction, and still she pulled at him, tugged at him, wanting more and more of him, wanting him, not his mouth, not his hands working their fiendish magic, she wanted all of him.

She was scarcely aware that he'd released her. Not until he covered her trembling, shivering body with his, wrapping her in his arms against his own tense, damp body did she realize that despite the contractions still rippling through her, he was no longer touching her.

She put her arms around his neck, burying her tear-damp face against his shoulder. Had she thought there was any chance at all she'd be able to hold some tiny part of her inviolate? It was a false hope. He'd taken her completely, and yet he hadn't even attempted his own satisfaction yet.

His hands reached to cup her face. The moon had gone behind a cloud and the tiny glow of light had vanished from the room, leaving them plunged into inky darkness. His long fingers brushed the tears from her face, and then his mouth followed, kissing salty dampness from her cheeks, her eyelids, her mouth. She didn't need to hear the words; he didn't need to speak them. *You're mine. Forever.* She knew it in her heart, in her soul. There was no longer any chance of running.

She turned her mouth to meet his, and his long thick hair fell around them, closing them within a curtain of it. Once more darkness surrounded them, cocooning them in a world of sensation and midnight glory. He shifted her beneath him, parting her legs so that he rested against her, the heat and hardness and need of him, and she trembled, uncertain that she could take much more.

His slow, inexorable possession of her body was something she couldn't deny. It seemed endless, over-whelming, consuming, as her body shifted to accommodate him, and she knew from her initial twinge of discomfort that he was far more than what she was used to. Far more of everything. When he finally rested inside her, he pulled her legs up around his hips, settling in even deeper, and she couldn't contain a little gasp of dismay.

She could feel the iron hard muscles against her, feel the fierce control that tightened his body. ''Did I hurt you?'' he asked softly, urgently, and she knew if she said one word, he would pull away, leave her. And she would die.

But she wouldn't lie. Never would she lie to him. Instead, she kissed his mouth, silencing the question, and tightened her legs around him, pulling him in deeper still.

Now it was his turn to shudder, to tremble and shiver in reaction. The control that he'd kept so tightly began to slip, as he slowly pulled away from her, only to fill her again. She winced in the darkness, keeping still, determined not to flinch from the fierce possession of his body.

She wasn't quite sure when it changed. When the last trace of discomfort vanished and she was reaching for him, clutching at him, sobbing and weeping as he strained against her. He was so strong, so powerful, that her entire body felt invaded, overwhelmed by his possession, a possession she didn't want to end. She arched up against him, knowing that nothing could possibly reach the heights she had earlier, but reaching anyway when the moon came out from behind the clouds, filling the room with silvery light.

He had his face turned away from her so that all she could see was his unmarked profile, the sheath of long hair between them. His muscles were bunched, slippery with sweat beneath her hands, and she was loath to give up holding him, touching him, but she had to. Reaching up, she caught his face, turning him to look down at her, full face, his bisected beauty mesmerizing her. She kissed his mouth, his nose, she kissed the marked side of his face. Pushing his hair out of the way, she kissed the side of his neck where the mark continued down between their joined bodies.

For a moment, he stilled the hypnotic, powerful rhythm of his body and she was afraid she'd gone too far. She met his gaze fearlessly and she said the words she'd only thought, the words that would be her death knell. "I love you."

He closed his eyes, an expression of pain and something else she couldn't read washing over him. And then, flinging his head back, he began to move again, slow, deliberate thrusts that she met with every last ounce of her strength. Until the tempo increased, until he was thrusting into her with a fierceness that should have frightened her. She held on desperately, somehow wanting to absorb him into her very skin. She knew he was on the absolute edge of his climax; she could feel it in the shivering tension of his body and she wondered why he held off, why he waited.

And then she knew, as suddenly, without warning, her own body convulsed again, around him, with a power that seemed to stop the earth in its orbit. She could feel him, rigid against her, she could hear her name, a curse of despair and triumph, as he joined her, spilling into her, giving the last that he'd kept from her in a timeless, endless dance of desire and satisfaction that she was certain would destroy her. And she would have gone willingly.

When reality returned, it was minutes, hours later. He was lying on top of her, his marked face hidden in the white pillow beside her, and his body was cool and shivery and very tense. She knew he was going to move away, and she couldn't let him go. Threading her arms around him, she clung tightly, unaware of her tear-streaked face, the desperation in her embrace.

His tense muscles relaxed against her, and his hand came up to gently caress her face. In a moment, he was asleep, pinning her beneath his much larger body, and she found, to her amazement, that she was smiling through her tears.

He was human after all, and just as prone as any other damned man to fall asleep after making love. It was a tiny measure of relief to know that even he wasn't always astonishing.

She lay beneath him, accommodating herself to his weight, knowing she couldn't possibly be smothered, even though it felt like it. As the tumult in her heart and body subsided, the tumult in her mind increased. It made no sense. Her experience hadn't been extensive, but enough to know what she liked and didn't like, of what her own body was or was not capable. And he'd proven her wrong on every point, taken her on a trip of such mysterious, mesmerizing proportions that she doubted she'd ever be the same again.

Now he slept in her arms, weighing her down, his silken hair around them both. And not for the first time she wondered whether she'd stepped into a fairy tale or a nightmare. Or a bewildering combination of both.

There was no answer to that. Not in the middle of a moon-shadowed night with a man in her arms who not only meant more to her than anything else. He was the only thing that mattered to her. The only thing at all.

She didn't know how it happened. What strange flaw in her character made her become totally obsessed by a man who'd essentially kidnapped her, terrorized her, seduced and enchanted her. It didn't do any good to wonder. For the first time in her twenty-seven years, she was in love, irrationally, completely. Eternally. She was just going to have to figure out a way to live with it.

Live with him.

If he'd let her.

Chapter Thirteen

Watching Meg while she slept had become an obsession for Ethan. Lying in the bed beside her didn't lessen the potency of that pastime. Her eyes were closed, her sunlit hair was a tangle around her face, and he could see the trace of dried tears in the faint glow. The moon had set long ago, but he was accustomed to the dark, welcomed it. The brightness of the full moon had been almost intrusive. He preferred it this way, with the shadows all around them, enclosing them in the bed just as the muslin curtains did.

At some point during the night, they'd shifted. She lay curled up beside him, not touching him, her hands tucked under her chin, her body hunched slightly beneath the sheet that covered them. He wanted to touch her. He wanted to lift a strand of hair and kiss it, follow the peachy texture of her skin with his mouth, he wanted everything, and he wanted it so much, he shook with need. But he held himself distant, remote, a tense occupant of the huge bed, knowing his time was drawing to its damnable, inevitable conclusion.

He hadn't even let her touch him. She wanted to, he knew that. But he was afraid if she'd touched him, if she'd been more than a recipient of his overwhelming passion, then he might not be able to follow through on his determination.

He shouldn't have gone this far, he knew. But he couldn't let her go, not without having her, just once. Not without tasting that silken, peachy flesh of hers. Not without watching the passion, the astonishment, the shimmering delight in her face as he made love to her.

He'd remember that look for the rest of his life, and he had no doubt that even if, God help him, he lived to be ninety years old, his body would still respond to the memory.

It would be all that he had. A few moments more of watching her, of breathing in the flowery perfume of her body, feeling the warmth of her breath against his skin, and that would be the end. This life, this existence he'd been handed was rough enough. If his punishment for unnamed crimes including living another fifty-some years without her, he didn't think he could stand it.

He couldn't bear to let her go, but that was exactly what he intended. He'd always known he had to. For the past ten days, he'd been trying to steel himself to do just that, trying and getting nowhere. Tonight had stiffened his resolution. He'd given in to temptation, to the silent cry for him that he alone could hear. He'd gone to her, called to her, and she'd come without hesitation, without questions, without demands, with only that one, damnable protestation of love.

And it had been perfect. No, not perfect. Life wasn't perfect. It had been something close to heaven. No wonder the French called it *le petit mort,* the little death. Making love to Megan had felt like the cataclysm of everything he'd known flaming into nothingness, a death that was its own sort of triumph. Nothing else could ever come close.

She murmured something in her sleep, rubbing her face against the pillow, and then she smiled in her dreams. He wanted to reach out and pull her into his arms, his hands were shaking with the need to touch her, and still he didn't move, prolonging his torment, prolonging his agony. And then, even his formidable resolve failed and he made himself leave the bed before he gave in.

She made a tiny sound, a small, weak sound of protest, and her arms reached out for the empty space where he had lain. But she slept on, only in her dreams did she know that he'd abandoned her.

His clothes were in a tumbled heap at his feet. He pulled them on slowly, his eyes never leaving her sleeping face. She had a mark beneath her chin, a faint bruise that must have come from him. He found himself wishing that mark would never leave her. That she would look at the small mark and think of the man who'd given it to her. That even when she was back in her safe, controlled world and her sojourn here was nothing more than a distant dream, she'd find something and remember.

The wind had picked up and the muslin curtains surrounding the bed tumbled in the air, flapping against him. He could feel the approach of dawn with its glaring sunlight. It had been so long since he'd felt the sun's warmth on his face. Maybe Salvatore was right. Maybe he should go back to the island. Maybe then he'd forget about her.

It didn't take him long at all. He worked quickly, efficiently, ignoring the pain in his hands as the thorns lacerated his fingers. She slept on, oblivious, as he stepped back into the bedroom, behind the billowing bed curtains. And she only smiled faintly in her sleep as he covered her with the petals of a thousand white flowers, their scent filling the room, blending with her own flowery fragrance and the raw, erotic smell of sex.

He wanted to take her in the midst of all those creamy white petals. He wanted to lie in the flowers with her, devouring her, body and soul. He wanted her so much and in so many ways that he had only one choice. He left her.

He went straight to the computer room in the bowels of the house, comfortable in the utter darkness, welcoming it. The candles had long since burned down, but he found his way to the huge, thronelike chair with unerring instinct, sinking down into it. A trace of her flowery scent clung to him, to his skin, to his hair, to his hands. Alone in his room, he knew what he had to do. He just didn't know how he could do it.

He leaned forward and put his face in his hands. His long hair covered him, wrapping him in a curtain of her scent. And he began to shake with pain.

MEGAN WAS ALONE. The scent of flowers was all around her, but still she felt oddly bereft. She knew Ethan was gone from her, knew it without having to reach for him. She just didn't know how far away he'd gone.

The early lavender-and-coral light of dawn was threading through the billowing muslin curtains. She sat up in the bed, shivering slightly in the early-morning chill, and looked at the flowers he'd strewn over the bed. Sudden, inexplicable tears filled her eyes, and as she reached to pick up a silky white petal, the dull gold of the Janus ring gleamed on her hand.

She pulled up the sheet around her. There was nothing to worry about, she told herself. He didn't like the sunlight, she knew that. It didn't matter that she'd seen him. He'd made love to her in total darkness, and she had the insight to know that the darkness was more than a way to hide. And if he did use it to hide, it wasn't from her. It was from himself.

And he'd left her flowers. A garden of flowers, a blanket of flowers, covering her body. Why did she have a tiny, frightening feeling that those flowers were his way of saying goodbye?

Time had little meaning since she'd taken up residence in Ethan's strange house. If she had any sense at all, she should try to sleep some more, but she couldn't. She told herself it was sheer happiness dancing across her nerves, and to try to sleep would be a waste of time. She couldn't wait till he came to her again, until he touched her again. Until she touched him.

Salvatore usually came with her breakfast in the late morning, and he usually moved her to another room by early afternoon. She could tell by the rumbling in her stomach and the position of the sun overhead that he hadn't appeared by noon, and the door to the hall was securely locked. Her doubts started then, the first niggling worry beginning to creep though her intense well-being and anticipation.

The garden looked different in daylight, not nearly as mysterious. The white blossoms glowed less in daylight, and the shallow pool no longer reflected the brilliant moon. Megan stepped out, glancing at the high walls and wondering whether she could manage to shimmy up one, when she saw a familiar figure in the far corner. Joseph.

She picked her way carefully through the lush greenery, glad that she wasn't wearing one of those filmy dresses. The rose bushes had thorns that managed to scratch even through the heavy denim of her jeans, and there was an unnatural chill in the air, making her glad she'd pulled on her sweater.

Joseph was kneeling in the dirt, digging beneath a huge white rose bush, seemingly oblivious to her approach, but she knew better. For days, he'd been frustratingly absent. His appearance today wasn't a coincidence.

She wanted to take his arm, to touch another human being, to remind herself that he was flesh and blood, but she resisted the impulse. There was a touch-me-not quality about Joseph, despite his kindly expression and concern. So she simply halted a few feet away, rubbing her chilled arms briskly, and waited.

Finally, he lifted his head, and there was no reading the expression on his seamed old face. ''Don't you hurt the boy,'' he said.

She stared at him in confusion. ''The boy?''

''Ethan. I know he's a grown man. I just can't help thinking of him as a child.''

Megan sank down cross-legged in the grass. It was dry, warmed by the overhead sun, and she wondered why she was still so cold. ''Did you know him when he was a child?''

''I was there when he was born. I remember his mother's scream of horror. I imagine he does, too.''

''People don't remember things from that long ago.''

''Don't they?'' Joseph asked. ''Haven't you figured out yet that Ethan isn't like other people? It doesn't matter. If he's forgotten that, he's had plenty of time since to face people's rejections, his mother's included. I don't know that he can stand much more of it.''

''I didn't reject him,'' Megan said in a low, quiet voice.

Joseph stared at her for a moment. And then he sighed. "These are bad times, Megan. Very bad times. Even if you could give Ethan what he needed, I don't know if he'd be able to accept it. He's a man with an overwhelming rage inside him, and it's eating him up. I'm afraid he's going to destroy himself if something or someone doesn't stop him."

"I don't understand."

Joseph shook his head. "The people of Oak Grove aren't ordinary, either. They've been too isolated, too preyed upon by crazies like Pastor Lincoln. They believe in Satan, and they think Ethan is hand in hand with him, and nothing and no one is going to convince them otherwise. Especially when Ethan goes out of his way to goad them. But he's going to push them too far. They're already losing control."

"I still don't understand."

"He owns most of this town, you know. His family has for generations. And he's planning on giving about two thirds of it, some forty thousand acres, to a non-profit organization. He's even going to build their headquarters and conference center."

"It sounds noble enough."

Joseph laughed, but the sound was mirthless. "Ethan's not one for nobility. The world hasn't taught him to be noble. He's planning on building the Center for Psychic Research. Bringing the devil right into the home of all those rabid fundamentalists. They're even going to have dormitories, communal living quarters for those interested in following New Age stuff."

"Oh, God."

"Exactly," Joseph said. "Now, somewhere in the Northeast, or along the West Coast, something like that'll do just fine. Here in the heart of America, with a group of people who see Satan in every blade of grass, he's asking for disaster. And he's getting it. They've been burning crosses out here almost every night.''

"Every night?" she echoed faintly.

"Every night. They've been holding meetings out at the building site, threatening all sorts of things in the name of their own personal, vengeful god. Ethan won't stop until they're out of their minds. And they won't stop until they've destroyed him.''

If Megan felt chilled before, she felt absolutely icy inside. "But why?"

"Because he feels they killed his father. Because revenge is the only thing that keeps him going. What else does he have? A wife, family, a life of any sort at all? He's lived his life in the darkness, and now it's part of him.''

"Someone's got to make him see reason!"

"Sal tries. But Ethan's not a man to listen to anyone."

"But what about you? Why don't you try to talk to him?"

The expression on Joseph's face was so sorrowful that it almost made Megan weep to see it. For an odd, eerie moment, he reminded her of Ethan. Something about his pain-filled eyes, the desolation in the set of his shoulders. "He'd never listen to me, least of all."

She didn't question the certainty in his voice. Here was one more person who'd betrayed Ethan, either as a child or an adult. "Then I'll have to be the one to do it."

Joseph looked at her for a long moment. "I think it may be too late."

"Don't be ridiculous...."

"I think that the best thing that could happen would be for you to leave before things explode. Things have gone too far—the people in town won't listen to reason. They wouldn't even recognize it. The only way you could help Ethan would be to leave.''

"I won't."

"I don't think you're going to have much choice," Joseph said. He looked past her to the open French door to her room. Ruth stood there, framed by the flowing white curtains, a curious stillness in her stance.

Megan clambered to her feet, reluctant to face her, reluctant to see anyone. Anyone but Ethan. She turned back to say something to Joseph, but to her amazement, he'd disappeared, vanished without a sound. Somewhere, hidden in that stone wall must be a door on hinges so well-oiled that someone could come and go in complete silence. She stared at the spot where he'd been, bemused, as the sun beat down on her, warming her. And then she turned and walked slowly down the crushed stone path toward Ruth's waiting figure. As she went, she turned the ring on her finger, letting it hang loosely, clinging to it as a protection against some sort of nameless evil. Or maybe the evil wasn't that nameless. Maybe it was simply the pain of a broken heart.

"SORRY I'M LATE." Sal's voice was muffled in the darkness. Ethan didn't move. It was a testament to the sheer anguish he was going through that he hadn't even noticed Sal's failure to return.

"What time is it?" he asked, turning around in his chair and staring through the darkness at his friend's silhouetted figure.

"Sometime after six. At night. Your girlfriend's probably climbing the walls. I better get her something to eat, then I'll come back."

"What's wrong?" Ethan asked sharply, setting his hands on the table in front of him.

Sal hesitated. "I ran into a little trouble in town."

"You went in last night and you don't come back for more than twenty-four hours? I'd think it was more than a little trouble. Turn on the light."

"Let it go, Ethan."

"Turn on the light, Sally."

Salvatore had never failed to obey a direct order in his life, no matter how much he argued. Ethan instinctively shut his eyes as the dimly-watted bulbs blazed forth, giving himself a moment to accustom his night-dim gaze to the glare. When he could, he looked at Sal's battered face and he began to curse.

"It looks worse than it feels," Sal said, moving forward with utmost care.

"What happened?"

"A bunch of guys jumped me at the construction site. They were up to their usual mischief, smearing the machinery with chicken blood, tacking up signs that say Repent or Perish." He shook his head in disgust. "Some of Pastor Lincoln's minions, I'd guess. I can't believe I was dumb enough to let them get the drop on me."

"What did they do?"

"Just beat the living daylights out of me. I would have been back sooner, but they cracked a rib. I figured I'd better have it taped, and there was no way in hell I was going to let Doc put his drunken paws on me. 'Specially since I thought I saw him there watching."

"I'll kill him."

"Calm down, Ethan. Lord knows I've had worse. If I hadn't let my guard drop, they wouldn't have been able to do more than bang me up a bit." He took a step nearer. "Are you certain you're doing the right thing?

Can't you just let it go? Let the town go? Let's get out of here, go back to Saint Anne. You can even bring the girl if you have to. But let's get the hell away from here."

Ethan shook his head, a faint negation. "It's too late for that, Sally. Too late for everything."

"What happened while I was gone?" Sal's voice was sharp with suspicion.

Ethan looked at him from behind the curtain of hair. "Not a thing," he said, not even wondering why he lied. He'd never lied to Sally, not in the decades they'd been together, from the time Sally had been a father figure, teacher and bodyguard all rolled into one. But he was lying to him now. He didn't want anyone's opinion, even anyone's knowledge, tainting the hours he'd spent in Megan's bed. It was over, sealed away forever in his heart. It was for him alone.

Sal took him at his word. "So what's next?"

Ethan leaned back, making a little temple of his fingertips. Fingertips that trembled slightly. "You get her out of here."

"When?"

"Just as soon as you can make arrangements. Tonight, if possible. Tomorrow at the latest."

"I'll make it tonight," Sal said. "As long as you're certain."

"I'm certain. Get her out of here, Sally. Please." He didn't bother to disguise the raw pain in his voice. He'd managed to lie to Sally once—any more would be pushing it.

"She's gone," Sal said evenly, spinning around and heading back to the door, a new purpose in his stride. Ethan wasn't the slightest bit surprised. Sal was possessive—after years of being almost everything to Ethan, he felt jealous of anyone interfering in their relationship.

He kept his own romantic entanglements to a healthy minimum, and while he was more than happy to make those same arrangements for Ethan, for someone healthy and energetic to come to him in the dark, he wouldn't have wanted Ethan's heart involved.

He'd disliked Megan the moment she'd arrived, and Ethan had been under no delusions as to why. He'd known, as Ethan had known, that Megan was going to change their lives. That she was going to matter, more than any other woman ever had. And the thought had frightened Salvatore almost as much as it had frightened Ethan.

He'd never see her again. He'd have to resist the temptation to have Sal check up on her, see how she was doing over the ensuing years. If he heard she married, had children, it would tear him apart. If he heard she kept herself remote, mourning something long past, it would be even worse.

Maybe it would all be moot. He hadn't needed the proof of Sal's battered countenance to know that the people of Oak Grove were getting riled to a point of madness. He'd planned it that way. Sooner or later, they weren't going to be content with burning crosses. Sooner or later, they were going to march on this house with flaming torches, setting it ablaze as some sort of fiery sacrifice to the vengeful god they worshiped. He only hoped he'd be trapped inside.

The construction crews were coming in two days, ready to break ground on the research center. The greedy denizens of Oak Grove had their limits—this time, they wouldn't take his money to work on his project. No one had come out to the house in two days, no one but Ruth. They were planning a bloody uprising that might very well take all of them with it.

Another reason to get Megan safely out of here. He guessed he had a few days' grace before the town imploded, but there were no guarantees. He wanted her far gone, off on her aborted trip to Europe, before it did.

Fifty years without her. They stretched ahead of him, an endless desert of unbearable pain. If they didn't torch the building, he might very well do it himself.

MEGAN SAT IN THE MIDDLE OF the huge bed, her legs drawn up to her body, shivering slightly. She'd lost count of how long she'd been in residence in Ethan Winslowe's rambling old house, but of one thing she was certain. This was the first time they hadn't moved her to a new room by midday. _

It was a good sign, she told herself, but she didn't believe it. He wanted her there, he wanted to join her in the huge white bed again, but she didn't believe it. Disaster loomed over her like a huge, dark bird. He wasn't going to come to her again.

She hadn't touched the food Ruth had brought her. She hadn't responded to Ruth's cheerful conversation. She'd made the bed herself so that Ruth wouldn't realize those pristine white sheets had seen more than just sleep. But she'd kept her secrets to herself. She wasn't ready for an audience, someone to share the earth-shattering moments of the night before. Particularly not someone who'd already shared Ethan Winslowe's bed.

It was irrational and unfair of her, but she didn't want to look at Ruth, didn't want to talk to her, didn't want to be anywhere around her. What had been simple, unacknowledged jealousy before had taken on soul-eating proportions. The thought that Ethan had touched Ruth the way he'd touched her made Megan want to scream.

Except that she knew, deep in her heart of hearts, that he hadn't. He might have had sex with Ruth over a period of years—she wouldn't deny that. He might have even made love to her. But he hadn't shared what he'd shared with Megan. Those few hours with her were more important than years with Ruth. Meg didn't know how she knew that. But she did with unshakable certainty.

She rocked back and forth on the bed, her arms wrapped tightly around her knees, as the night fell around her. She didn't bother to turn on the meager lights in the white room. He wouldn't come to her in the light. And all that mattered was that he come to her. She was trembling with need, with longing. She could do nothing but sit and wait and fight the dread that filled her.

She heard the key in the door leading to the hall, and that dread spilled over. Ethan wouldn't use a key. He wouldn't need one. She huddled deeper into herself, dropping her head down, refusing to face what she knew she'd have to.

A pool of lights spread into the room and she could see his shadow there. "Get your things together," Sal said, his voice faintly muffled and infinitely hostile.

She looked up, then, into his battered face and angry eyes. "You're moving me to another room?" she asked, already knowing the answer to the question, hoping and praying she was wrong. He was going to move her to Ethan's room, Ethan's bed, so that she never had to be far from him. *Please, God, let it be that.*

Sal shook his head. "You're leaving. Getting out of here, back to your own safe world. Tonight."

She didn't move. Wouldn't, couldn't move. "How?"

"I've got a car for you. A four-wheel-drive Blazer with enough gas to get you wherever you need to go.

Nothing will stop you. By tomorrow morning, you'll think this is just a nightmare.''

"And if I refuse to go?"

He stared at her. "You've been begging and pleading and complaining since you got here. You're finally getting your wish.''

"And if I refuse to go?'' she repeated.

"Then I'll carry you out to the car, drive you to the nearest airport and drop you there. You'll never find your way back here. And if you do, it'll probably be too late.''

"Too late?''

"Either this place will be gone or we will. Face it, girly. He doesn't want you. He's finished playing his little games with you. He wants you gone.''

Megan didn't move as rage and pain battled for control deep inside. Rage was beginning to win. "When?''

"I'll have to get the car ready, get it gassed up. I'll be back for you in an hour. And don't think you can go find him on your own and plead your case. This house is too convoluted for anyone to find anything. He doesn't want to see you, and there's no way you'll be able to force him. You're leaving, either willingly or not. Be ready.'' The door banged closed behind him, bouncing against the door jam. Bouncing before the automatic lock could click into place.

She waited until his heavy footsteps faded into the distance. And then she pulled herself from the bed, absolutely vibrating with rage.

Her hands were shaking as she ripped off the filmy gown she'd been wearing and pulled on her jeans and sweater. Ethan thought he could simply dismiss her, did he? He thought he could kidnap her, hold her hostage, make love to her and then simply send her on her way without a word?

He was in for a rude awakening. Never in her life had she suffered the ignominy of a one-night stand, and she wasn't about to start with her personal phantom. If he wanted to get rid of her, he was going to have to tell her himself.

As for the ability to find him in this maze of passageways, she had no doubt at all. She had a sixth sense about him, one that would take her directly to him. He'd have to tell her himself. Full face, with the lights blazing. He'd have to send her away himself. And then maybe she'd go.

Chapter Fourteen

Ethan could hear the distant rumble of thunder, far above him, through the stories of concrete and steel, wood and plaster. He sat alone in the center of the rambling mansion, alone in the darkness, and waited for her to leave.

He'd know when she was gone. It was very simple—his heart would be torn out. The pain that rippled beneath his skin would overwhelm him, blind him, wipe out all conscious thought. He would sit there, alone in the darkness, and die of grief.

He wasn't naive enough to think she'd leave easily. She'd be bound to have mixed feelings. On the one hand, she wanted to escape, had wanted nothing else since she'd arrived.

On the other hand, he knew perfectly well that what had passed between them last night was out of the ordinary. For both of them. He'd seen it in the shattered expression in her deep blue eyes, the tremulous mouth, the tears, heard it in her strangled, helpless expression of love.

She'd get over it, he thought, trying to summon up his customary ruthlessness. She was temporarily enchanted by the place, by the circumstances, by the man. Once she got back to her own life, to the harsh brightness of the sun and the noise of the cities, she'd count herself lucky in her escape.

There was even the remote possibility that he might get over it, too. He could listen to Sal's good advice, leave this place, leave his revenge, leave Joseph and Ruth and go back to the island. Where no one stared at him or even looked twice, where he could sit in the sun-dappled shadows and swim in the ocean, where he could breathe the air and feel the cool tropical breezes on his skin. Where the sunlight wasn't harsh and cruel, but soft and gentle, where the nights were warm and peaceful.

But he didn't want the breezes, the sun, the water. He didn't want anything but the one thing he couldn't have. Megan Carey.

Leaning back, he shut his eyes in the inky darkness. *Let her leave quickly,* he prayed to a distant, distrusted God.

MEGAN WAS HOPELESSLY LOST. She'd been so certain she could find him. Her sense of direction had always been excellent, and she'd been taken down to his lair enough times that it should have been child's play to find it again.

Instead, she just went deeper and deeper into the cavernous old house, turning corner after corner, passing gaslights and candles and dim electric lights, torches and kerosene lanterns and miner's lamps, heading down into total darkness. She thought she could hear the distant scratching, scuttling sound of something she'd rather not even contemplate. Rats, Salvatore had told her the day she arrived, and she hadn't been sure whether to believe him or not. Alone in the darkness, she had no doubt at all.

She recognized the squeaky sound, too. High pitched, with an ominous fluttering overhead. Bats. She put a nervous hand to her tangled hair. Did bats really fly into people's hair? Did rats really climb up their clothes?

There was still a faint glow of light in the long, tunnellike ramp that led down into the bowels of the house. In the distance she could hear the rumble of thunder, and she managed to summon forth a nervous laugh. She should have stayed in the flowing white robe and kept the candlestick in her hand. Then she would have been the perfect Gothic heroine. Gothic heroines didn't wear jeans and sweaters and Reeboks. They weren't consumed with rage at being seduced and abandoned. Ethan had mocked her for being a virginal heroine. She was far from it now. She was a woman filled with rage and determination.

One thing she was absolutely determined about. She wasn't going to leave this place until Ethan himself told her to go.

She wasn't sure when the uneasiness slid over into fright. And when the fright sizzled into panic. The final clap of thunder did it, loud enough to shake a building that seemed to cover acres, rattling the windows, the walls, Megan's teeth and bones. She screamed, alone in the darkness as the last faint trace of light abruptly disappeared, and she knew that whatever power the house boasted had been abruptly terminated. She was alone in the darkness, with rats and mice and bats. She was lost and terrified.

She couldn't take another step into the inky darkness of the hallway. She didn't know what she might find, and she didn't allow her panicked imagination to even think about it. She sank down on her haunches, leaning against the stone wall, and then slid farther, curling her legs up underneath her. She was cold, so very cold. And alone.

Ethan, she thought, the name a cry of grief and longing. *Ethan, I'm frightened.*

There was no light. No sound. No warning at all but the brush of air against her skin. And then his hands were on her arms—she knew they could be no hands but his—hauling her upward, into his arms, strong hands, hurtful hands.

She didn't mind. She went to him, weeping with relief, yanking her arms free and sliding them around his neck, reaching up on tiptoes to find his mouth.

He tried to jerk away, but she caught his long hair, entwining her fingers through it, and held him still for her desperate kiss. And as if he couldn't help it, he kissed her back, a kiss fraught with anger and despair.

She moved her hands down between them. She could feel his loose shirt, and without thinking, she yanked at it, ripping it open so that the buttons went flying, exposing his warm, smooth skin to her touch. She pulled her mouth away from his, sinking down, kissing his chest, the smoothly muscled torso, as her hands caught his belt buckle and began fumbling with it.

He groaned, a sound of pain and pleasure, as she dropped to her knees in front of him, and then his hands caught her, the fingers hard and painful on her shoulders; and he hauled her up, away from him, shoving her against the wall and pinning her there.

"Don't," he said, and the one word was a rasp of agony.

She was trembling with reaction, with need. She wanted to touch him, press her face against his bare stomach, take him into her mouth and love him. She wanted to do things to him that she'd never contemplated; she wanted to love him in every possible way. And she was frightened...frightened....

"Don't send me away," she said brokenly. "Don't make me leave. You don't really want me to go, I know you don't."

The fingers on her shoulders tightened painfully for a moment, and then released her as he stepped back into the darkness. "You know nothing," he said, and it sounded as if each word was infinitely painful. "The game is over. Go back to your safe little world, your lovers, your father. Forget about this place. Forget about me."

"I can't. Ethan, I love—"

"No!" he said, drowning out her declaration. "It's over, Megan. I got what I wanted. And now I want you to go away."

He meant it, she thought numbly. He meant every word of it. His voice was cold, harsh, and that painful yearning that was tearing her heart apart had to come from her alone.

The wall was cold and solid at her back. She could hear the thunder rumbling overhead, an angry god muttering in the distance. And she knew her choice was simple. She could throw herself at his feet and beg him. Or she could run.

But she'd already begged and it had done her no good. He could see in the dark quite clearly. He could see her white, stricken face, the pain and sorrow. Whereas she could see nothing at all.

The silence was brief and endless. And then she broke it. She couldn't see him, but she knew where he was in the dark. She crossed the black space between them, reached up and pulled his marked face down to hers. "Damn you, Ethan," she said, her voice a strangled cry.

And she kissed him, the tears flowing down her face, she kissed his cold, unresponsive mouth with hopeless desperation. And then as she felt him lift his hands toward her, she shoved him away, knocking him off balance, as she began to run.

The sense of direction that had failed her chose then to reappear. Too soon she found herself back in the Victorian section of the house, the front parlor with its stuffy furniture, the front door and the porch. She hoped, she prayed the door would be locked, just as she'd hoped and prayed that Ethan would follow her through her headlong flight through the tunnels. But he hadn't; he'd let her run. And the door opened beneath her trembling fingertips, opened to the storm-tossed night.

It was inky black, the full moon covered by the thick, ominous clouds. She could hear the soughing of the wind, the crack of thunder, the sound of trees bending and creaking. A streak of lightning split the sky, illuminating the car that sat directly in front of the entrance. The Blazer Sal had promised.

She had no doubt it would be filled with her suitcases. The key would be in the ignition, the gas tank would be filled. Her sendoff would be complete.

Another crack of thunder, following close upon the lightning, and she shut her eyes, feeling her body vibrate with pain. She could feel him calling her, but she ignored it. It had to be her own desperate wanting. He'd sent her away. She had no choice but to go.

She didn't dare hesitate any longer. Running down the steps, she crossed the drive and jumped into the Blazer. It roared to life when she turned the key, and her last hope was gone. She would have to leave. Unless a beneficent God dropped a tree in front of the car and halted her reluctant escape.

Lightning flashed, illuminating the stormy landscape, and she could see the trees bending in the wind. But they held fast, and she knew she had no choice but to ignore the cry that echoed in her heart, ignore her own despair, and leave.

She shoved the Blazer into gear, tears pouring down her face. The rain started, fat, angry drops splattering the windshield, moments later obscuring everything beyond the headlights. Megan ignored it, blinded by her own tears, and shoved the car into Drive, stomping on the accelerator and taking off with a fishtailed swerve in the mud.

Megan. It wasn't the sound of her name. It was a roar of anguish, like an animal in pain. It wasn't in her ears, it was in her heart, filling her, clawing at her, ripping her apart. *Megan,* he cried, *if you leave me, I'll die. Megan,* he cried.

She slammed on the brakes, but the car kept going, sliding across the rain-slick drive and ending in a water-filled ditch by the side of the road. The headlights were glinting crazily through the heavy rain, but she ignored it, leaping from the car and running back. Back to Ethan.

She didn't go back into the house. This time she listened to her instincts, to her heart, knowing where to find him. She went to the left, skirting the rambling structure, fighting her way through the gardens, brambles tearing at her hair, scratching her tear-streaked face. She slid once, falling in the mud, and she cursed the fact that it slowed her down. But she was on her feet, running, her heart bursting in her chest, running to him as she heard his roar of pain and grief vibrate through her soul.

He was standing in the middle of a garden she'd never seen before. She stopped in the entrance, still in the darkness, knowing he was there before she could see him, and then the lightning flashed again, illuminating him. He was wearing dark pants, and the white shirt she'd ripped open was plastered against his strong body, wet with rain. His face was turned up to the angry sky, his long hair rippled down his back, and the perfect half of his face was stark with despair. And then he turned to her, and she could see both sides of his face, the darkness and the beauty, and she could see the grief, the longing. The need. And the love.

"Megan," he cried, and this time she heard the word with her ears as well as her heart.

She ran to him, across the rain-swept garden, and he caught her in his arms, in an embrace so fierce she thought she might be crushed. He kissed her, raining kisses across her face, across the tears and rain, and she kissed him back, clinging to him fiercely.

"Don't listen to me," he said in her ear. "Don't leave me. If you leave me, I'll die."

"I'll never leave you."

"I tried to let you go. I tried to send you away, I know I should—"

"Hush," she said, covering his mouth with hers, silencing him with hurried kisses. "You can't send me away. Wherever you are, I'll hear you, I'll come to you. You can't get rid of me, Ethan. I love you. Forever."

And then there was no more need for words. She pushed his torn shirt off his shoulder, following his rain-slick skin with her mouth, tasting his flesh, cool with rain, letting her tongue dance off the soft tendrils of hair as she undid his belt, releasing him into her hands.

He hadn't let her touch him last night. Now, in the rain, in the stormy garden, he held himself still, his hands threaded through her hair as she kissed him, held him, loved him, and words tumbled from his mouth as his fingers clenched against her scalp, part curse, part plea. She could feel the heat in his body, the swelling ebb and flow, and when he could stand it no more, he pulled her up against him and covered her mouth with his as he lifted her into his arms, wrapping her arms and legs around him as he carried her into the house.

She had no sense of where they were, and she didn't care. Inside the door, he released her, ripping off her clothes with the same shaking passion that suffused her body. She was trembling so hard, she couldn't help him, didn't want to help him. All she wanted was to touch and kiss his body, to possess it, possess him, until there was nothing left between them, no secrets, nothing held back.

And then she was naked, wet with rain and sweat, shaking with fear and desire, and he was naked, wet with rain and sweat, and he lifted her up in his arms, pushing her back against an unseen wall and entered her, driving deep with a fierce thrust that made her cry out in instant, shuddering satisfaction. He wrapped her legs around him, holding on to her hips as he drove in and out, in and out, like someone possessed, and his mouth against hers, the words that tumbled forth, love words, sex words, angry and despairing and tender, simply fanned the flame higher and hotter until she thought she might explode from the power of his thrusts, the power of his love.

And then she did, again and again and again, as the madness closed around her, beating at her brain, at her heart, like the wings of angels. And she felt him burst within her, filling her with the hot wet tumult of his love.

He was shaking too hard to hold her. She was too weak to support herself. Together, they slid to the floor, a tangle of arms and legs and racing hearts, a tangle of love-slick bodies and lovesick souls. He pulled her against him, and his strong hands were tender, gentle, protective on her sensitized flesh. She rested her head against his shoulder, closing her eyes and drawing in a deep, shaky breath, too overwhelmed to speak. She had no experience with these feelings, these needs, these desires. And lying there in the cradle of his arms, still trembling with the aftermath of their explosive joining, she wanted him again. She wanted him in every way possible. She wanted to make love again, to experience that conflagration. She wanted to hold him, to give in to the unexpected tears that were burning at the back of her eyes. She wanted to tease him, to laugh with him, to have his babies and heal his soul.

"Are we...going to sleep on the...floor?" she managed to ask, her voice still shaky.

There was a long silence, only his hand stroking her shoulder, deep, strong strokes that were as soothing as they were arousing. Finally he spoke. "Only until I get enough strength to get us over to the bed. You wear a man out, Megan."

She laughed, a soft, gentle sound. "What are we going to do when we make it to the bed?"

His hand moved up her neck to cup her face, and his lips danced across hers. "I imagine we'll make love again. Unless you feel like letting me sleep."

"Do you want to sleep?"

His own laugh was equally gentle. "Not in this life-time." His muscles bunched beneath her hands, and he scooped her up in his arms, swinging her through the darkness so that she felt oddly weightless, disoriented, before he set her down on a bed. The room was pitch black, only the streaks of lightning penetrating into the darkness, and they were gone as soon as they started. She felt him sitting beside her supine body, leaning over her, and she opened her mouth to ask him, then shut it again, afraid to drive him away.

But he could see in the dark, feel her response. "What?" he asked. "What do you want from me? If I can, I'll give it."

The heat was already starting to build again, that burning, yearning ache that centered between her legs and spread up through her belly to her breasts, her mouth, her body and soul. She didn't want to lose him, but she had to ask.

"Could we make love with the lights on?"

The utter stillness in the room was deafening. Even the pouring rain, the fading thunder seemed to have van-ished, and for a moment, she was afraid Ethan had vanished, too, gone back to his subterranean lair, never to surface again. He didn't say a word, and she could feel the torment she'd put him through, and she cursed herself, but she didn't withdraw the request.

The bed creaked, shifted, and she thought he was leaving her. And then the room was flooded with a blinding light, a white-hot blaze of brilliance that hurt the eyes. She shut hers with a little gasp, unused to the brightness, but his hands were on her wrists, pulling them away.

She blinked rapidly as her eyes grew accustomed to the brilliance. And then she looked up at him, at his utterly still body and expressionless face.

The mark was as she remembered, bisecting his face, turning it into a thing of tragic beauty. What she hadn't known was that the mark spread down his body, his neck, one shoulder, and his torso, ending just above his hip. The mottled, liver-colored flesh contrasted to the lightly golden tone of the rest of him, once more emphasizing the contrast, and beneath that skin was a strong, leanly muscled body, And he was the most erotic thing she'd ever seen in her life.

She sat up, still shaky with effort, and leaned forward, pressing her mouth against his. Then she kissed his neck, the marked side. She kissed his shoulder, using her tongue, she kissed the flat, tight male nipple, she kissed his stomach and his waist and his hip as he sat there, utterly still and unmoving.

She looked up at him, wondering if he wanted her to go further, wondering if he was angry or disappointed with her request and her reaction. Belatedly, she realized that the brightness did more than expose him to her curious eyes. It exposed her, too, extra ten pounds, too-rounded hips, too-full thighs and all. And she started to retreat in sudden uncertainty, back against the sheets, and she knew her expression must have signaled some of her self-doubt.

He smiled then, a faint, rueful upturning of his mouth. "You're right," he said in his soft, beguiling voice. "There's something to be said for being able to see. Especially when it's someone as beautiful as you are."

"I'm not—" she began, prepared to point out all her deficiencies, but he stopped her mouth with his, stretching out beside her in the glaring midnight light. And then she realized those ten pounds didn't matter, not one bit. To him, she really was beautiful. And if he thought so, she did, too.

They did sleep, at least for a while. They awoke to make love again, then slept, then awoke. The bright glare of the electric light was joined by the approaching lights of dawn, filling the room with a murky gray light. Megan cuddled in Ethan's arms, too content to sleep, and surveyed the room.

It was one she hadn't seen, one that wasn't part of the game of musical rooms Ethan had been sending her on. The sheets beneath them were a pearly gray, the walls a similar muted color, and the rug that they'd tumbled onto earlier was a beautiful Oriental with shades of gray and rose. Candlesticks were mounted on the walls, on the dresser, and the pile of books beside the bed was a haphazard tower. She knew without question that this was Ethan's bedroom, Ethan's bed, not one more in a line of secret rooms. She looked up at the walls, squinting through the darkness to decipher the one shadowed painting that adorned the bare stucco. It was a chiaroscuro of light and shadows, and she squinted, then found herself sitting up, pulling herself carefully out of Ethan's sleeping arms to focus on the painting.

It was a life-size nude. And it was unquestionably her. He'd painted her from memory in the act of doing her defiant striptease in front of the video camera. He'd captured her anger, her challenge, every ripe curve to perfection. But he'd also captured her vulnerability. An expression in the back of her eyes as she stared out at the world, daring him to come to her. Daring him to love her.

He was awake, of course. "Do you like it?"

"Did you paint it?"

"Did you think I would have let anyone else see you?"

"You had Sal lie to me. Why?" She knew the answer, but she had to hear it from him.

"I wanted to make you angry. To drive you away. To somehow lessen the power you had over me."

She looked down at him, lying back against the pearly gray pillow. "Did it work?"

"What do you think?"

She glanced back at the painting, at the woman who was here, and yet far more than she'd ever thought she could be. "I think you really do love me," she said. "I think—"

Her words were interrupted by a thunderous pounding on the hall door. With a little shriek, she dived down in the bed, pulling the covers around her, huddling against him.

"Why the hell's the door locked?" Sal's voice demanded from the other side, a rough urgency filling it.

"Because I wanted to lock it," Ethan replied, his voice cool as his hand gently stroked Megan's huddled form. "What do you want?"

"We got trouble. Plenty of it. For one thing, and that's the least of our worries, the girl didn't leave last night. She must be wandering around the place looking for trouble. The car was left in a ditch with the lights on. The battery's dead, and it's going to take hours to recharge it, and—"

"You said that was the least of our worries," Ethan reminded him, his hand dipping beneath the sheet to stroke the smooth line of Meg's back.

"Yeah. She'll turn up like a bad penny. It's Ruth."

Ethan's hand stopped its slow, erotic motion. "What about Ruth?"

"She's been taken to the hospital in Millers Fork. Burt says she's in stable condition, but he's staying over there."

"What happened to her? Who took her to the hospital?"

"Burt drove her. Doc was too drunk to help. And the others…" There was a strangled pause on the other side of the heavy door. "They stoned her, Ethan," Sal said in a broken voice. "Pastor Lincoln got everyone convinced she was the whore of Babylon, consorting with the Satan that lives on their doorstep, and they went after her with rocks."

Ethan had pulled himself upright in the bed, a dark, unreadable expression on his face. "They hurt her because of me."

"No, Ethan. They hurt her because they're crazy and wicked and stupid," Megan said urgently, putting her hand on his arm. He didn't yank it away, he just sat there.

She'd forgotten Sal didn't know where she was until she'd spoken. "She's in there with you, isn't she?" he said finally, his voice heavy with disapproval and something else.

"Yes," Ethan said.

There was a pause. "Then you'd better keep her with you. There's no telling what that mob will do at this point. Once they've tasted blood, there may be no stopping them. Or maybe they're so frightened and ashamed of what they've done that they'll lie low for a while. Long enough for us to get away from this place. You'll go, won't you, Ethan?"

Ethan looked at Megan's pale, questioning face. And then he put out his hand, pushing the tangled sheaf of hair away from her eyes. "Yes," he said. "I'll go."

Megan, hearing the defeat and acceptance in his voice, wondered whether he'd be going alone. Or whether he'd take her with him.

Chapter Fifteen

Ethan left her then. She hadn't expected him to stay with her. Without a word, he left the bed, moving with unselfconscious grace and disappearing into an adjoining room that she assumed was a bathroom.

With a sigh, she rose, grabbing the pearl gray top sheet from its spot on the floor and wrapping it around her like a toga. She went to the hall door, unlocking it, bracing herself to meet Sal's disapproving eyes.

In the light of day, he wasn't looking any too good himself. The livid bruises that had adorned his face had turned even brighter, and she could only assume they'd come from an encounter with the same crazed group of townspeople. He was right, they had to get out of there as fast as they could, before the whole thing exploded around them.

"Sorry about the car," she said inanely.

He just stared at her. "You should have left while you still could," he said, his rough voice somber.

She glanced over her shoulder at the tightly shut door. "I couldn't," she said, more to herself than to him.

Sal followed her gaze. "No," he said. "I guess you couldn't." He moved past her, not touching her, but she could sense his mental dismissal. "I put your suitcases back in your room. You'll probably want to change." His gaze raked the sheet she had pulled around her. "And Ethan and I will need some time alone."

"All right." She couldn't think of an argument. And she desperately longed for a shower and a change of clothes. Maybe then she wouldn't feel so weak and shaky, so helpless. She wasn't used to feeling helpless— it was an unpleasant feeling, but one she couldn't shake. She was at the mercy of emotions, events that she couldn't control, couldn't even influence. She was at the mercy of a man who mystified as much as he enchanted her.

"Just keep turning right and you'll come to your room," Sal said, sensing her hesitation. "Anyone with your ability to get into places where you shouldn't be won't have any trouble finding it. And once you're there, for God's sake, stay put. Ethan will know where to find you. I'll be going into town to find out exactly how bad things are. I wouldn't want you to be wandering around alone if Pastor Lincoln decided to make one last try at converting you."

Megan shivered. "I'll stay in my room. At least until Ethan comes to get me."

Salvatore's answering snort was far from encouraging.

ETHAN DIDN'T COME TO get her. She made up a dozen excuses for him. He had to be as tired as she was after their sleepless night. She was able to sleep for several hours on the muslin-enclosed bed, hoping, dreaming that when she awoke, Ethan would be lying beside her. But when a nightmare yanked her into sweating, heart-pounding wakefulness, she was alone in the darkening afternoon.

The thunder was back, a distant, ominous rumble, and the wind had picked up once more. She climbed off the huge bed, stretched her cramped, sore muscles and walked over to the French doors. The white-flowered garden was empty—no elderly gardener was stooped over the fragrant blossoms. She'd have to remember to ask Ethan about the old man. For some reason, she'd always been too overwhelmed by the here and now to think of anything, anyone but the two of them. When she was with him, all other people seemed to fade into the distance.

She glanced around the darkening room, looking in vain for food. She couldn't remember when she'd last eaten, and while food had certainly been a low priority while she'd been in residence, she realized quite suddenly that she was famished.

In her wanderings around the convoluted old house she'd never found anything as remotely practical as a kitchen, but then, she'd never been looking. Maybe her sense of direction would work as well for cheese and crackers as it worked for Ethan. Except that she didn't think it was going to be that simple. She needed Ethan far more than she needed food to stay alive.

Maybe she'd go in search of him, and together, they could invade the kitchen. She could manage a decent omelet if she could find the right pan. The thought of cooking for him, of a tiny, normal morsel of domesticity, was alluring. And somehow, very unlikely.

The hall door was tightly locked. She stared at it in disbelief, unwilling to accept the fact that last night had made no difference at all. But then, Sal was perfectly capable of taking it upon himself to lock her in. Ethan was probably wondering why she was gone so long, why she hadn't come to him.

No, he was wondering no such thing. He could come to her, as he had before. If he wanted to.

Where was Sal? It had been midmorning when he said he was going to check on what was happening in Oak Grove. Though she had no way of telling time, she could only guess that it was early evening, six or seven. He'd been gone a long, long time.

And she wasn't going to sit there a minute longer like a passive little lady. If she couldn't get through the door to the house, she could go over the garden wall. And if Ethan came to rescue her while she was gone, then he'd have only himself to blame.

The wind was picking up, knocking the white-budded flowers this way and that. She went first in search of the door Joseph had used just yesterday, but that stretch of wall was smooth and unblemished. There'd been no way he could have simply vanished in front of her eyes, but there was no other practical explanation, either.

The white climbing rose ran up a trellis. She tore her hands climbing, snarled her hair, but nothing could make her stop, not the wind howling overhead, not the distant crackle of lightning, not the threatening roll of thunder. She dropped down lightly on the other side into a Zen-like garden of swirling sand patterns and miniature fir trees, then up and over another wall, her anger at odds with her quickly building panic. Something was wrong, something was very wrong, and she had the sense that danger was all around her. She could smell smoke in the air, a sweet, piny-pitch smoke, and the rumble of thunder sounded ominously like the rumble of voices.

The next garden had no walls. Instead, there was a maze made of boxwood that reached over her head, a maze she had no choice but to enter. There was no way around it, and she sure as hell wasn't going back.

The chanting was louder inside the maze, and she knew with sudden grim fear that Pastor Lincoln and his loyal crew of followers had to be nearby. Hadn't Sal warned her? Hadn't Ruth already ended up in the hospital, an innocent victim of their deranged sense of justice?

The voices grew louder, closer, and the smell of fire was stronger than ever. Torches, she thought, panicked. They used to burn witches, didn't they? Hadn't Pastor Lincoln accused her of being something perilously close to a witch?

She turned back, panicked, but the maze split in two directions, and she had no idea which way to go. She started down one path when something or someone seemed to call to her. Looking back, she saw Joseph, as if from a great distance, beckoning to her.

Without hesitation, she wheeled around and ran to him. He was gone by the time she got there, but she kept on in that direction, blind with panic and fright, the voices behind her growing louder and louder.

Another split in the path, and Joseph was there again, leading her to safety. She no longer thought she'd reach him, she was happy just to follow him, away from those droning voices, those evil minds. He'd take her to Ethan, she knew he would, and Ethan would keep her safe. Ethan was all-powerful, dark and menacing and mysterious to people whose limited minds couldn't understand him, and he loved her. He wouldn't let anyone touch her.

She almost made it. The end of the maze was in sight and she began to run toward Joseph's patiently waiting figure, slipping in the dew-wet grass, racing as fast as her beating heart would allow her, when she felt the hands behind her, reaching out for her, gnarled, clawlike hands, catching at her clothes, pulling her down, down. She screamed, Ethan's name a helpless cry that was silenced as it began as a hand clamped over her mouth, followed quickly by a foul-tasting rag. Something pungent and acrid covered her nose, and she held her breath, struggling, fighting with all her strength.

"Ether'll do the trick." She recognized Doc Bailey's slurred tones with horror. "She'll either have to take a breath or she'll pass out on her own accord."

"Evil!" Pastor Lincoln intoned from overhead, and she knew they were his hands holding her down, hurting her breasts with perverse deliberation. "She'll be purified by fire and blood...."

Megan could smell the fire, see the flames of the torches against the darkening sky. Why didn't Joseph help her? She turned her head and saw him at the edge of the maze, watching her struggle, making no move to help her.

She kicked hard, connecting with the good pastor, forcing him to release his painful hold as he rolled to the ground. But there were too many willing hands ready to take his place, and her lungs were about to burst. She opened her mouth against the rag in one last attempt to scream, but the drug poured into her, blackness surrounded her, and the last thing she saw was Joseph watching her, standing close, a sorrowing expression on his ancient face. And the odd thing was, no one else seemed to notice him at all.

ETHAN SAT BOLT UPRIGHT in his chair, his hands clenched into fists. For five long hours he'd sat in darkness, fighting his need to go to Megan, fighting his own guilt and rage. She wasn't safe. He'd known that, known that once he'd put his own convoluted plans for revenge in gear, nothing would stop them. Not an innocent woman who stood in his way, not his own, belated second thoughts. He'd gone too far to change his mind, to back down. And now Ruth lay in a hospital, Sal was missing, and Megan . . . Megan . . .

She was safe for now, locked in that room, with the locked garden beyond. No one could get to her, most of all him.

When had things shifted beyond his control? He'd managed his life so carefully, using his money, his brilliance, the gifts a stingy God had given him in return for deformity, to run his life. No one was able to touch him, to hurt him. Those who had managed would pay the price.

First Reese Carey, with his greedy tactics that endangered people in order to line his own pockets. A man worthy of punishment, yes. But not Ethan Winslowe's punishment. If Ethan had simply been interested in justice, he would have sent his information directly to the investigators looking into Carey Enterprises. Instead, he'd planned to keep the man a prisoner, playing his own sadistic cat-and-mouse game, to make the man suffer.

It had backfired when Carey had been despicable enough to sacrifice his daughter, instead. And Ethan had fallen in love with that daughter, despite his best efforts. Megan Carey was everything her father wasn't. Brave, honest, compassionate and loyal. She also looked at him without flinching. No, it was even worse than that. She looked at him with love.

He had no defense against that love. His experience with Jean Marshall, with Ruth, with various carefully made professional arrangements had left him unprepared for the magnitude of falling in love for the first time in his life. And for the last, he realized. Life was no longer as he chose to make it. It had fled from him, leaving him an angry, struggling victim.

And who was he to wreak vengeance on a town so small and poor and miserable and inbred that its inhabitants no longer knew right from wrong? Who was he to sit in judgment? He'd chosen to stay here knowing his presence filled their superstitious souls with fear and torment, and when that wasn't revenge enough for the death of his father, he'd upped the ante, turning most of their barren little town over to what they'd consider Satan himself. And he'd done so with malicious relish.

But he'd pushed them beyond their limited lease on sanity. And they hadn't hurt him. They'd hurt Sal. They'd hurt Ruth. And he knew that if they could, they'd hurt Megan.

He didn't want to let it go. He didn't want to take Megan and turn his back on them, letting them off scot-free for their escalating violence. He wanted to punish them, destroy them, squash them into the ground like malevolent bugs. And much as he loved Megan, he couldn't give up the one thing that had kept him going through the long, dark years. That hatred had kept him alive—it was as important to him as his love for Megan.

But he couldn't have both. He didn't need an ultimatum from Megan to know that. He'd made his own ultimatum. The damnable thing was he couldn't decide.

Deep in the center of the house, it was too dark to tell the time, but his internal clock told him it was late, and still Sal hadn't returned. Megan would be locked in her room. Probably ravenously hungry and mad as hell. He was sorry he'd been gentlemanly enough to disconnect the video monitors. He'd done it for his sake as well as hers. He'd known, subconsciously if not otherwise, that he was going to join her in that room, take her on that wide white bed. And he didn't even want the computer watching.

Maybe he should have taped it. Maybe once she left, he could sit and watch the tape, watch their bodies join, over and over and over again. But he didn't need that. He'd watch the tape in his mind, endlessly, a helpless voyeur to his own pain.

It sliced through him with a sudden, shocking savagery. She screamed for him. Megan's voice, Megan's soul, calling out for him in panic. He'd heard her call before, and had answered that call, but never had he heard such bone-shattering terror.

He knocked over his thronelike chair as he went, not bothering with lights when he was so accustomed to the thick blackness that surrounded him. There were secret passageways and tunnels, shortcuts through the maze of hallways and ramps. Within minutes, he was outside the door of the white room. The room that was locked, the key back in his basement lair.

He smashed through the door, ignoring the pain in his shoulder. The room was deserted, the white muslin curtains billowing in the fierce breeze, and he raced into the garden, dreading what he'd find.

It was empty. The rose-covered trellis had been pulled from the wall, signifying her escape route. For a moment, he didn't move, wondering if she'd simply made up her mind to leave him after all.

And then he knew, with no doubt at all, that she hadn't been running away from him. She'd been running to him.

He was over the garden wall in two seconds flat, dropping down lightly into the Zen garden. The wind was whipping the sand up, stinging his eyes, and still his heart was racing, his blood throbbing through him, feeling her panic, her need.

The door in the north wall was standing open. The door ahead of him was still locked. It made no sense that she would have gone straight ahead, but he hesitated, torn.

It had been years since he'd seen Joseph. He'd thought that he never would again—he'd given up hoping or even caring. But suddenly, he was there, standing in front of the closed door, beckoning to Ethan.

Beckoning to his son.

Ethan didn't bother with the wall this time. His shoulder could stand up to more punishment, and besides, that door was flimsy. It splintered beneath him, and he stumbled out into the maze.

He let out a groan of anguish. The house and gardens were so convoluted that even he forgot which part adjoined which. He knew the way through the maze, but there was always the chance that Megan and her enemies—his enemies—were lost somewhere in one of the blind turns.

''Megan!'' he called, and the wind took his voice and hurled it up into the bending trees. No answer at all, not a sound beyond the violence of nature.

There was no sign of her in the maze, no sound at all, and no sign of any intruder. When he came through the other side, he saw the open door and allowed himself a moment of relief. Maybe she'd simply gotten lost in the maze and been frightened. Maybe Joseph had shown her the way to safety and even now she was lying curled up in his bed, waiting for him.

And then he stumbled over it. Bending down, he picked up the shoe, holding it in his big hand. It wasn't one of her silly high heels, the ones he found ridiculously erotic. It was her bright red running shoe, lying in the dirt. He could smell the pitchy scent of torches mixed with kerosene, and he knew they'd taken her.

A darkness closed over him. Not the warm, beneficent darkness that cradled and protected him. This was a darkness of murderous rage so intense that it seemed it would never lift. He sank to his knees in the dirt, cursing, as he held her shoe like a talisman.

And then he looked up. Joseph was there, distant, indistinct, remote as he'd been since the day Ethan was born.

"The grove," he said, his faint voice fading on the wind. "They took her to the old grove." He started to fade.

"How long?" Ethan demanded, pulling him back. "How long ago?"

Joseph simply shook his head, growing ever fainter.

"Wait!" Ethan called, but Joseph had already disappeared into the stormy evening air.

WHEN THEY'D CARRIED HER away, Megan couldn't see, couldn't hear, could scarcely breathe. She guessed that they'd thrown her in the back of a battered pickup truck, one without springs. That, or it was Pastor Lincoln's old school bus with the Repent or Perish slogan on the back.

The smell of kerosene lingered in the air, mingling with the smell of stale sweat and cheap after-shave. What kind of person wore after-shave to a mob scene, she wondered dizzily.

She had no sense of time. She could have been unconscious for minutes or hours before she came to, trapped in that rattling vehicle. She could hear the sizzle and crackle of lightning, the angry roar of the thunder. Could she hear Ethan? Would he find her in time? Would he save her?

Maybe she didn't need to be so frightened. Maybe they were just going to lecture her, throw her in a ducking pond, maybe make her confess her sins. But she didn't think so. The fanaticism of the people of Oak Grove was deep and twisted. A simple repentance wouldn't sate their warped, hungry souls.

The vehicle came to an abrupt stop, and she was flung forward against a tangle of legs. She heard the nervous laughter, felt the hands pull her upright, lingering on her breasts, her buttocks, and then she was pushed out into the darkness and the blindfold was taken from her eyes.

Night had fallen, a dark, dangerous night. Lightning sizzled all around them. The wind was whipping her hair into her face as she tried to focus on the place they'd taken her.

It was an oak grove, presumably the place from which the town had taken its name. High on a hilltop, it overlooked the rolling Arkansas landscape, and the trees huddled in a circle looked oddly like Stonehenge. In the center of that circle was a broad, flat boulder, just the perfect spot for a picnic, she thought dizzily. Or a sacrifice.

She could see the huddled shapes of construction equipment in the distance. This was where Ethan planned his spite house, his psychic-research center. It was no wonder they'd brought her here. What better place to leave Ethan Winslowe a message?

Pastor Lincoln came up to her. They'd tied her wrists together with leather thongs, had bound her ankles, too. She'd lost one of her Reeboks in the battle, and she thought, idiotically, of Cinderella. Would Ethan find the glass slipper?

She was punchy from panic and whatever filthy drug they'd given her. It took all her self-control to look calmly at Pastor Lincoln and wish she wasn't gagged. So that she could spit in his face.

"Are you ready to repent, sister?" he screamed into the rising wind. "We've brought you to the godless place to heal the sickness that's invaded our community. We've brought you to the place of witches so that you may join your evil horde or else be washed clean by the blood."

Whose blood, she thought, glancing once again at that flat boulder.

"You recognize the place, don't you, Hecate? Your sisters danced here one hundred years ago. They put a curse on our town that has lasted to this day. And their master, Ethan Winslowe, is the culmination of that curse. But we're going to put a stop to it. By blood and by fire, we'll cleanse this town of its evil."

Megan didn't move. She couldn't. She was afraid she was going to throw up, and then she'd doubtless choke to death with that gag in her mouth. She simply stared at Lincoln, too frightened to show her fear. She stared and he took a step backward, holding up his hands as if to ward off the evil eye.

"Unclean!" he screamed. "But we have your punishment. Not the rock. Not the ways of your ancestors. But the ways of ours. You'll be cleansed by the fire."

And then she saw it. A sturdy piece of wood driven deep in the ground, looking like a foreshortened telephone pole. At its base was a well-laid pile of twigs, branches and logs, with an ominous gas can nearby. And she knew then what they'd planned for her.

She tried to run, but the ropes around her ankles sent her sprawling. They half carried, half dragged her over to one of the oak trees, tying her there as she struggled.

"Doc, you and Ferdy watch her while we go back for Winslowe. It's not quite three hours till midnight. These things have got to be done right."

Megan glared at them, at the drunken doctor who was swaying slightly, at the spry, evil figure of the man who'd filled her gas tank when she'd first arrived at this misbegotten town so long ago. "Don't let her trick you, boys. Keep her tied up, and when midnight comes, she'll be ready."

For a moment, Megan simply stared: at the pastor, with his robes and saintly demeanor, at the crowd of men behind him, normal enough looking, with their after-shave and their flannel shirts and their sweaty faces. This couldn't be real, couldn't be happening. But it was.

She closed her eyes, sinking her face against the rough bark of the oak tree.

"That's it. In a couple of hours, you'll be meeting your master. I hope for your sake it's your eternal savior and not the one who's bought your soul."

And moments later, she was alone on the hilltop, alone with a drunken doctor and an evil old man. Alone with the stake and the firewood carefully prepared, all set for her punishment, waiting only for a match. And a victim. Alone.

Chapter Sixteen

Sal had taken the Mercedes, Ethan realized with a frantic curse. Of course he had, he'd had no choice. The Blazer's battery had run down after Megan left it in a ditch. Sal was thorough in all matters—the battery would be somewhere in the garages being recharged. But where the hell it was and whether Ethan, who'd done very little driving in his reclusive life, would be able to reconnect it was a moot point.

That left the huge black '57 Thunderbird that had been his mother's pride and joy, complete with spiky tail fins and enough shiny chrome to dazzle a blind man. It would have a full tank, of course, and start right up, but whether it could navigate the rain-washed back roads was another matter. And whether it would make it up the rough construction road to the old oak grove was even more questionable.

What wasn't questionable was where they'd taken her. Even if Joseph hadn't broken his silence and told Ethan, the answer was obvious. He'd chosen the site for the research center with malicious care, planning to set it on the very spot where the ancestors of the people of Oak Grove used to hold their witches' sabbath. The sin-obsessed parishioners of Pastor Lincoln would choose that spot for their revenge.

Lightning spit and crackled overhead, slicing the darkening sky, and the wind whipped his long hair into his face. Ethan could see the knoll from the distance, but it was too far away to tell whether anyone was up there. He cursed as he started the huge old car. He cursed his mother for her addiction to flash and prettiness and her resounding rejection of her tarnished son. He cursed his father for his vacillating weakness. He cursed Pastor Lincoln for his evil and the townspeople for their hidebound stupidity. He cursed Megan for leaving her room, he cursed her for coming there in the first place and upsetting his careful, vengeful plans. But most of all, he cursed himself, slowly, savagely, as he spun the wheels and tore off into the night, a deformed knight in tarnished armor, the Thunderbird instead of a white charger beneath him. The woman he loved might very well die because of his single-minded quest for revenge.

He had to stop them. He had to get to her before they hurt her. He had to put an end, once and for all, to the madness that infected this town, that was out of place, out of time. Or die trying.

His eyes, so accustomed to darkness, saw the faint glimmer of the headlights from miles away, far enough for him to jerk the wheel, slide the huge old car into a stand of woods and kill the engine. He sat there, his strong hands clenched around the steering wheel, waiting, listening.

He knew Pastor Lincoln's old school bus by sound. When it finally pulled into view, he could see that it was covered with men, sitting on the top, hanging out the windows, some even clinging to the hood as it bounced and jounced down the road. Back toward his house. The convoy of ancient pickup trucks followed, each one filled with townspeople. Not just the men. Some of the women were there, too, the hatchet-faced, sourspirited matrons of Oak Grove. The ones whose children left as soon as they were old enough to come to Ethan and ask for bus fare out of there. All the faces looked alike. Blank, almost hypnotized, no sign of life at all in their expressions. Except for the gleaming hatred in their eyes.

He waited until they passed. Megan wasn't with them; he knew that even without seeing. They must have left her up on the hillside when they went after him.

They wouldn't find him. He was going after her. He'd find her, get her safely away from this place, and they'd never come back. He didn't even spare a thought for the house he'd lived in, hidden in, for most of his thirty-four years. It had been in his family for almost a century and he could leave it without a twinge, watch its certain destruction without a qualm. As long as Megan was safe.

He turned the key in the ignition again, and nothing happened. The first real tendrils of panic began to filter through as he turned the key again and again and again. There was no answering rumble at all from the old engine. The car was dead and he was stuck in the middle of nowhere, Megan on one side, a murdering horde of maniacs on the other.

He had never in his life run anywhere but on the small indoor track he had built in the east wing of the house. Never had he run outside, where people might see him, with the cool night air in his face. He did so now, uncertain how good his stamina was, how long he could last. He was strong, very strong, from swimming, from the various machines Sal had bought and installed in that same wing. But whether he could run the eight or so miles up to the knoll in time to get Megan away from there was a question he couldn't answer. All he could do was try.

He'd always loved the night, the thick black darkness that covered him. Not now. Not anymore. The darkness hid evil, it covered the foul deeds of Lincoln and his followers. As long as the night lasted, Megan was in danger. Once the sun rose, she'd be safe. From the crazed people of Oak Grove. And from him.

He ran down the rutted, rain-slick road, the lightning snaking down around him, the wind whipping past him. He ran, pacing himself, trying to force to manageable levels the fear that filled his heart. He ran, knowing he had to save her. Knowing he had to set her free. He ran, feeling the sweat run down his face. And he knew that it wasn't sweat. It was tears.

THE ODD THING WAS, Megan wasn't afraid. Her wrists were tied too tightly, bound together, her ankles throbbed, the bark of the old oak tree was rough against her face, and yet, she wasn't afraid. Alone on a hilltop, the thunder and lightning all around her, a hideous fate awaiting her at the hands of a mob, and yet she wasn't frightened.

At least she'd managed to spit out the foul-tasting gag. Neither of her two guards had paid any attention—they knew her screams wouldn't be heard. She felt sick and dizzy from the drug, and her head ached abominably. And she knew that that was the least of her worries.

The doctor was mumbling. Sitting on the other side of the clearing, propped against an incongruous yellow bulldozer, he had his flask in his hand, and she could tell by the angle that it was almost empty. The old man from the filling station, Ferdy, was stalking around, practically prancing with ghoulish glee, and she knew he was just looking for an excuse to tighten her bonds. To touch her again. She wouldn't give him that excuse.

Closing her eyes, she breathed in the earthy, rich smell of the bark still damp from the last rainfall, and she considered her odd, abstracted state of mind. Maybe she simply accepted death. Maybe she knew there was no escape, not with a town of crazies yapping at her heels, and that the more she struggled and panicked, the worse it would be.

Maybe she simply didn't believe it. Death was unreal to her—someone strong and young and healthy didn't have her life ripped away from her without warning. This was all something out of a Gothic nightmare—terribly melodramatic and all that, but surely just a little too overblown.

She opened her eyes a crack to see Ferdy taking a deep swig of Doc's flask. She could smell the keroseney odor of the torches, and she could see the silhouette of the stake in the shadowy night. And she knew it was no joke.

She shut her eyes again, letting the cool, damp breeze of the approaching storm wash over her. It had been a night like this when she'd gone to Ethan's bed. Outside, the world had crashed and burned. Inside, their lives had exploded with a passion that managed to distract and weaken her even in her current situation.

She smiled wryly against the trunk of the tree. She was in a sorry state when erotic memories could make her forget that she was going to die a hideous death in a few hours. Still, what better thing to think about? A fate that she wasn't sure she could escape? Or Ethan's beautiful, long-limbed body, his wicked, knowing hands and mouth, his beautiful marked face...

"What are you smiling about?" Ferdy demanded in an angry screech. He'd moved over there on his spry little feet. Doc was leaning against the bulldozer, eyes closed, snoring slightly, peacefully passed out. Not that he would have been any protection from Ferdy.

She simply looked up at him, keeping her expression carefully blank, and Ferdy's rage exploded. "Don't look at me out of those witch's eyes! I know your kind. Wicked, godless strumpets, leading men to their doom, ripping away their holiness, making them burn." He grabbed a stick from the ground, a long, pointed one, and held it in the flame of one of those torches. "I can put out those eyes. I can stop you from watching, from seducing. It won't matter to Pastor Lincoln. He'll praise me. Yes, he'll praise me for seeing the devil and blinding her. Yes," Ferdy mumbled, drooling slightly as he advanced on her. "Yes," he said. "He'll praise me...."

And then he stopped. The flaming brand was in one upraised hand, and his twisted expression of malevolent determination suddenly altered.

She'd watched his approach with that same, detached curiosity, knowing her danger and yet not feeling it. Even as she felt the heat in that flaming stick, she didn't whimper or panic. She just waited, very still, watching him out of expressionless eyes.

He dropped the stick to the ground with a pain-filled moan of his own. "No!" he said in a hushed whisper, sheer horror filling his voice. "No." But this time it was a strangled scream as he stumbled backward, not looking where he was going.

She couldn't say anything. She watched it happen with that same remote curiosity, knowing that in a few more steps, he was going to go over the edge of the cliff. She had no idea how far down it was, whether it was simply a short, gentle slope or a murderous drop-off. It wouldn't matter. She opened her mouth to speak, to warn him, but no sound came out. He was looking past her in terror, and the noises from his ancient throat were garbled, unintelligible sounds of panic.

He tripped backward, over the carefully-laid bonfire. And then he disappeared over the side of the hill. Without a sound. Just the silent dropping away from sight, and Ferdy was gone. Leaving her alone in the darkness with only the comatose doctor for company.

She began to struggle at her bonds then, knowing that she'd somehow been granted a reprieve. She didn't know how long she'd have—whether Ferdy would manage to struggle back up from his precipitous drop, whether Doc would reemerge from his drunken stupor, whether Pastor Lincoln and his brigade would return from their mission. Were they going to bring Ethan back? Or destroy him where he stood?

But the ropes that bound her wrists were tighter than she'd realized, and the more she struggled, the tighter they got, rubbing her wrists until she thought she could see blood in the wavering torchlight. The wind was howling, whipping the light into strange, dangerous shadows, and the threatening thunder rumbled overhead, a ghostly counterpoint to the darkness.

And yet for some reason, the night didn't close down into inky blackness. There was a glow to the north, a bright glow, enough to be a good sized town. And then she smelled fire in the air, and she knew they were burning Ethan's house.

And then she knew why she hadn't been frightened. Somehow, deep inside, she'd been sure that Ethan would come, Ethan would rescue her in time. Now that certainty had vanished, doubt for the first time creeping in and terrifying her. He was probably deep in the center of the huge octopus of a building, deep within, not hearing anything. He probably still assumed she was safely locked in that bedroom, that Sal was on patrol, that everything was all right. He wouldn't know until he smelled the smoke, and then it would be too late.

She had to get back to him. Had to warn him. Except the glow in the sky told her it was already too late. The house was burning, filling the sky with an unearthly light. And Ethan might be dead already, caught in the conflagration, his beautiful flesh in torment....

The hand holding hers was solid, cool, and strong. Flowing through that hand were courage and hope, flooding her once more, so that she raised her head, her tear-drenched face, and looked into nothingness.

There was no one there. Someone was holding her hand in a firm, reassuring grip, and there was no one there.

She tightened her fingers and the unseen comforter tightened back, and reassurance flowed through her. She waited, patient, unmoving. And there was Joseph, sitting cross-legged in the dirt beside her, holding her hand.

"Did they hurt him...?"

Joseph shook his head. "He'd already left. He's coming to get you, Megan. He's coming to get you away from here."

"But the others..."

"They can't hurt you. No one will hurt you," Joseph said with infinite gentleness.

She glanced uneasily over her shoulder. "Ferdy..."

"He's dead. That's a sixty-foot drop onto rocks below. A hundred years ago, when a group of bored and lonely women came out here and played harmless games, the other townspeople rose up against them, led by Pastor Lincoln's grandfather. They came and they drove those poor women over the cliff. The two who survived wished they hadn't."

Megan shivered, cold on this hot, stormy night. "Can you untie me, Joseph?"

"No," he said, with great regret.

She looked down at their clasped hands. She only saw hers. He sat distant and apart, his ancient face creased in sorrow, and she knew.

It wasn't a conscious knowledge. It wasn't something she wanted to think about, to understand. Instead, she simply accepted what was unbelievable, letting her hand rest in his reassuring, unseen grip while she waited for Ethan.

She might have, unbelievably, slept. Or merely let her mind drift, overloaded by the danger and terror that surrounded her. At one point, Doc stumbled to his feet, wandered over to the edge of the cliff and relieved himself. Whether he noticed Ferdy's body beneath didn't make any difference at that point. And then he went back to his spot by the bulldozer.

The flask was empty by then, and he flung it away in disgust. He glanced over at Megan with no more than casual interest, and then he froze.

She'd seen that expression before. On Ferdy's face, just before he died trying to escape from whatever had frightened him.

Doc didn't move. He couldn't. He sat there, his face pale in the storm-whipped night, his mouth moving and not a word coming out. And Megan knew it wasn't her who had frightened him. It was Joseph.

She glanced back at her distant companion and comforter to see what was so frightening about him. He looked the same, old and harmless and slightly wavering in the night air. Nothing to terrify two old men.

Doc rose again on unsteady feet, coming marginally closer, as if he couldn't believe his eyes. "You're dead," he said flatly.

For a moment, Megan thought he meant her, and the notion was chilling. And then Joseph spoke, and his unseen hand still gripped hers tightly.

"Yes," he said in that peaceful voice of his. "You did your part in killing me."

Doc swayed slightly, and his eyes were bulging. And then a shiver went through his body like a massive electric current, and he collapsed, almost at Megan's feet, his hand outstretched, clutching the hypodermic needle he'd been holding broken in the dirt.

"Tried to...make it easier for...you," he gasped. "Can't stop Lincoln. Can only make it...less..." And then he stopped. His breathing was loud, tortured in the moonlight, but his eyes were staring blindly, his mouth moving without a sound issuing forth.

She looked down at the broken needle. "What was it?" she asked in a hushed voice.

"Some kind of narcotic, I suppose," Joseph murmured. "Something to make you oblivious to Lincoln's plans." He didn't bother looking at Doc's comatose body. Instead, he glanced skyward at the rolling clouds. "Storm's getting closer."

"Yes," she said.

"So's the mob."

"Yes," she said again, clinging tightly. Waiting. Waiting for death. Or waiting for Ethan. She had no choice. Doc's breathing grew more erratic as he struggled and gasped, like a fish out of water, flopping slightly on the damp ground. And then Megan realized he wasn't making any noise at all. He lay there, still and cold, and his breathing had stopped.

Even as the darkness descended around them, the brightness grew, and she knew it was the headlights of Pastor Lincoln's brigade. They were going to make it back before Ethan found them. And she knew there was no hope for her.

She considered trying to reach the broken hypodermic, then dismissed the notion. She wasn't going to die a coward. The hand holding hers told her she wasn't going to die at all. Though at the moment, she wouldn't have put any money on that certainty.

It seemed as if there were more trucks returning than had left. In the wind-tossed darkness, the clearing seemed covered with blinding headlights, and yet the crowd of people moving toward the grove seemed diminished. She didn't stop to consider why. She simply clung to Joseph, keeping her head high and her gaze steady as Pastor Lincoln advanced on her.

He looked straight at her, unaware that she wasn't alone. "What have you done, you harlot? Where's Ferdy? What's happened to Doc? Answer me, or God's wrath will pour down upon you...."

She was getting a little tired of his direct connection to God's wrath. As far as she was concerned, she was of equal value in His eyes. "I gave them the evil eye and they both dropped dead," she snapped, trying to dredge up her courage.

Definitely a major mistake, she knew that immediately. Pastor Lincoln began to shriek, calling upon God and all his saints to strike her dead, ordering his faithful followers to punish her.

His faithful followers were already looking a little uneasy. Mob frenzy could only last so long, and the drive between the knoll and Ethan's house was a long one. The fire seemed to have sated their blood lust, for no one moved.

"She's murdered Doc!" Lincoln shrieked, his face red with fury. "With her witchcraft, she's broken every holy ordinance. She must die."

Still no one came close. They were looking at what Pastor Lincoln couldn't see. The man sitting in the dirt behind her. The old man, watching, warning them away.

The knife glittered in the darkness as Lincoln slashed through her bonds. She could feel the hot, sticky wetness of her own blood as he hauled her to her feet, but she no longer wondered why Joseph didn't stop him. He couldn't.

Lincoln dragged her over to the stake, shrieking prayers that were both macabre and eerily familiar. On that hilltop, they were the only two people moving, the others were transfixed, watching the gory tableau as Megan kicked and fought and scratched, ignoring the vicious blade in the pastor's deft hand. "Help me," he called to the others, panting as he struggled with her desperate fury, but no one moved. No one helped him, but no one stopped him, either. They stood there, transfixed, watching.

He slapped her hard across the face, momentarily stunning her, and she fell back against the hard, wooden stake. He had ropes in his hands, to bind her to her funeral pyre, and as he advanced on her, she screamed.

She felt his presence before she saw him. The lightning was all around, snaking down on the high, exposed place, with the thunder shaking the ground. From over the cliff, he appeared, climbing up the sheer rock face, and as the bolt of lightning illuminated him, Megan felt a sudden, superstitious terror.

Ethan looked like Lucifer, the fallen angel. His long black hair flowed around his narrow, marked face, the beauty and the deformity a contrast in rage. He was dressed in black, and he stood there at the edge of the cliff, intent on Pastor Lincoln's mesmerized figure.

"Get away from her."

Lincoln dropped the ropes in sudden superstitious terror. And then he managed to regain his fury. "Kill the ungodly!" he screeched to the skies. "Send your lightning down and kill the evil ones."

The slashing sizzle of fire was instantaneous, followed immediately by a thunder that shook the valley below. The bolt of lightning snaked down, a direct hit. Slicing through the upraised arm of Pastor Lincoln. Killing him instantly.

It was a moment of speechless horror. The smell of fire and electricity, the sudden finality of it. For an endless moment, he stood there as the very air around him crackled. And then he fell, face forward. His body spread-eagled across the pile of kindling he'd planned for Megan's execution.

Chapter Seventeen

Someone took her arm. Megan couldn't remember when she'd managed to struggle to her feet. Pastor Lincoln's body was nearby, but she kept her gaze averted, watching Ethan's distant face.

Now that she was on her feet, she could see the conflagration in the distance as Ethan's house went up in flames. The lightning seemed to have vanished, that final, murderous bolt the end, and now rain began to fall, a steady, soaking rain. She looked at Ethan, wanting to run to him, but the hand on her arm held her steady. And then he turned his back to her, to stare out into the rain-swept night toward his burning home.

"Come with me, Megan.' The voice was gentle, familiar, and she half expected it to be Joseph. But it was Sal, his face bruised and battered almost beyond recognition, with more kindness than she'd ever heard from him. "You're bleeding. You need to get to the hospital and have someone check you over. And the police are going to want a statement."

"Hospital?" she echoed, dazed. "Police?" She looked around her and realized that the members of the motley crowd who'd been out for her blood just hours ago weren't subdued simply by their leader's shocking death. They were subdued by an astonishing number of uniformed policemen.

"Come along," Sal said again, tugging her toward a police car.

She tried to pull back. "But Ethan..."

"I'll take care of him. I always have. Go with Lieutenant Dixon. Now." The shove was not as gentle as his hands had been, pushing her toward the waiting police officer.

She turned back, wondering if she could break away, but Ethan's back was still turned. Tall, remote, he'd shut everything out. Including her.

The ride to the hospital in Millers Fork was endless. She sat in the back of the police car, staring blindly at the blinking lights on the dashboard, and answered questions in a dull monotone. And had her own unasked ones answered.

Sal had gone for help the moment he'd realized how far things had transpired in town. Pastor Lincoln had left him tied up in front of the altar in the old church, but the bonds had been looser than Megan's, and he'd managed to escape, stealing a car and heading for Millers Fork and the nearest police station. It hadn't taken much to convince the authorities—his own beaten face and Ruth Wilkins's presence in the hospital were proof enough, and the stories about Oak Grove had been rampant.

They were too late to save Ethan's house, but the crowd was so het up that it hadn't noticed a phalanx of anonymous sedans had joined the convoy back to the old oak grove. Lieutenant Dixon was just about to make his own move when Pastor Lincoln had met his abrupt end. Megan didn't listen to the excuses or explanations. They no longer mattered. What mattered was that Ethan had come to save her. And once she was safe, he'd turned his back on her.

It took too long, too damned long at the hospital. Lincoln had managed to give her a substantial gash across her ribs, one that required several stitches, and she had various scratches, bumps and bruises that needed attending to. At three in the morning, she didn't have the option of visiting Ruth, but she was told Ruth was recuperating quite nicely and would be released in another day. Though why anyone would want to go back to the town of Oak Grove was beyond Megan's comprehension.

Except that was exactly where she was desperate to go. And she still had to wait, and wait, and wait while the inexorable Lieutenant Dixon drove her to the police station and plied the sleepy stenographer and himself with coffee that Megan steadfastly refused. She was already about to fly apart—she didn't need caffeine on top of her monumental case of burgeoning hysteria.

The sun was rising when they finally decided they'd asked enough questions. There were three bodies that needed accounting for. They'd all been horrified witnesses to the Pastor's demise, but Ferdy and Doc were a little more problematic. Dixon had seen for himself that Megan was still securely bound when they'd arrived and that both men were dead. But she knew he wouldn't understand about Joseph. And she didn't bother trying to explain.

It made the whole inquisition last longer, and Dixon was far from satisfied when he finally let her go. But there was nothing more she could say, not when she didn't understand herself.

They offered to drive her to the nearest airport or, failing that, to the nearest car-rental place, but she turned them down. For one thing, she had no purse, no identification and no one she could call for help. She'd be damned if she'd ask her father for anything.

The same held for Rob Palmer. There was no one she could turn to, no one she wanted to turn to. Except Ethan. And he'd turned his back on her.

In the end, she called her future stepmother, thanking heaven a few minutes later for the inspiration. Madeleine asked no questions other than to ascertain that Megan was all right, and offered no information that Megan didn't want to hear. A thousand dollars would be wired immediately, and Megan could come home and Madeleine would take care of everything.

For the first time that night, Meg started crying. She wanted a mother, someone to take care of her, tuck her in bed, scare away the demons. But she didn't want them all scared away. What she wanted most of all was her phantom. And she was horribly afraid she'd never see him again.

She had to wait until seven in the morning to rent a car, and even then, they weren't pleased with cash and no credit card, insisting on calling the police for verification. The car they rented her was not much better than the old clunker that had taken her to Ethan Winslowe. She thought briefly about that car, destroyed at the hands of Pastor Lincoln and his gang. She was going to have a fun time explaining that to the insurance company.

The storm of the night before had blown through, leaving the landscape sodden and clear. The endless trip from Millers Fork seemed twice as long as it had long hours before, and Oak Grove looked even more like a ghost town than it had when she'd first arrived. Except for the police cars patrolling the streets.

The smell in the air was unmistakable as she drove the long, twisting driveway back to Ethan's house. She knew even before she got there what she'd find, but the reality of it was devastating. She pulled the car to a stop in front of the vast, smoldering ruins, and she felt like crying.

There was no one in sight, and she wondered why she would have expected otherwise. Even the outbuildings were destroyed, only some of the gardens having survived the scorching flames. She found herself hoping the maze had been reduced to cinders.

She stepped out of the car, shivering slightly in the cool air. She didn't look for Joseph—he was gone. But Ethan was here, somewhere. And she couldn't leave until she'd seen him. Until he told her to go.

He was in the moon garden. The white flowers had shriveled in the intense heat, the shrubbery blackened and stunted, and the shallow pool was filled with half-burned timbers. He was sitting in the back, still and silent in the fitful sunlight, and he didn't move when she entered the garden, even though he was as aware of her as she was of him.

She was reminded of Joseph—there but remote. And like Joseph, Ethan's bearing kept her at a distance.

She crossed the cinder-strewn paths, stopping a few feet away from him, waiting for him to look at her. She'd never seen him in full daylight. The mark across his face was a cruel travesty for a man blessed with such beauty, and the contrast was, as always, heartbreaking.

"Who is Joseph?" she asked, surprised that that should be the first question.

He looked up at her and his long hair flowed down his back. "My father."

"Your father's dead. He's been dead for twenty years."

"Yes."

It explained everything and nothing. "Where is he?"

"Gone. This time for good, I imagine." Ethan's low, once-beguiling voice sounded lifeless, dead.

She moved closer, ignoring his unspoken need to keep her at a distance. "What are you going to do now? Are you going to rebuild?"

That startled him into a bitter laugh. "I don't see much point in it, do you?"

She looked around her at the smoldering ruins. "Then what will you do?"

"Go back to the islands, I suppose. I own most of a tiny little island off Martinique. It's very remote, very secluded, and the people there accept me for what I am." He looked up at her then, and his eyes were dark with a pain she couldn't understand. "What are you going to do?"

It shouldn't have hurt so sharply. So deep a pain that she wanted to crawl away and hide, as Ethan had hidden most of his life. She wasn't going to give up so easily, she told herself, bracing against the pain. She'd come back to fight, and fight she would. "Ask me," she said. "Ask me to come with you."

"I can't do that." The words were a death knell in her heart.

"Why not? Don't you want me?"

He laughed, the sound bitter and uneasy in the morning light. "Not want you?" he echoed. "I'm not crazy, Megan. But I'm not going to have you."

"Why not? All you have to do is ask me." She sank onto her knees beside him in the mud, not touching him, afraid to touch him, afraid if she were to do so and he sent her away, she might hate him.

"I can't ask you."

She shivered, sinking back onto her heels. "And I can't go unless you do. I can't chase after you, throwing myself at you. You have to love me enough to tell me. You have to make that one small sacrifice. You have to commit yourself enough to just ask me." Her voice was pleading. She hated the sound of it, but she had to.

"No." The word was low, flat, final.

For a moment, she didn't move, kneeling at his feet in the mud. Slowly, she pulled the Janus ring from her finger, her fingers caressing it one last time as she didn't dare caress him. And then, dropping it in his lap, she rose, blinking back the tears.

It didn't matter. He no longer looked at her. He'd dismissed her, wiped her out of his mind, out of his life.

"One word," she said, her voice thick with grief. "One sign, and I'll come to you."

He looked up, remote, devil and angel side by side in his extraordinary face, and spoke one word.

"Goodbye."

MEGAN KEPT WAITING for life to resume some semblance of normalcy. She stayed with Madeleine for a couple of weeks after she flew back to Chicago, but she felt as if she were only treading water. She reopened her apartment, she visited the foundering Carey Enterprises offices, she fired Rob Palmer, and she visited her father. But still she moved through the days in a fog.

She'd wake up at night, alone in her bed, and reach out for Ethan. It was absurd, after twenty-seven years of sleeping alone, two nights had forever changed her life. She'd walk down a busy street and imagine she saw

Ethan reflected in a shop window. Ethan, who'd probably never walked down a busy city street in his life.

She kept her father uncomplaining, silent company as he went through his pretrial hearings and plea bargaining, saying nothing as he tried to wheedle his way out of the mess his greed had gotten him into. And when it was finally clear to him that there was no way out, he accepted his disgrace with his daughter standing beside him.

She waited until he married the ever-faithful Madeleine. She waited until he'd begun his three-month term at a place just a little bit fancier than the country club he paid thousands of dollars in dues to, waited until he was already beginning to improve his tennis game. And then she packed once more, ready to leave.

Maybe Ethan wouldn't haunt her by the canals of Venice. Maybe he wouldn't be at her shoulder along the Champs-Élysées. Maybe he wouldn't walk with her in Devon, hike with her in the Scottish Highlands, whisper to her in Vienna. But she doubted it.

She had no choice. Ethan was gone, disappearing from her life as effectively as his father had. She was fully alone for the first time in her life, and she was running away from the pain of it.

She wasn't even pregnant. That had been her secret, wicked hope when she first returned to Chicago. Neither of them had used any precautions, and a pregnancy would have forced her to go after him.

But there was no pregnancy, no easy way out. He'd left her, and in this life, there was neither hope nor joy. He had to want her enough to risk his heart or in the end, he would destroy her. Because who could live with a broken heart and a broken life?

Her happy ending was so obvious to her. He could design his extraordinary buildings; she could build them. Together, they could do anything, anything at all—no obstacle was too great. But he didn't believe that.

The early-morning flight from Chicago to New York seemed longer than usual. The three-hour layover was a pain, but one Megan was prepared to endure. She'd had to endure far worse during the last two months.

She was going to be trapped on a plane for six more hours—she certainly had no intention of spending the time waiting for her next flight sitting on her behind. She walked up and down the corridors, watching the travelers at each gate. The businessmen, the vacationers, the families and the lovers. The airline she favored flew everywhere. She passed each gate, thinking about the various destinations. Iowa, San Francisco, Honolulu. Tokyo, Vancouver, Martinique. Paris, Rome...

The plane to Martinique left in forty-five minutes. The waiting area wasn't crowded—mid-June wasn't prime time for the Caribbean. Megan stood there in the middle of the terminal, staring at the counter, at the sleek silver plane through the windows beyond.

Turning on her heel, she spun around, moving away from temptation, moving away at something close to a run. In the corner of her vision, she thought she saw a familiar figure, but she didn't dare turn and check. Too often she thought she'd seen Ethan near her, only to find out it was a heart-tearing fantasy prompted by a longing so intense, it was going to kill her. She wouldn't give in to weakness this time and look.

Her own gate was half the terminal away. A few transatlantic passengers were already there, but the area was empty enough so that there was no missing the figure waiting for her. The same, hauntingly familiar figure she'd seen at the other gate.

She looked at Joseph across the rows of orange plastic seats. No one else could see him, of that she was certain. She even wondered whether she could, or whether she'd just managed to conjure him up out of intense longing.

It didn't matter. He simply looked at her, expressionless, waiting for her decision. And all hesitation left her as she nodded.

"Are there any seats left on this flight?" she asked the attendant outside the Martinique gate.

The woman smiled. "This must be your lucky day. We were booked solid, but we've just had two cancellations. How many?" Her eyes focused directly on Megan, not seeing the pale figure hovering at her shoulder.

"Just one."

"Will you be checking any luggage?" She glanced down at Megan's unencumbered hands.

Megan shrugged. "I'm afraid my luggage is on its way to London. Again."

The attendant was all concern. "We'll do our best to get it back to you as quickly as possible."

"That's all right," Megan said as a belated confidence began to fill her. "I don't expect I'll be wearing much clothing when I get there."

The woman blinked for a moment, and then she grinned, a conspiratorial grin. "Lucky you. Is he absolutely gorgeous?"

Megan smiled back, thinking of Ethan's divided face. "Absolutely."

She buckled herself into the window seat, impatient to be off, half afraid reason would rear its ugly head and send her tearing off the plane. She stared out at the tarmac, not looking when someone sat down beside her, rubbing her arms against the sudden chill on the air-conditioned plane.

"He needs you," Joseph said, his voice soft and fading in her ear.

She didn't bother to turn. She knew she wouldn't see him if she did, just as she knew he was there with her, as he'd been that terrible night so long ago on the hilltop. *I need him,* she said without speaking.

"Go to him."

She turned then, just in time to see a fat, sweating businessman lower his bulk into the seat beside her. He caught her scrutiny, gave her a bored leer and buckled his seat belt around his impressive bulk. Closing her eyes, Megan leaned back and waited for the silver bird to take her to Ethan.

THE TWO-HOUR FLIGHT FROM Chicago had been endless. The five-hour flight to Martinique was far too brief, despite the presence of the flirtatious Harley Beamer beside her. She had no idea what she'd find when she got to the island. She had no idea where Ethan was. He'd said something about another island, a smaller one, but she imagined there'd be quite a number to choose from. If people had actually seen Ethan, they'd remember him, but he had a talent for keeping hidden. He'd probably arrived in the dead of night, on a private plane, and Sal would have whisked him past any witnesses.

She'd have to be prepared to search. It would be getting on toward sunset when she arrived, and she probably had little choice but to find a hotel and start in the next morning. If she'd had any sense at all, she would have waited till she found out exactly where he was. The police in Millers Fork would have to know.

But she hadn't had any sense, and if she'd waited, she might have chickened out. She couldn't keep asking for something he wasn't ready to give. It was time for her to take the risk herself.

In the end, it was astonishingly, fatefully easy. When she walked into the small airport terminal on the island of Martinique, she looked across the crowded space and saw a familiar, burly figure at a counter offering charter services. She moved swiftly through the crowds, afraid he might disappear before she caught up with him, but when she tapped him on the shoulder, he turned and looked at her with such glowering horror that she was afraid she'd made the worst mistake in a mistake-strewn life.

And then she realized it wasn't horror on Sal's face, it was shock. "What the hell are you doing here?" he demanded roughly.

She wasn't going to let him scare her away. "What do you think I'm doing here?" she countered, sounding more self-assured than she felt. "What are you doing here?"

To her amazement, he laughed. "Chartering a plane. So Ethan can come and find you." He shook his head in amazement. "I guess the two of you got the right idea at the same time. If he hadn't decided to go, I swear I would have drowned him to put him out of his misery. I knew you'd destroy him sooner or later. You've come back to him, haven't you?"

"I've come back to him. If he wants me."

"You never struck me as particularly stupid," Sal drawled. "Are you going to stay?"

"As long as he lets me."

He nodded, satisfied. "There's a boat waiting to take me back to the island. It can take you instead." He looked past her. "Got any luggage?"

"None."

He made that odd, wheezing sort of laugh again, and she realized that during her timeless sojourn at the strange old house, she'd never heard him laugh. "Don't imagine you'll need any. Come along."

The boat was waiting at one of the jetties, a laconic native behind the wheel. Salvatore helped her into it, then stepped back.

She looked up at him. "Aren't you coming?"

"Nope. He doesn't need me anymore."

She looked for signs of sorrow, of jealousy, of anger in Sal's swarthy face. They were all there, but strongest of all was acceptance. "Will you ever come back?"

"Sometime. Right now I've got to find my own life. Take care of him, Megan."

She spoke past the pain in her throat. "I will."

"I know you will. Otherwise, I wouldn't leave him to you." He tossed her a box. "I was picking this up for him to bring to you. You might as well wear it." And without another word, he turned his back and disappeared into the gathering twilight.

She knew what she'd find in the box. The Janus ring had been cut down, sized perfectly for her slender fingers. She slid it on the ring finger of her left hand, where it belonged, knowing a moment of irrational regret for the piece of lavender yarn that had held it in place. The fit was perfect, but when she tried to pull it off, it stuck fast. She looked down at the twin faces in the dusk and smiled.

There was no conversation as the boat crossed the darkening waters of the Caribbean. Megan sat huddled in a corner of the boat as night fell around her, marveling at the lopsided way the quarter moon hung in the sky, the brightness of the stars overhead.

The island seemed small enough as they approached through the dark waters. She expected the operator to dock at one of the quays, but instead, he circled the island, and pulled up at an expanse of moon-silvered beach, then helped her alight.

"He's here someplace," the man said in his liquid voice. "you find the mon or he find you, it makes no difference." And then he pushed off, leaving her alone on the sand.

She started walking up the beach, her high heels sinking into the sand before she pulled them off and tossed them away. The sand stuck in the feet of her pantyhose, and she pulled them off, too, tossing her linen jacket, her purse, her belt and her earrings onto the pile of discarded clothing, so that she was dressed in nothing but a silk dress that flowed loosely around her, white in the moonlight. And then she started out in search of Ethan, her heart pounding.

She saw him long before he saw her. He was standing at the edge of the water, barefoot, shirtless, his dark hair tied at his neck, his marked face illuminated by the bright moonlight. The flowers growing in fragrant profusion around him were white, the same flowers that had filled that moon garden centuries ago. The same flowers that had covered her bed. And suddenly, Megan was afraid.

"Go to him," Joseph said, his voice a whisper of sound on the soft trade wind. "Be with him. Hurt with him if you must. But stay with him."

And then he left. This time forever. And with his passing went Megan's last doubt. She'd wanted Ethan to ask, and the ring on her finger was enough.

"Ethan," she called, her voice strong and sure on the moonlit air.

And he turned, already knowing she had come back to him, and held out his arms.

Back by Popular Demand

Janet Dailey
Americana

A romantic tour of America through fifty favorite Harlequin Presents, each set in a different state researched by Janet and her husband, Bill. A journey of a lifetime in one cherished collection.

In August, don't miss the exciting states featured in:

Title #13 — ILLINOIS
     The Lyon's Share

#14 — INDIANA
     The Indy Man

Available wherever
Harlequin books are sold.

JD-AUG